ALSO BY J. CARSON BLACK

The Shop

Darkness on the Edge of Town

Dark Side of the Moon

The Devil's Hour

Dark Horse

Darkscope

The Desert Waits

The Tombstone Rose

ICON

Text copyright ©2012 by Margaret Falk
All rights reserved.
Printed in the United States of America.

Published by Thomas & Mercer
P.O. Box 400818
Las Vegas, NV 89140

ISBN-13: 9781612182704
ISBN-10: 1612182704

ICON

J. CARSON BLACK

To my fellow author and good friend William Simon,
who can always talk me down from the ledge.

Acknowledgments

Many thanks to the people who helped make this book a reality: Deborah Schneider of Gelfman-Schneider Literary Agency; my editors, Courtney Miller of Thomas & Mercer and Charlotte Herscher; and to my friends and fellow writers for their helpfulness and unbending support: Sinclair Browning, Elizabeth Gunn, J.M. "Mike" Hayes, Carol Davis Luce, Susan Cummins Miller, Michael Prescott, Cheryl Shireman, and William Simon.

Thanks to my husband and publisher, Glenn McCreedy, and my wonderful mother, Mary Veronica Falk.

Prologue

Big Bear Lake, California

When he considered all he'd had were textbooks, some of which he'd written himself, and a slide rule, retractable measuring tape, calculator, drafting pencil, and reams of notebook paper, Dr. Stephen DePaulentis was quite proud.

Stephen DePaulentis, MD, PhD, chief forensic pathologist with the Los Angeles Police Department (retired), member in good standing with the National Board of Medical Examiners, and frequent crime-scene expert on CNN, was well aware that his thirty-plus years of accumulated knowledge would go unappreciated in the cabin at Big Bear Lake.

But for the moment, he savored the magnitude of his accomplishment.

He'd discarded three prospective scenarios as impossible and stuck with the simplest solution to the problem presented him. Over a two-day period, he had gone over his projections from stem to stern. There were no holes.

He peered out the half-closed blinds of his cabin. A speedboat arrowed across the lake. Sunlight glistened on blue water. He wished he could be out there—

And realized, for the first time in eight months, he actually *wanted* to live. The heart bypass had kneecapped him, *shrunk* him, and the depression that followed was crushing. Now he felt useful again.

He heard a motion behind him. His captor.

"I didn't hear you come in," he said. "It's all done."

"Good," his captor said.

"Everything's worked out, the blood spatter, the trajectories, where to place the…" He looked at the still, quiet eyes and faltered. "At any rate, mission accomplished. You can simulate it on a computer. I've given you all the measurements, probabilities, forensics—everything."

Abruptly, he felt deflated. Nothing left to say.

His captor held a takeout bag from The Lodge. Last night Dr. DePaulentis had asked for Kobe beef, and had gotten it. Not as good as you'd get in the restaurant, but good enough for takeout. Today it was poached salmon.

He tucked in while his captor read over his notes. They finished about the same time. His captor said, "Remarkable."

"I think so." He wiped his chin with the linen napkin that had come with the food. Wondered what his pals in the forensic biz would think.

As he set down his fork, he heard a snap behind him. It was a snap he recognized from years of donning latex gloves. He spun around. "What—?"

His captor looked at him with that stone face, eyes immovable in her head. One gloved hand held a semiautomatic. She nodded in the direction of the bathroom. He capitulated, walking ahead of her, his heart ramming its way up into his throat. He could hear the motorboat whining across the water, see the sun filter through the ponderosas between the blinds. The sky outside was a perfect, crystalline blue.

She stopped at the bathroom doorway. "Take off your clothes."

"Can't we talk about this? I have two grown daughters—"

She raised the gun to chest level. No point arguing. He removed his clothes, embarrassed by his white, flabby body, the scars on his chest. Covered himself with shaking hands.

"Get in the bathtub."

He stepped in. What else could he do? The water had once been warm, but it was tepid now. She must have run it before she went to get his lunch.

"Sit."

He sat in the tub, tried to keep his voice calm. "You don't have to do this. I promised I'd keep quiet, and I will."

She reached down by the sink and handed him a full bottle of wine. Good wine too, he noticed. "Drink," she said.

"You can monitor my phone, my e-mails. I promise I won't say anything."

"Drink."

No choice. He drank. Good wine or not, he barely tasted it. His mouth was sour with fear. He swallowed rapidly, like drinking from a fountain, wanting to be as drunk as possible.

His captor emptied a vial of pills into her hand. He recognized them immediately: secobarbital. He stared at the red capsules for a long time, his heart hammering in his ears. He wouldn't get through this alive. His only choice was *how*.

He took a deep breath and reached out with surprisingly steady fingers. Picked the pills up delicately, one by one, from her outstretched palm and transferred them to his own, then placed them in his mouth.

Thinking, *I did truly fine work.*

He almost choked, his mouth was so dry.

But eventually, he swallowed them all.

I: DESERT CREATURES

Chapter One

THE WOMAN AND THE BOY CAME FROM LA. THEY DROVE A white 1999 Toyota Camry, which looked like a million other Toyota Camrys all over the West. The woman, who'd bought the car two days previously from a man in Anaheim, wanted something that would slip under the radar.

There was an "AAA" sticker on the back bumper. They'd argued about it. The woman for, the boy against. The boy thought that someone might notice the Triple A sticker, but the woman said the sticker hinted at solidity. Besides, she said, people don't see Triple A stickers.

The woman won. She always won—she was the boss.

They'd started out at dawn, stopping in Banning for breakfast. No hurry. Detoured off I-10 to drive into Palm Springs. For five dollars, the woman bought a map of the stars' homes. They drove past Frank Sinatra's Twin Palms, which you could rent for $2,600 a night, and the honeymoon house of Elvis and Priscilla Presley on Ladera Circle, and Marilyn Monroe's house. The Palm Springs Tram was closed for repairs or they would have taken it to the top of San Jacinto. The boy got a souvenir, though—a Palm Springs traveling cup.

He had quite an accumulation of souvenirs from their travels, mostly cheap things. In Indio, he insisted they stop at a roadside stand for a bag of dates. Not to eat, but to add to his stash.

"When we dump the car," the woman said, "you can't take all this stuff with you."

The boy shrugged. He knew better than most that life was a transient proposition.

The boy was twelve going on twenty. Quiet. He kept his feelings to himself. But the woman knew that behind the subdued facade was a land mine waiting to explode. You just needed the right thing to trigger it.

He *wanted*.

The woman knew what he wanted, and she would have liked to give it to him, but this was serious business. The job came first.

He was lucky she was taking him at all.

Chapter Two

WELL INTO THE SECOND HOUR OF MAX CONROY'S incarceration, the arresting officer came to release him from this stinking hellhole. About time.

From the outside, the courthouse in Paradox, Arizona, was nineteenth-century ornate, but that didn't fool anybody. The inside was moldering, cramped, and oven-hot. It smelled of urine, alcohol, and BO. His cell mate hadn't moved in the two and a half hours Max had been in here; he just lay on the one bunk with his face to the wall, snoring like a gas generator.

The alcohol fumes were getting to him. He couldn't stand the stench. Sometimes his mind would drift—this had happened a lot in the last couple of weeks—and when he came back into his body he imagined he could smell it on himself.

But he was clean. Alcohol and drug free.

Reborn.

A couple of hours later, the deputy who arrested him unlocked the cell door. Her nameplate said "Tess McCrae." Tan uniform, twenty pounds of leather and weaponry girding her hips and ruining what was probably a nice line. She had good posture, though. Squared away, no nonsense. Efficient too, the way she'd had him handcuffed and shoved up against her sheriff's cruiser in one fluid motion.

She led him through intake, which was also output, just a shabby corner hidden from view by a flimsy partition. The whole inside of the third floor of the courthouse was like a stage set. Even the guard by the door seemed like a cardboard cutout—adding to the unreality that floated around Max most of the time now.

She returned his possessions, including his belt and shoelaces, which had been taken in case he'd gotten it in his mind to hang himself. He waited for her to say something. You'd think, in this backwater, not having ID would be a capital crime—maybe even a hanging offense. But she didn't bring it up.

"That it?" he asked. "I'm free to go?"

She nodded.

He gave her his best Max-as-charming-con-man voice. "What did I do? Officially."

She looked at him sideways through calm, hazel eyes. "You loitered."

"Seriously?"

"It's on the books. You can look it up."

Loitering was as good a trumped-up charge as any, Max guessed. He was grateful to her for saving him from the two guys in the limo, even if it meant spending a couple of hours in the pokey.

Who knew what they were after? If it hadn't been for the deputy's resourcefulness, he might have been a rotting corpse in the middle of the desert by now.

Although more likely, he'd be on a jet headed back for LA.

Tess McCrae walked him down the stairs and out through the echoing, empty first floor to the double wooden doors.

The door screeched as it scuffed over the sill. Sunlight spotlighted him. He blinked and realized again that although he didn't have a hangover, it sure felt like one.

Outside, the street looked like someone had run an iron over it. His heart sped up for a moment or two, then slowed back to its normal pace when he saw there were no suits in a black stretch limo. In fact, nobody at all.

They could be around the corner, watching and waiting.

The unreality of it was dizzying. For a moment, his thoughts started to fly away again, and he pictured himself holding the M-1 rifle, the one in *Man Down*, how he'd liked the heavy feel of it cradled in his hands, liked the shooting, the casings pinging around him. He pictured holding a pistol muzzle to his head, those many times he'd wished hard for the percussive sound that would obliterate it all.

But now, he marveled, those thoughts had lost their potency. Realized he just thought them out of habit.

"I'm free," he said.

She looked at him. "Of course you're free. I said you were."

He stepped outside, getting his sea legs. The sun bearing down, blinding, he could swear he smelled alcohol—he'd been pickled in it for so long—and the smell of sex with countless women he didn't know, and the dry mouth and seizing heartbeat from the prescription drugs. Sweat beaded under his hair. "You know a good place for lunch?"

"I know a place for lunch," she said. "But it isn't good. Nothing's good around here."

"The diner?"

She nodded again. That straight spine. No leeway there for all the silly stuff most people did with their hands and expressions and body language when they realized who he was.

Then she spoiled it. "I'll go with you."

"Why? You said I was free to go."

"I'm hungry. How's that?"

* * *

THE DINER HAD A WESTERN THEME, LIKE EVERYTHING IN the town. Old movie posters on the walls, bustling waitresses with raccoon eyes and beauty-shop hairdos, clicking down the plastic plates and banging the ceramic coffee mugs. The deputy caught the door he held out for her. He could feel her calm presence even though they weren't touching. He wondered if he'd been mistaken—that maybe she *didn't* know who he was. The beard helped. He'd been living in these clothes since yesterday morning, and with the hundred-degree heat and the hitchhiking and the rainstorms he knew he was pretty ripe. During his two weeks at the Desert Oasis Healing Center, he'd learned the hard way that the hippie deodorant they provided didn't work for shit.

The waitress didn't make eye contact with him. Amazing how that worked. Nobody saw the homeless.

She sat them by the window away from everyone else. Fine by him. He could look at the street. He caught the deputy noting that. The deputy noted everything. After the waitress left with their order, the deputy leaned forward, setting her hands palms-down on the paper place mat. She wore clear polish and her trimmed nails were little half-moons. Her gaze was so steady it made him want to look away.

"So," she said. "Who's after you?"

"No one's after me."

"Those guys in the limo—why did they want you to go with them?"

"Beats me."

She said nothing, just continued to watch him. No recognition in her eyes, though. Her face didn't betray her real feelings about him, if there were any.

The silence was oppressive. He felt he had to say something. "What's it to you?"

"Frankly, I don't see why they'd want to get their car dirty."

He gave her his most winning smile. "I can't explain it."

"You can't."

"Nope." He added, "Maybe they were aliens come down to abduct me."

She stared into his eyes, searching. Her half-moon nails solidly on the place mat.

Max realized he liked her.

She tapped her fingers on the place mat. "I guess it's your business," she said.

The diner was beginning to fill up—starting to get noisy.

A short, stocky man came in and approached their booth. The man wore a knit polo shirt and jeans and a lanyard around his neck. "Push over, doll," the man said to the deputy, sliding into the booth next to her. He thumped union-boss elbows on the counter and leveled his gaze at Max. "Who're you?"

"Who are *you*?"

"I asked first."

The deputy said, "This is Pat. He's Bajada County's one and only detective, so don't make him mad."

"No kidding." Pat lifted the paper place mat up close to his face and studied the menu printed on it. "Tess, you know if they got peekin' pie today?"

"Think so," the deputy said.

"So who is this guy?" Pat asked.

"Says his name is Dave."

"Dave?" Pat looked up, his blue eyes startled in his pink Irish face. Something changed in his expression, but he hid it well.

The waitress took their orders, standing upwind and doing her best to ignore Max.

After the waitress left, Pat leaned forward on his stout elbows. "So, *Dave*. What's a genuine, honest-to-God, bleeding-heart, liberal *movie star* like you doing in this piss-water town?"

"You're mistaking me for someone else."

"Uh-huh. Tess, you ever see this guy's movies?"

"Some of them."

"What was the first one you saw?"

"*The Slab.*"

Pat leaned forward. "When was that?"

Tess sighed. "June twenty-second, two thousand nine."

"And that was…"

"A Monday."

"You sure, now? How do you know it was a Monday?"

"It just was."

Pat settled in deeper in the booth and stared at her avidly. "Anything special about that day?"

Tess looked at Max. "Two Metro trains in Washington, DC, collided."

"Oh?" Pat leaned forward, cupped his chin in his hands, sang, "Tell me more, tell me more, tell me more."

Tess held Max's gaze. Those calm hazel eyes. "Nine people died."

"Anything else?"

"Eighty people were injured."

"Do tell. Where was this?"

"Tahoma Station."

The waitress came over with their food. "You playin' that game again, Pat? I'm sure this girl is tired of bein' your one-trick pony."

Max said to Tess, "Someone you knew died in the wreck?"

"Permit me," Pat said to the deputy, then turned to Max. "She didn't know any of them. As a matter of fact, I doubt she even knew there *was* a Tahoma station."

A loud beep emanated from Pat's belt. He shifted away from them and called in, his voice low. Closed his battered flip phone and looked at the deputy. "We gotta go. Somebody fighting over a goat—I kid you not. Knowing those two mean-ass lesbians, it could turn into a homo-cide for sure."

Deputy McCrae was already on her feet.

Pat stood up, guzzled the rest of his coffee, and tossed a few bills on the table. "See you around, *Max*."

Chapter Three

WHEN THE WOMAN SPOTTED THE TURNOFF FOR JOSHUA TREE National Park, she exited the freeway and took the road under the overpass.

"Why are we stopping here?" asked the boy.

"I think you should see this."

"See what? It's just a bunch of rocks and cactus."

The woman said nothing, just followed the road to the Cottonwood Visitor Center, and parked out front.

"We haven't made it very far," the boy said as they got out of the car.

"We're in no hurry."

"Jesus, it's hot out here!"

"Mouth," she reminded him.

"Yeah, yeah. OK." He started up the walkway to the visitor center, turned back. "You coming?"

She motioned to her mobile phone, which was vibrating. "In a minute."

The number on the readout belonged to Gordon White Eagle. When she answered he said, "Dammit! I've been trying to reach you since yesterday afternoon!"

"What time in the afternoon?"

"How should I know?" He paused. "Around five o'clock, six at the latest."

"I don't answer after five. You didn't leave a message, did you, Gordon?"

Gordon ignored this. "Where are you now?"

"Joshua Tree National Park. I think we're going to camp here."

"No you're not. There's been a change of plans." Gordon paused. The woman had never known Gordon to pause.

There was no ambiguity to Gordon. He was certain of things. In fact, he was a know-it-all. She'd seen him intimidate people—he was big, with a shiny bald head like Mr. Clean. She knew it was all calculated to get the upper hand, but no one got the upper hand with her. Right now, surprisingly, she heard indecision in his voice like play in a steering wheel. "Our, er...*resident* went out on his own yesterday and hasn't come back. I've had a couple of my men looking for him since early yesterday evening. I need you here."

The woman looked at the new black pavement and the desert beyond. "What do you want *me* to do?"

"Get here ASAP! This isn't a scenic trip. How long will it take you to get here?"

Shaun estimated: Yucca Valley to Blythe, Blythe to Quartzite, Quartzite to Phoenix. Phoenix up I-17 to Cottonwood, then to Desert Oasis. "Late."

"Late? What does *that* mean?"

"Night."

"I'll send a jet. Where's the nearest airport? Indio, right?"

After the arrangements were made, Shaun closed the phone and walked to the visitor center. The road trip, the national parks and scenic vistas and campgrounds, would have to wait. It was something kids should have in their childhood. Her best friend from elementary school, Lisa Ann Davenport, had traveled all over the country with her parents every summer, and it had set her up for life. Lisa Ann was married to a handsome, successful businessman. She ran her own business, and they had two children, a boy and a girl. No doubt, she and her husband took them to national parks, where they made s'mores and told ghost stories around the campfire. Shaun wanted those kinds of experiences for Jimmy.

He was far too obsessed with killing.

She found him pawing through the Joshua Tree hats. There were plenty of souvenirs at the Cottonwood Visitor Center, and she let him pick out half a dozen. Paid for them in cash without complaint.

They took a short loop drive, photographed a couple of Joshua trees, then drove back to Indio to wait for Gordon's jet.

* * *

AFTER THE DEPUTY AND THE DETECTIVE LEFT HIM ALONE at the table, the waitress kept looking at him. He knew she was wondering where she'd seen him before.

Time to get out of here. He shifted in his seat to reach for his wallet.

It wasn't there.

From her place by the lunch counter, the waitress watched him like a hawk watches a weasel.

Where was his wallet?

She started in his direction.

He looked at the money Pat had thrown on the table. Not enough to cover the bill. Cheap son of a bitch.

The waitress was standing over him.

He tried the other back pocket of his jeans. Her voice assaulted his ears, shutting out all thought. Her lips were moving but he couldn't hear anything but the band-saw shriek.

He squinted up at her, tried to read her lips.

"Don't worry about that. Deputy has it covered."

She was looking at him quizzically, as if wondering why Tess would bring a stinking bum into her place.

"Thanks."

"Thank her."

He kept his eyes down. In his years of going out in public, Max had noticed people didn't really see you if you looked like a kicked dog. But he had to ask. "What was that about the train crash? What the deputy was talking about?"

"Oh, that." She waved a hand. "She's got some weird kind of memory. Perfect recall or something like that—she remembers every little thing." She added, "Since you're all paid up, you can go now."

And don't let the door hit you on the way out.

He went outside and turned into the alley beside the diner. He was only exposed on the main street for a few seconds, but his heart pounded so hard he thought it would explode. He stopped in the shade of the diner. The building opposite him was windowless; a few cars were parked nose-in. Nothing stirred. The town drowsed in the heat and the flies.

No limo.

No wallet either. He shoved his hand into in his jeans pocket, thinking he might at least have some change. Instead, his fingers closed around a tight wad of bills. Somewhere along the line—he couldn't remember exactly when—he'd stuffed cash in both pockets, plenty of it. Max had no idea when that had happened; his space-time continuum was completely disrupted.

Then he remembered. When the deputy processed him into the jail, she'd taken cash from his pockets. He'd signed for it with the name of one of his lesser-known characters. Here in the alley, he pictured the cash falling onto the desk, loose change and a wad of crinkled bills. The deputy had him count it.

There were holes in his memory. Max had become accustomed to that in the last week or so.

But what had happened to his wallet?

Relax. Don't think about it and it will come to you.

* * *

MAX REMEMBERED MOST OF THE DAY BEFORE—HIS ESCAPE from the Desert Oasis Healing Center in the laundry truck, the guy letting him out on I-17, thumbing rides. Just wanting to get away from the paparazzi and be a nobody for a while. He remembered taking shelter from the thunderstorm inside a Texaco mini-mart in some town along the freeway. He'd just come from a thrift store down the street, having tried to hire on there. But the owner recognized him and called in his buddies to look at him like he was an animal in a zoo. The owner said, "Job? You serious? What is this? Is this a reality show? Like *Candid Camera*?"

"Huh," said the owner's buddy.

The thrift store owner looked past Max in the direction of the front doors. "Where's the camera?"

"There is no camera. I want to work here."

"You can't work here."

"Why not?"

"Why not?" The guy stared at him. "Are you serious?"

The idea he could get work had seemed reasonable at the time. From the moment he'd left the Desert Oasis Healing Center, Max had seen his escape as a second chance. He was sober for the first time in years. He wanted to make a clean break. Leave his old life behind and be a normal guy like his father was. Your average Joe. Even when he drifted in and out of awareness, that goal remained constant—his north star. Max wasn't asking for much, just a regular job. Something he could do with his hands, maybe. No autograph seekers, no cameras, no paparazzi. No public that saw him through the prism of its own needs, wants, or desires.

But he couldn't escape who he was. People recognized him. They gawked. They yelled his name. Took photos of him with their phones.

The funny thing? He used to pretend he was a regular citizen all the time in LA—and half the time he got away with it. But now, when Max really *wanted* to be anonymous, it didn't work quite so well. Maybe it was because it meant so much to him. Maybe he was trying too hard.

So it had been raining, really coming down, and he'd gone from the thrift store to the Texaco mini-mart next door, thinking he might try there. Hard rain pelted the roof and steam rose from the pavement. He was sopping wet and shivering. He'd wait out the storm by pretending to look for items aisle by aisle.

Suddenly his ringtone blasted, howling, "Now you're messing with a son of a bitch!" from "Hair of the Dog" by Nazareth.

He fumbled in his pocket, and the phone skated out of his wet hand and hit the floor. The kid behind the counter stared at him, his face pale under the fluorescents. Max picked up the phone and turned away, lowering his voice. "Hello?"

"Max. Ah, glad I found you."

Jerry.

Max said nothing. He felt like the cottontails he used to shoot at when he was a kid. How they'd hunker down in plain sight and hope you didn't see them. Their ears lit up like stained glass windows—bright pink.

"Max? You there?"

He didn't answer.

"I have some stuff for you to sign," Max's business manager said. "That last little escapade of yours is costing us. Audemars Piguet is making noises about backing out of the endorsement deal, but I promised him there wouldn't be a repeat. There's a new clause I'm faxing over, no biggie."

Max said nothing.

Jerry said, "Max, I can see why you're angry." Max didn't reply. "I know you hate the place, and I'm sorry about that." Max said nothing. "But you're going to thank me later. Once this is all over, we'll have a big laugh about it…are you listening? You didn't lose your voice, did you? If so, we need to get hold of the vocal coach. Shooting starts in three weeks—"

"I won't be there in three weeks."

"What? Are you crazy? What are you saying? You have a contract!"

It went on like that for a while. First shock, then anger, then denial—skipping right over grief. Max listened, wondering why he didn't just cut Jerry off. Shut the phone and that would be the end of it. But he couldn't. He clamped the cell hard against his ear, every muscle tense. Maybe listening to Jerry Gold was the beginning of catharsis. Maybe he needed to remind himself what was in the rearview mirror, and why he was leaving it all behind.

Jerry was talking faster now. "You're due on the set August first! You can't just turn your back on this and act like it's some kind of stupid *game*. This is real life, Jacko, and you'd better get that through your head right now. People are *depending* on you. You know how much this is costing already? So stop with the prima donna *bullshit* and get back with the program!"

A calmness came over him. His fingers loosened. "I quit," he said.

Silence. Then, "You quit? You *quit*?" A tirade followed. Max let the phone drop through his hands to the floor, heard the case crack.

Serenity bloomed inside him. He turned to look at the attendant, who was staring at him, eyes wide.

"Dude, you broke your phone!"

The ringtone once again filled the small mini-mart: "Now you're messin' with a—" beat, beat, "Son of a *bitch*, you're messin' with a—"

Max picked the phone up off the floor. Noticed the dried swirls from a mop—place was dirty as hell.

When Max answered, he heard "You are in big fucking trouble! You—"

He ended the call. It was difficult because the edges didn't true up. The smile inside him was warm and welcoming, like a sunrise.

The phone sounded again. Max wondered if his darling wife was with Jerry right now. Wondered if she was hearing all this. If so, he hoped she was worried.

Lightning strobed the interior of the mini-mart. Thunder crashed.

The phone stayed quiet in his hand.

"Dude, I mean, seriously…" The kid trailed off. "Hey, man, I seen you before?"

Outside, headlights flared up behind the needles of rain. Water funneled off the windshield of a dark car with a menacing grille. Windshield wipers slashed.

The kid behind the counter said, "You're…Hey, man, I know you…"

Max stepped toward the door and peered outside. He suddenly became aware how completely soaked he was. When he moved, his jeans rasped together like sandpaper.

No one got out of the car in front. The windshield wipers whipped back and forth, sluicing off the buckets of water coming out of the sky. Max couldn't see past the wipers, past the water brimming on the windshield, but he could almost feel whoever it was peering out at him, peering into the brightly lit store.

The glare of the overhead lights was getting to him. He felt exposed in here.

There were times Max was hyperalert. Times when he could tell something was wrong—a sixth sense. He'd always had it. It felt, right now, like someone had taken a comb and run it over the hairs on the back of his neck.

He felt the tingle in his belly, a low humming. A warning.

Did Jerry know where he was? Had they sent someone after him? Pinpointed his position by GPS through his phone?

"Dude," he said to the kid behind the counter. "You got a back way out of here?"

"Yeah, sure." He nodded at a door near the beer case. "Why?"

There wasn't much time. Max opened the door to the rear of the store, looked up the hall to the exit, and saw the open doorway to the back room.

He returned to the front of the store just as a car door slammed outside. "Hey, man," he said. "You got a good lock on the door to the back room?"

"Uh, sure."

Outside, feet pelted on wet pavement. "Take my advice and go lock yourself in there now."

"What're you—?"

Max didn't hear what else the kid said. He was out the back door and gone.

Chapter Four

TURNED OUT NO ONE HAD BEEN COMING FOR HIM—AT LEAST not at the mini-mart. But Max's instincts had been right. There had been trouble brewing, he'd just mistaken the nature of that trouble.

The mini-mart was the target of a simple robbery. The robber left with the contents of the cash register and a case of beer. The kid was shaken, but unhurt. The security camera tape that they played on the news showed a guy wearing a dark hoodie. You couldn't see his face.

Max watched the nightly news while sitting on the sway-backed bed of the Riata Motel farther south in Paradox.

The bed smelled of feet.

Fortunately, the kid at the mini-mart didn't mention that he had, moments before, pointed the back way out to the famous actor, Max Conroy.

Too shaken from the experience, probably.

Max felt he'd dodged a bullet. He'd been the kid on the trestle who managed to jump off before the train hit him. The old sixth sense had worked out...

Except the guy in the hoodie hadn't been coming for him. He was just some asshole holding up a mini-mart.

But *someone* was coming. He could feel it.

Max had put eighty miles between himself and the Texaco mini-mart. By then, the rain had stopped, and he'd been bone tired when the trucker had dropped him off in Paradox. He'd staggered as far as the Riata and peeled off some cash for one night's stay.

Couldn't use a credit card even if he wanted to. He'd buried his wallet last night, in a fit of paranoia after the incident at the Texaco—wrapped it in a plastic produce bag and dropped it into the hole he'd dug by a fence somewhere in the desert. His credit cards, his Triple A card, his SAG card. Everything. A clean sweep.

He'd ditched the cell phone too.

Sitting on the lumpy bed in the Riata Motel, Max thought, why the hell did I do *that*?

But he knew. In the throes of some paranoid delusion, he really *had* tried to burn his bridges.

After a long shower, Max opened the door and leaned in the doorway of Room 3 of the Riata Motel. The place was old enough to have a neon sign, buzzing and sizzling a weak yellow: the R, the A, the T. Rat. Like someone did it on purpose as a joke.

Standing out there in the freshness after the rain, the sweet but slightly acrid smell of wet creosote in his nostrils, he tried to remember where exactly he'd buried his wallet. Just in case he needed to go back and find it again.

Unfortunately, he drew a blank.

The burying tactic was nothing new for him. He'd have his doctors write prescriptions for oxy and other drugs, and stockpile them. Sometimes, when he hated what he was doing, he'd bury them in his yard and try to forget where they were. He did that with liquor too. Max had always hoped that if he was shit-faced, or drugged out of his mind, he wouldn't remember where he'd hidden them.

Many times, it worked. There were caches of drugs and liquor all over his backyard he didn't know about—stuff he'd forgotten. Salted throughout his yard like land mines.

* * *

THE NEXT MORNING MAX AWOKE FROM A TERRIBLE DREAM. In the dream, he was standing on the ledge of the Jumeirah Essex House in New York, looking down twenty-five stories at the street. And he was naked.

Somebody down below—looked like an ant next to a Tonka truck—yelled into a bullhorn, but he couldn't hear what the guy said.

He sat up in bed in the Rat Motel. The sun filtered in through the cheesy orange curtains. The nightmare reminded him of something he'd seen on a TV show—he thought it was *Dateline NBC*. An in-depth look at the ill effects of some intensive self-help seminars. A rash of people had developed a sort of "mental break," many of them ending up shivering naked on a ledge somewhere, more than a few leaping to their deaths.

The story, which he could barely remember, must have influenced his dreams. But he wondered. If he'd stayed at the Healing Center, would he have ended up like that?

The worst, though, were the hallucinations: gigantic birds of prey coming at him from out of the sky, or rats running up his legs. There were harmless visions, as well—a man rowing a boat a couple of feet off the ground.

Funny: for all the drugs and alcohol he'd consumed over the years, he'd never had a hallucination before his time at the Desert Oasis Healing Center.

Sitting there in the squalid room of the Rat Motel, Max knew he needed help. He needed to talk to his closest friend.

When he dialed the number to the motorcycle shop, Dave's wife, Karen, answered.

He almost hung up. Instead, he asked, "Is Dave there?"

"Max?"

"Yeah. Is Dave around?"

Her voice sounded tinny—distant. She avoided him when she could. "Dave's gone all day. What's going on?"

"Nothing's going on."

"We heard you left rehab."

"Where'd you hear that? Is it all over the media?"

"No, there's been nothing on TV. Jerry called Dave this morning, hoping he'd know where you were."

Earlier this morning Max had turned on the television. He hadn't seen anything either. They'd somehow managed to keep his escape from the rehab center quiet—Jerry was good at that kind of thing. Max knew Jerry would find a way to keep it quiet until he could woo him back.

But Jerry didn't know Max was unwooable.

Karen was talking again. "Where are you?"

"Here and there." He laughed, but it came out forced. The guy in the rowboat was back. He was right outside Max's window.

"Max? Did you hear me? Once Dave gets off, he could come for you. All you have to do is tell us where you are."

The guy in the rowboat looked the same as he had the last time Max had seen him—the same shower cap and granny glasses, tinted pink like the specs in that famous picture of Janis Joplin. He rowed past and waved.

What did they *do* to him?

"Max? Just tell us where. Dave will come and get you. We're worried."

Max didn't buy the "we're worried" part. Dave would be worried—no doubt about that—but Karen would just as soon never see Max again after what had happened in Nautilus Canyon.

The canyon, which the three of them had hiked in southern Utah last summer, wasn't named for the nautilus shell without reason. The trail ran through an intricate labyrinth of red-rock chambers. Dave had gone off ahead—he was always an adventurous sort. Max and Karen followed at a slower pace, taking in the stunning play of light and shadow. Then Karen found an offshoot chamber that glowed like St. Patrick's Cathedral at Christmas. She eased through a narrow passage in the rock to take a photograph—and her leg got stuck up to the thigh. Max worked assiduously to get her out; he used sunscreen on her leg to help it slide.

And Max being Max, it didn't stop there.

Afterward, Max and Karen agreed. As long as Dave didn't know what happened, things would be fine. What was done was done. Why go out of their way to hurt him?

And so Max and Karen stayed away from each other as much as possible, their dislike for each other growing along with the residual self-loathing.

Max felt bad about the whole thing, but the damage was done. It would only hurt Dave to know the truth. He and Dave had been best friends since high school. One mistake wasn't going to sabotage that.

And Max knew without a doubt that Dave would help him now. He would come and get him and together they'd work something out. Dave was the ultimate wingman. He would keep his secret.

And Karen—she was good at keeping secrets too.

Max suddenly felt small. He looked out the window. The guy in the rowboat rested his oars in the locks and held a conversation with a middle-aged couple in matching Sun Devils T-shirts.

Max looked away. He needed to make a decision here.

Then Karen said, "Jerry's fit to be tied. He needs to know what you're going to do."

"Do?"

"About *V.A.M.Pyre*. It's not fair to the cast and crew… to everybody. We're depending on, well, you know. It's hard for everybody, not knowing if we're going to have that job."

He knew then that Karen wouldn't let it go. She'd keep pushing. She'd try to get him to go back. It was economics to her, and rightfully so. She and Dave had to make a living. The motorcycle shop was more of a hobby than anything else, and while Dave had plenty of other stunt work, their bottom line depended on Max.

Everyone depended on Max.

He should do the right thing. He should think of somebody else besides himself. But right now he just…couldn't.

"Just tell him I'm all right, OK? Just tell him that." He set the phone in the cradle and stared out the window.

Mercifully, the man in the rowboat was gone.

After his talk with Karen, Max turned on the TV and clicked through the channels, looking for references to his escape the day before. He saw nothing on the cable news shows. Max figured Gordon White Eagle didn't want it known that a high-end, exclusive dry-out center like the Desert Oasis had misplaced one of its high-profile celebrities.

He went looking for breakfast, walking the one block to Paradox's main drag. The place was unreal. There were boardwalks, like you'd see in the movie *Tombstone*. One-story buildings, streets you could drive a cattle herd through.

He felt oily, grainy, and dirty. He was clean but his clothes weren't. He should have washed them in the sink, but it hadn't occurred to him until he'd put them on this morning. He kept forgetting things.

Kept *seeing* things.

He turned the corner and he was walking back to the motel when he heard someone calling his name.

Across the street, a guy in a suit leaned against the driver's door of a black limo, arms folded. Sunglasses, buzz cut, Bluetooth.

Out of place in a town like this.

"Max!" the guy called again. Max ignored him and kept walking. He didn't look back, just kept moving, picking up the pace.

His heart going like a jackhammer.

Knew he was going down the moment before the guy landed on him like a pile of bricks.

Chapter Five

ON THE WAY OVER TO THE TRAILER COURT WHERE THE domestic over the goat had taken place, Pat said to Tess, "What's the story with the movie star?"

"I helped him out this morning. Did you see the stretch limo?"

"Stretch limo? Woweeeee," Pat said. "I told you this place was a gold mine. All those rich sons of bitches moving in to take in the desert air and prison view."

"There were two guys, arguing with the homeless guy."

"That would be Max."

"Right. At first I thought maybe the transient was doing the squeegee thing on their windshield, and the guy in the limo didn't like it."

"Huh." He shook his head. "Can't see that happening around here. As many cars come down this street, it wouldn't be worth the initial cost of the squeegee. This tough economy, you want to avoid any unnecessary startup costs. So then what happened?"

"They were trying to load him into the back of the limo."

"Hope they had one of those pine tree air fresheners hangin' from the rearview mirror."

Tess had stopped and asked what the trouble was. The limo driver had been annoyingly obsequious. "No trouble, Officer."

Tess said to the homeless man, "You want to go with them?"

"No, I don't."

"His wife wants him to come to the hospital," said the big guy with the earpiece. "She's having a baby."

Tess looked at the man. "That true?"

"No."

She focused on him, this piteous sight in the stinky clothes. Underneath the grime, she saw his facial structure—good health shining through. Even, white teeth. An athletic frame. She knew who he was immediately.

"Listen, Deputy," the big guy said. "Frank here goes on binges, forgets himself. His wife is having a baby and she wants him there. We thought we'd clean him up—"

"You two friends of his?"

The guy stared at her. "We're friends of the wife."

"Would you mind telling me her name? His wife."

He glared at her. "Sally."

She pulled out her pad, did the officious thing. "Last name?"

"Uh, Dor. Dor-man."

"Spell it?"

"D.O.R.M.A.N. Dorman." Sometime in his life, he'd participated in a spelling bee.

"She's at which hospital?"

"Ma'am, if you'll excuse us, we're just trying to help out a friend, and we have to get going—"

"I'm asking because if it's an emergency, I'll be happy to escort you."

"You know what? Never mind. If this jerk doesn't give a damn about his wife, then it's his problem."

The two men got in the car and drove away.

A welcome breeze blew through, spiraling around them in the early sun. The only freshness in what would be a very hot day.

"Thanks," the guy said.

"So what was that all about?"

He shrugged. She noticed, with that shrug, he not only had a good frame, but muscle layered over it. Muscle that came from hours in the gym—lean, but sculpted. Of course he would.

He was a little shorter in person but just as handsome, even under the five o'clock shadow. His head was big for his body—just a little. She noticed that because she'd read that celebrities' heads were often larger than their torsos—some-how it made them more photogenic.

In this case it was definitely true.

Most of what Tess knew about Max Conroy came from a *People* article she'd read at her doctor's office after she'd sprained her foot in April. She knew, for instance, that Conroy was what they called a "franchise" in the movie business. He'd starred in three *V.A.M.Pyre* films—big summer blockbusters. He had a contract to do at least two more. The films featured a "vampire version of a James Bond-like character," who righted wrongs and drank the blood of beautiful women. Together the films grossed $2.7 billion. Tess had not seen any of them, but her friend Marcy had a teenage daughter who was obsessed with the man. Teenage girls and handsome vampires—go figure. Tess herself thought from the look of him that Max was getting a little old for that kind of thing, and when she thought about it at all, wondered why he didn't make movies that appealed to a general audience. He was leading man material; that was for sure.

It was a nice spread in *People*, and included three photos. One of Max on the set of his new film, one of him horsing around with his wife, Talia, at their Malibu mansion, and one of him posing before the vintage motorcycle shop he co-owned with his best friend and stunt double, Dave Finley.

According to the *People* article, Max Conroy had married Hollywood star Talia L'Apel twice. Talia had this cute little mole under one eye. She had appeared in several chick flicks, the last one being *Lemon Aid*, about a woman whose child had cancer and the city that wanted to close the child's lemonade stand down. Tess saw that movie with her cousin on February eighth, when they'd driven down to Phoenix for the day. Max and Talia divorced in January, but four months later, after reconnecting at a Hollywood party at Charlie Sheen's house, they'd flown to Vegas and tied the knot again at the Desert Dreams Wedding Chapel. They'd grabbed tourists off the street for their witnesses. Tess knew their names and what they did—the man was grossly overweight—but she'd filed it away and didn't feel the need to retrieve it now. That was just background stuff, and over the years she'd learned to keep some of that information out of sight.

Some things, she relegated to footnotes.

"Am I free to go?" Conroy asked her after the limo was gone.

"Sure, you can go."

"Thanks."

He ambled away. Tried to act unperturbed, but Tess knew he'd been shaken by the experience.

* * *

"THAT IT?" PAT SCANNED THE ROAD FROM THE PASSENGER side. Cataloging what he was seeing as they talked.

"Nope," Tess said. "Half hour later I saw the limo again by the park. I could hear somebody pounding on the windows inside."

She stopped the limo. The driver got out. The back window buzzed down and this time Max Conroy spoke for himself. He wanted to go with them; he was worried about his wife.

"Why were you pounding on the window?"

Inside the limo, he shrugged those ripped shoulders of his. "Saw someone I knew."

The other guy, small, stocky, a Special Forces type, sat very close to Conroy. It was a big space, the back of the limo, plenty of places to sit and stretch out, but these two were joined at the hip.

She also thought there was a bruise on Conroy's face. Maybe it was just grime, but Tess thought it was a bruise.

She unsnapped the strap to her holster and kept her right hand near her weapon.

"Out of the car. Now."

They complied. Conroy and the guy with him still joined at the hip. Guy's hand on his arm.

"License and registration?" The driver handed it to her. His name was Hogart, and the limo belonged to a leasing company in Phoenix.

"Have we broken any laws?" Hogart asked, after she came back from her cruiser, having run the plate.

"No, sir."

"Good. Then we'll be leaving."

Tess looked at the guy. Max Conroy, the movie star.

Whatever else this was, it was a lie. There was no Sally "uh, Dorman," she of the fictional baby and the fictional hospital.

Tess moved fast, pulling Max around and walking him to the back fender and shoving him down against it. Secured him with cuffs. "Anything in your pockets?" she demanded.

He shook his head. She patted him down, careful with the pockets, worried about needles. Movie stars had been known to shoot up.

"Hey, what is this?" yelled Hogart.

Tess ignored him and said to her prisoner, "You have the right to remain silent. Anything you say can and will be used against you in a court of law..."

"Look, this is a misunderstanding," Hogart said, coming close to invading her space.

She drew her weapon and held it by her side. "Back up. Place your hands on your head."

He complied. Quickly, automatically.

"On your knees."

He sank to his knees immediately. Either he had really good knees, or he was used to taking the position.

"This man is under arrest. *You* are free to go."

"What's he charged with?"

"Are you interfering with the lawful duties of a duly sworn sheriff's deputy?" she said.

He backed off, as she knew he would. The two men got back into the limo and drove away. By then, Tess had her prisoner in the backseat of her cruiser.

And she didn't know what to do with him.

"So you put him in jail," Pat said.

"Safest place I could think of."

"That place has more holes than the Alamo."

"Yeah, but I didn't think those guys were gonna come storming in."

"You know they'll be back."

"Not much I can do about it. At least I bought him some time."

"You have any idea what they wanted?"

"Nope."

"And Hogart?"

"No wants or warrants. Same with the other guy."

"License number?"

Here we go again, Tess thought. He never tired of the game. She reeled the plate number off.

"What did Hogart's license say?"

She rattled off the info on his driver's license: five foot nine, one sixty, brown and brown, restricted to corrective lenses, his domicile in Flagstaff. She gave him the address.

"Wish I could get you on *Jeopardy!* We could split the winnings. You run Hogart?"

She nodded. "Works for the Desert Oasis Healing Center in Sedona."

"*Healing* center? One of those fancy-dancy places where celebrities go for the cure?"

"Maybe Max didn't want to be there anymore."

"You think they'd try to make him stay?"

"I have no idea."

Chapter Six

The Desert Oasis Healing Center

GORDON WHITE EAGLE DIDN'T SPOOK EASILY. HE WAS A master at assessing people—that was his stock in trade. But *this* one, the twelve-year-old kid…

Scared him.

Maybe it was the eyes. They were predator's eyes, which didn't surprise Gordon at all, because the boy's mother was more wolf than human. Two nights ago, he'd dreamed about her, that he was trapped in a deep fissure in the earth, his body impossibly broken, and she was staring down at him behind dark glasses, her face impassive.

Gordon White Eagle paid attention to dreams.

Funny, but he couldn't remember, during his interactions with Shaun over the last three years, if she'd ever mentioned a kid. He'd always assumed she was childless.

He shrugged. She lived in LA, and had done only a few jobs for him. She kept her private life private. Maternity aside, she was here now. And he needed her.

First thing, he gave them the tour. Gordon took every opportunity to show the place off to his visitors, even though

Shaun had been there many times. But the boy, Jimmy, barely looked up from fiddling with his phone.

"Can't he stop texting for one minute?"

"He's not bothering anybody."

"He's bothering *me*. I don't want him texting his friends. This is a private conversation."

"He won't." She looked at Jimmy. "You won't text your friends about where we are or what we're doing. Do you get that?"

He nodded dismissively, still thumbing the phone like a virtuoso.

Gordon didn't trust him. He bent down from his six-foot-four height and put his hands on his knees. "How'd you like to go for a swim, young man? Danny here can fix you up." He nodded to their attendant, a burnished Adonis in white linen drawstring pants and huaraches.

Danny, an actor studying his lines for the part of an Australian cow farmer at the Clarkdale Dinner Theatre, was still in character. He said, "Off we go, *moyte*," and steered Jimmy toward the cabanas.

The kid taken care of, Gordon led the way to a table shielded from the sun by a royal palm. "As I told you, things have changed."

Shaun said nothing, just stared at the vista. And why not? It was a beautiful vista. Most of the Desert Oasis was tucked away along a stream, but there was one place—it took some walking to get to—that yielded a limited view of the Verde Valley. An infinity pool, like a plane of dark glass, mirrored the massive mountains above and delineated the sheer drop-off to the valley below.

Gordon said, "Our erstwhile friend has flown the coop. Taken a powder. Made tracks, so to speak."

Shaun stared impassively at him from behind her Dolce & Gabbana aviators. Gordon shivered despite the heat. She always made him nervous. "Apparently, he bribed one of the laundry crew to drive him out in his truck."

Shaun said nothing. There was no curiosity at all. He realized for the hundredth time that she was a beautiful woman but she left him cold.

She had perfect features. A model's cheekbones and a model's posture. But Gordon, who was naturally attracted to pretty much every woman on earth, no matter how dumpy or plain, shuddered at the thought of fucking this one.

It wasn't that she came off a bit mannish. It wasn't even that god-awful haircut, a man's haircut, what you'd call a "fade," clipped close to her skull.

No. Sex, no matter if it was with one of the maids from housekeeping or an alcoholic socialite or the hottest movie star in LA, was special to him. Performance art in the sweetest possible way. But he knew, with this woman, it would just be…mating.

Shaun finally spoke. "What did Max see?"

Gordon didn't know for sure if Max Conroy saw *anything*. And frankly, it was a side issue. The fact that he saw anything at all was only relevant to the fact that it might have spurred him to leave.

"So what did he see?" Shaun repeated.

"Nothing that important." It was just another problem in a string of problems Gordon had to deal with. And problems invited scrutiny.

"He might have seen a body," Gordon said at last.

Deedee Wertman, an inbred socialite from Montauk, had come out to Arizona to recover from a bad love affair. It was easy to see why she got dumped. She was fat, loud, and abrasive.

She was also headstrong. She insisted on going into the sweat lodge.

Thing was, Gordon had put a temporary moratorium on sweat lodges after the tragedy at another self-help place just up the road. The insurance costs were way too high. But Deedee Wertman kept at him, hectoring like a magpie. She wanted the sweat lodge experience. She'd *paid* for the sweat lodge experience. It said "sweat lodge experience" right in the brochure—was this a case of false advertising?

He should have refunded her money. He should have told her to go to hell and never darken his doorway again. But Gordon had too much on his mind, and so he relented. He'd instructed Mike, his sweat lodge man (during the interim, Mike had been relegated to gardening and landscaping duties) to keep the temperature down and provide plenty of air vents. He insisted Deedee drink ten glasses of water before going inside, and if she was in there for more than fifteen minutes he would pull her out personally.

Deedee Wertman was so excited at the prospect of the sweat lodge experience, she didn't watch where she was going. She tripped over a tree root at the entrance to the lodge and speared herself on the finial of one of the two waist-high ceremonial lamps outside.

Deedee Wertman bled to death before they could summon the paramedics.

So they didn't. Summon the paramedics.

In a panic, Gordon directed her to be taken to the storage room and put on ice.

This was a liability problem he just couldn't face right now. It was his sixtieth birthday, there was a big party planned, and there was the Other Thing.

The timing was impossible.

Fortunately, Deedee Wertman had virtually no friends and, better yet, was estranged from her family. She was childless and hadn't spoken to her only sister in twenty years. Deedee loved "adventures"—she globe-trotted around the world by herself, spending her inheritance down.

It was amazing what Gordon could learn through hypnosis. From what she'd told him, he figured that Deedee had only a hundred thousand or so dollars left, and he'd planned for her to spend most of it here.

The best-laid plans…

"So you think Conroy saw her?" Shaun said.

"Why else would he take off like that?"

"Because he hated it here?"

Gordon had to admit that was a possibility. Not everyone took to the Desert Oasis Way.

"You said he wasn't right in the head."

"He was royally fucked up, all right. I did a pretty good job of screwing with his psyche, not to toot my own horn. Kids, don't try this at home."

Shaun ignored this. "Where is the dead woman now?"

"Don't you worry about that."

"So what do you want me to do? Kill him?"

"No, I don't want you to kill him!" He leaned toward her, trying to keep the pleading tone out of his voice. *"You have to get him back here."*

Chapter Seven

FROM THE ALLEY BEHIND THE DINER, MAX MADE HIS WAY to the motel. The place seemed quiet, no cars in front of the units. Certainly no stretch limos. After ten minutes or so watching the Rat Motel from a shaded yard across the street, he realized that he couldn't go back to his room. That was the first place they'd look.

Instead, he walked a block over to the Subway/Short Hop Trucking Center. There, he bought stick deodorant, a $2.99 pair of pull-on shorts, sunglasses, a ball cap, and an extra large T-shirt with the words "Arizona: Rattlesnake Capital of the World" printed on the front. He took his purchases into the restroom and came out a new man.

After dining on a sub sandwich while sitting in the back booth with a good view of the doors, he went looking for a place to think. He needed a dark place, a busy place, an anonymous place. It just so happened Paradox had a game arcade for the disaffected youths who were forced to grow up here. He found himself a dark corner to play a video game while he tried to think about what to do next.

Jerry wasn't giving up. All Jerry wanted was to get Max back to the gulag so he could stumble through another vampire epic. To Jerry, Max was an ATM machine.

The thugs were over the top, but Jerry always did have a flair for the dramatic. Max felt a little embarrassed by the way he'd overreacted. It was pretty clear to him that Jerry'd sent guys to scare him into going back to LA, but it wasn't going to work. What were they going to do to him, really? Break his kneecaps? He was a valuable commodity. No way they'd hurt him. The limo, the guys in suits—that was all for show, to intimidate him into doing what they wanted.

For the first time in days, Max asked himself if starring in another vampire epic was such a bad thing.

He was the luckiest man on earth. He was married to one of the most beautiful women in Hollywood. In two weeks' time, Talia would come winging her way back from Africa with their adopted baby girl, just in time for the premiere of the next installment of the *V.A.M.Pyre Chronicles*. Their reunion on Piers Morgan's show would be Hulued and YouTubed and TMZed.

Lots of red meat here. The rekindled romance with his former/current wife, the new theatrical release, the sweet orphan baby girl from Africa. And Max's stint in rehab was the icing on the cake. It was all about redemption—the bad boy movie star brought to heel by true love.

Fans—especially female fans—loved to see the bad boy tamed.

Max suddenly asked himself, why was he being so stubborn? What was so bad about his life? He wasn't an impoverished tenant farmer in Appalachia. He wasn't a starving child in Bangladesh. He was a star, for Christ's sake. He was *lucky*.

Would it hurt to be just a little bit thankful for all his good fortune?

He could go back to his old life, no problem. In fact, he could start now, by walking across the street and plunking down some of his hard-earned cash at the Branding Iron. Go from one cave to another, but that cave would be soothing and have that cool, slightly dank smell of beer. Budweiser signs, quiet darkness, middle of the day.

He pictured an icy bottle of Rolling Rock. OK, they wouldn't have Rolling Rock in a backwater like this. Heinie, maybe. They'd have Heineken, wouldn't they? He could see the green bottle, the amber waves of grain, the droplets of sweat cold and crisp in his hand. He pictured pouring it into a bar glass, lifting it to his lips—

Suddenly, something punctured his insides. At the same moment, a tide of nausea rose in his throat. The something hard and sharp seemed to spin out of control like a circular saw, cutting through his body, the pain excruciating. For a moment, Max remained upright, then fell to his knees.

Had he been stabbed? Light and dark specks danced before his eyes. He couldn't really tell what was going on. Everything happened in slow motion.

No one came to help him. The kids either ignored him completely or came to stand over him, mouths open.

The pain began to subside. He felt himself all over—no blood, no wounds.

The kids stared at him as if he were an animal in a zoo.

He managed to get to his feet. Managed to walk out the door into the blinding sunlight. Sweat encased him like a second skin. His new shirt was wringing wet. He was light-headed and sour-mouthed, but the pain in his gut was gone.

His head ached. He looked down and saw a spatter of drool on his Arizona tee.

They'd told him he would never, ever, drink or use again. No alcohol, no more oxy. He'd scoffed at the notion. How could they be so sure? As time had gone on at the Desert Oasis Healing Center, Max had become certain of one thing: the day he got out, he would head straight for the nearest bar he could find.

But when the time came, he didn't. In fact, it wasn't until just this moment that he'd even contemplated taking a drink.

Whatever they did at the Desert Oasis Healing Center, it wasn't aversion therapy. He knew people who had been through aversion therapy—they made you drink alcohol along with a concoction that would make you sick. The Desert Oasis Healing Center was nothing like other rehab centers he'd been to, and if Max had to put into words what they did or how they did it, he would have been at a loss. The program had seemed, well…half-assed. As if it was thought up on the spur of the moment.

They did New Age-type stuff, like leaving him floating in a sensory deprivation tank for hours at a time. Or locking him in a room with no way to see, hear, or feel anything, gloves like oven mitts over his hands. (He was allowed to use the facilities, allowed to eat, even allowed to leave the room, but he never did.) The only thing all those hours and days of "restricted environmental stimulation therapy" did for him was give him a major case of lassitude.

Yet *something* about the rehab center must have worked. Now he'd been treated to a definitive demonstration why going out for a beer wasn't such a great idea. He felt weak, as if he'd run twenty miles. He sat on the edge of the boardwalk and closed his eyes, waiting for the dizziness to clear.

"Hey," someone said near his ear. "You OK?"

Max looked back and saw the motel clerk who'd checked him in last night, standing on the boardwalk behind him, holding a bag of candy from The Apothecary Candy Store next door.

"I'm fine," Max said.

"Don't look like it to me." The guy settled on the bench outside the candy store and dug into the sack. "Horehound. Want some? Might settle your stomach."

"No thanks."

"Hey, I know you."

Max closed his eyes. *Wait* for it...

"You're Max Conroy. That wasn't the name you registered with, but you can't fool me." Guy just kept chatting merrily away, about the horehound candy—get it? *Hore*hound, funny, huh?—and about how this was a one-horse town where even the horse left, and all the time the sun beat down on Max's head and he knew he was going into a blood sugar nosedive...

"Some guys were asking for you. I told them you checked out. Although technically, you didn't—check out, I mean. You owe me for the long distance call."

Just another hole in the old memory. Would he always be like this? "How much?"

"A dollar twenty-eight. You weren't on long."

Max reached into his jeans pocket. He heard the motel clerk shift on the bench, and when he looked back, the guy was scrutinizing him. "I was wondering all day why you looked familiar. When those guys came by, that clinched it. Max Conroy, that's who you are."

Max's stomach ached, and he just wanted to get out of here. "If I was Max Conroy, would I be sitting here on this plank in Paradox, Arizona, getting ready to pay a one-dollar phone bill?"

The guy considered. "Maybe. You shooting a film here? Is that what you're doing? Scouting? Don't want anybody to know on account of people getting in your face asking for autographs? Hey, are you going to film one of the *V.A.M.Pyre*s here? My niece, she's thirteen—man oh man, she's in love with *you*, brother."

"I'm not Max Conroy!"

"The guys looking for you thought you were."

"What? What did they say?"

"Don't bite my head off. I report, you decide, is all. They said they were looking for Max Conroy, the actor. I said you checked out and were long gone."

"Why'd you do that?"

"I wanted to mess with them, I guess. But I thought you'd be nicer."

Max pushed his palm against his forehead. "Thanks," he said. "Did you see them go?"

"As a matter of fact, I did. Saw 'em get on the on-ramp headed north."

"Good."

The motel clerk, who introduced himself as Luther James ("Jesse James was my great-great-great-great-great-uncle") said, "If you want to stay here for a while, you know, *incognito*, I can fix you up."

"What do you mean?"

"Well, first, you gotta change your look. See, you're too obvious. You look like Max Conroy after a really bad night."

Max was floating now, his blood sugar in the basement, everything taking on a surreal tinge. "Could you get me some juice?"

"What kind? Orange juice? Apple?"

"Doesn't matter."

Luther returned with a bottle of apple juice from the drugstore, and Max drank it down. The blurred edges around his vision began to firm up. He still didn't feel like moving, though.

Luther sat on the bench again. "See, the best way to change your look is to shave your head. Then people will see you completely different. They'll be looking at your head, not your face."

Max stood up. "Thanks for your help, but I've got everything under control."

"Sure you do." Luther laughed. "Tell you what. You want to get a feel for this town, make your character accurate, what you ought to do is work for a living."

"I do work for a living."

"That's not really working, now, is it? Way I hear it, it's mostly waiting around. Then you say a couple of lines, and you wait around some more. That's not real man's work."

Max worked plenty—two hours in the gym six days a week, the time spent memorizing lines and researching his character, the long days and nights on the set. Not to mention his *other* job—promoting his films, making personal appearances and cameos. You had to work full time just to keep your name and face out there, or people would forget. "What I do is work."

Luther waved at him. "Oh, sure, I didn't mean to insult you or nothing."

"Seriously. It's hard work."

"Yeah, I get you. All's I'm saying is you seem to be looking for more. Am I right?"

He *was* right, but Max still felt insulted.

"You ever work with your hands? I need someone to finish putting up the rain gutters on my house. It's monsoon season and it's my number-one priority. But I have this bad back." He leaned even farther forward and lowered his voice. "Tell you what. I'll let you stay there if you'll help me out. How about that?"

Max realized this was what he had been aiming for. All he'd wanted was to escape the pressure, escape the fishbowl, and go back to his life before he became a movie star.

For a moment there, he'd lost his way. For a moment, he'd gone back to being what he'd been before—an addict. He'd faltered. Max knew if he went back to LA, he would go right back to the drugs, the alcohol, just to survive. This was the last, best chance he'd ever have to transform himself.

"OK."

"Ha *ha*," Luther said, patting Max on the back. "I knew it! Tell you what. Let's go to my place, OK? Let's get you all taken care of, get you started on those gutters. Then we'll see what's what."

As they walked, Max became aware of a car tracking them. He thought about walking into the nearest store when Luther said under his breath, "Should've known."

A seventies-era Cadillac in mint condition pulled up beside them. A large man bounced out and opened his arms wide. "Luther, my boy! How are you faring?"

Luther stayed where he was and said, "I'm good, Unc."

"Motel receipts?"

"Up."

"Excellent! Give me a hug, boy, and introduce me to your friend."

Luther introduced his uncle as Sam P. Noon.

"Call me Sam P. That's what everyone calls me, son," he said.

Max looked from one to the other. Luther had long stringy hair. His uncle had long stringy hair. Luther was shaped like a pear. His uncle was shaped like a pear. Sam P. looked like one of those inflatable clowns you'd hit and they'd spring back at you.

Sam P. was looking at Max. His eyes narrowed. Then he smiled. "Luther, my boy, we've got to talk. Why don't you tell your handsome friend here you'll meet up later?"

Luther glanced at Max. "Go ahead over to the motel. I'll meet you there soon as I can."

* * *

MAX APPROACHED THE RAT MOTEL CAUTIOUSLY, FROM THE alley, and melted into the shade of the same tree he'd hidden under last time.

Good thing he did. The limo was back—parked outside the motel office, engine running, probably to keep the air conditioner on. A few moments later, his two former captors marched outside, clearly in a foul mood.

Seeing them walk out angry made Max feel better. He remained in shadow and watched as the limo turned the corner and accelerated away.

He was about to walk over when the sound of an engine starting up caught his attention.

A white truck was parked half a block up—a shiny new Chevy. The truck executed a U-turn and turned onto the street the limo had taken a few moments before.

Max hung back in the shade, his heart pounding.

He had the definite impression the white truck had been waiting for the limo. Were the people in the truck following the limo because they were looking for *him*?

Max wondered if he was getting just a little bit paranoid. *Better safe than sorry.* And so he waited.

And waited some more.

Finally, Luther drove up to the motel and Max walked across the street to meet him.

They drove out of town past a clutter of houses and businesses and up a dirt road between scruffy five-acre spreads to a place partially hidden by a fence of live bamboo. The white brick ranch could have belonged to the Rat Pack—if they'd been on a budget.

Luther opened the door to the house. "What do you think?"

He took in the sixties-era furniture arranged on a beaten-down white carpet.

"Nice," Max murmured, to be polite. Frigid air-conditioning blasted the sunken living room. Luther showed him the house. It didn't take long. Lots of white, lots of threadbare, lots of old.

"We can go out by the pool," Luther said, motioning to the yard beyond the floor-to-ceiling windows. "I have extra swim trunks, if you want to take a dip."

Max declined.

He was glad, though, to be outside that frigid house, even in July. They sat in the shade of the terrace. Luther asked him the usual questions. What was it like to be a rich, famous movie star?

Did he really have a Vincent Black Shadow motorcycle? (Yes.) And was it true it once belonged to James Dean? (No.) What was it like to sleep with a babe like Talia L'Apel? Were they really going to adopt a baby from Africa like it said in the tabloids? Wasn't he just in rehab? As the questions got more personal and prurient, Luther pulled a bottle of Coca-Cola from the antique vending machine and held it up. "Coke?" Max nodded. It looked like the original bottle, the heavy greenish glass shaped like a woman.

"Sure."

Luther turned away to open the bottle on the door and asked if Max ever had three-ways with Paris Hilton. With Lindsay Lohan? Were there ever guys? The questions were insulting, but he was used to that. Everybody thought his life belonged to them, and they could tell him how badly he was fucking up and give him all kinds of advice and ask rude questions. He hated that shit, but it was nothing unusual.

At least the Coke tasted good.

Luther disappeared inside the house and returned with a baking sheet of heated-over taquitos, the frozen kind, like Max's mother used to make. He realized he was ravenously hungry. He ate four or five in a row and tried to keep up with the conversation. Luther handed him another Coke. Max watched the ice lumps clinging to the bottle, watched them slide down and drip between his fingers. He thought about telling Luther he could mind his own fucking business, but forgot about it when he heard a loud voice say, "Freeze!"

It was as if someone had spoken forcefully in his ear. A man's voice, authoritative. But Max turned his head and no one was there. It was just the two of them here. He really was losing it.

"Max? You all right, buddy?"

Max focused on Luther, who was still proffering the cookie sheet. Luther's voice was bright and uncommonly loud.

"Why did you say that?" Max asked Luther.

"Say what?"

" 'Freeze.' Why'd you say it?"

Luther stared at Max, clearly puzzled. "I didn't say 'freeze.' Why would I say that?"

"I don't know," Max said, suddenly weary. It was probably another hallucination—this time an audible one.

"I didn't say 'freeze.' " Luther said again.

"OK."

Luther held out the cookie sheet. "Taquito?"

Max wanted to rip the smirk right off Luther's face, but he couldn't. He just sat there, the ice water tricking through his fingers. Feeling he was untethered from the earth—not an unusual sensation at all.

A little different this time, though.

And that was his last coherent thought.

* * *

"That clerk was lying," Hogart said to Riis as he gunned the limo out of the motel parking lot. "He was stonewalling us."

"How do you know?"

"I just do, that's all."

The radio crackled. It was Gordon White Eagle, telling them to quit Paradox and drive to the Sunset Point Rest Area.

"This is bullshit," Hogart said, taking the interstate going north. "He's still in Paradox. I can feel it." The actor had gone to ground like a scared rabbit, about what you'd expect from a guy who made his living pretending to be fictional characters.

The rest area at Sunset Point was closed, orange cones blocking the roads in and out; place looked like an abandoned prison camp.

"Arizona's so lame," Riis said. "You can't even find someplace to take a leak anymore."

"Gotta do it the old-fashioned way," observed Hogart. "Find a bush."

"Yeah, well, the wife don't like it. She's got to pee like every five minutes when we're on the road. Money's tight, and now we gotta go to a McDonald's or something, and it's getting so those kids at the counter are looking for people just coming in for the facilities. I'm sick of the dirty looks."

"Times we live in. Gordon said to keep your eye peeled for a new white Chevy truck."

"Every other car on the road is a new white Chevy truck."

"Well, there's no truck over there—the rest area's blocked off. I'm turning around. We've spent enough time on this—"

He didn't finish his thought, because a massive truck suddenly loomed up in his rearview.

"What the…?"

The white Chevy's giant grille hugged his bumper, even though they were going eighty-five.

What was the guy doing?

Hogart punched in Gordon's number. It went to voice mail. They were on their own. About a half mile before the next overpass, the Chevy's right flasher came on. Telling him to turn off.

Hogart's phone chimed—Gordon. "Is there a white Chevy truck behind you?"

"Yeah, and let me tell you—"

"Follow their instructions. This is the rendezvous I was telling you about."

The call terminated.

Hogart saw the exit up ahead. He looked over at Riis and saw his own fear reflected there. But he signaled and slowed for the exit, the Chevy's grille practically crawling up his ass.

Riis shot him a glance. "I don't think this is such a good idea."

"Orders."

"Yeah," Riis said at last. "What can you do?"

* * *

TESS McCRAE ATE HER LUNCH AT HOME. OTHER THAN arresting an honest-to-God movie star after an attempted kidnapping by two tough guys in a stretch limo (not the usual thing that happened in a town like Paradox) the place had reverted to business as usual. It was hot, and people kept to themselves. There were meth labs out in the desert she didn't know about. There were petty thefts and bad-tempered

people with hair triggers who would ward off anyone tres-
passing on their land with a rifle. But no calls came in. Bajada
County was quiet.

After lunch, Tess powered up her MacBook and did a
little research on Max Conroy. She looked at celebrity sites
like TMZ and Entertainment Tonight.

The articles on these sites were long on sensational-
ism and short on information. They regurgitated the same
themes: Max's bad boy ways; an unnamed source at Maxima
Entertainment speculating that Conroy might not make the
first day of shooting *V.A.M.Pyre: The Target*; a quote from
Max's publicist, Diane Scarafone, that he was busy from dawn
until dusk preparing for the part, and was in "the best shape
of his life." There were some candid shots. One purportedly
at the Desert Oasis Healing Center, taken with a telephoto
lens. It was blurry and showed a man from the back, diving
into a pool. There was another photo of a man who *could* be
Max Conroy at a dry-out clinic in Sonoma, California. The
irony that a dry-out clinic was smack in the middle of wine
country was not lost on her.

Max's publicist was quoted in several places, putting a
great spin on her client's prospects. This was a very exciting
time. Max and his wife, actress Talia L'Apel, would soon be
welcoming a baby girl from Nigeria.

But the driver of the limo, Hogart, worked for the Desert
Oasis Healing Center. This led her to believe that the Desert
Oasis wanted Max back in the fold.

She wondered why Conroy couldn't just walk out the
door, get into a limo of his own choosing, and fly back to
LA if he wanted to. Instead, the man was wandering around

like a derelict, waylaid by Hogart and Riis in broad daylight on a public street.

Which, in Tess's opinion, was unlawful imprisonment. Now she wished she'd detained the men in the limo.

She looked up the Desert Oasis Healing Center's website. It looked like a resort. She read some of the literature. There was plenty of language about treating addiction, and Sedona buzzwords like "guided vortex tours," "spiritual awakening," and something called "aura Polaroids."

Max did not seem crazy. He was articulate enough, even if he looked shabby. He seemed OK to her.

He must be staying here in town. There were three motels in Paradox. One of them was a rent-by-the-month affair, an old motor court called the Sunland. Tess called the Sunland and described Max to the proprietor. All his units were full and had been for a long time. She called the Riata and the Regal 8 up the freeway. The Regal 8, not surprisingly, wouldn't say either way—she expected that from a chain. Jan, who was working the desk at the Riata, said there was no record of anyone going by the name "Max Conroy" staying there.

He might have used an alias, but Tess supposed he'd just moved on. No doubt, he would crop up soon, probably on a late show being interviewed for the new movie, which was coming out two weeks after he started shooting the fourth *V.A.M.Pyre* in the series.

Still, she made two more calls. One to Max's publicist, Diane Scarafone in LA, and one to the Desert Oasis Healing Center. She got a voice message at the publicist's office, and an administrative assistant gave her a canned response at the Healing Center. They did not disclose the names of their clients. She asked to talk to the director, but was told he was "indisposed."

In the afternoon, as she patrolled the roads of Bajada County, Tess kept an eye out for Max, but didn't see him.

She'd done all she could.

Chapter Eight

GORDON WHITE EAGLE TIGHTENED HIS GRIP ON HIS PHONE, staring at the Verde Valley below. A massive jolt of adrenaline hurtled through every synapse and nerve. "You did *what*?"

"Don't worry, no one will find them."

Gordon had to hyperventilate before he was able to squeak out one word: "*Why*?"

"Because they were inept? Because they were greedy? You really get an idea what people are like when they're staring death in the face, Gordo. You know what that bald guy, Bogart, said?"

"Hogart," Gordon said automatically. He pressed the phone harder to his ear as he paced around and around the pool, oblivious to the searing sun. The headache lowering over his eyes like a thick black curtain.

"Hogart," said Shaun. "Good to know. Anyway, after he was done pleading, he tried to bribe us. He said we could take Conroy ourselves and hold him for ransom. He wanted to double-cross you."

"He wouldn't have said that if you hadn't threatened to kill him!"

"I don't threaten, Gordo."

Gordon gripped the phone tighter. His fingers were sweating and the cell was slippery in his hand. "This is not what I wanted. I told you to relieve them. I told you to send them back here and I'd pay them. What part of that didn't you get? The last thing I need is to draw attention to this... this, ah, *situation*. I've got a dead woman on ice and a rock star saying he can't write songs anymore because I cured his heroin habit and now he's going to *sue* me. That's the kind of crap I deal with on a daily basis, and now you just wantonly shoot two men in the head? For no sane reason I can see?"

"Calm down, Gordo, they're not gonna be found. This road is miles from anywhere, and the car's at the bottom of a slag heap. No one's going to see it."

Gordon knew, of course, that *someone* would find them. He only hoped it would be later rather than sooner—and would never be tracked back to him. "Why'd you kill them, Shaun? I don't understand. *Why?*"

"Why? Because they didn't deserve to live."

* * *

SHAUN LOOKED AT HER PHONE AND HIT END. GORDON WAS a hypocrite. She liked him—liked him as much as she liked anybody—but she knew he thought he was better than she was. He kept his hands clean. He didn't kill anyone. He once told her he was a moral person in an immoral world, and while he appreciated the struggle for the survival of the fittest, he chose not to participate.

He let others do that for him.

In the last three years of their "association"—that's what Gordo called it—she'd been contracted for two hits. Gordo liked to talk about morality, but he was just as corrupt as his father had been. Her granddad had been Gordon's father's closest friend, and it was common knowledge that the high and mighty Eli Gould wasn't just a successful businessman—he did business with the mob. In fact, he couldn't get enough of mobsters, inviting them to his house for parties with the movie stars. Her dad said Eli was starstruck by Carmen Fratiano. He even tried to interest Gordon in Fratiano's niece.

And Gordo sure called her quickly enough when he got himself in trouble. He'd say he "had a situation" that needed taking care of, in that prissy little way he had. Gordo could intimidate movie stars and rock stars, but there were some situations he couldn't deal with on his own. And that's where she came in.

Gordo's favorite expression—in fact, he'd had it engraved on the wall in the Palm Garden at the Desert Oasis—was "denial ain't just a river in Egypt." You'd think once in a while he'd read what he put on his own wall. He seemed to think that sticking his fingers in his ears and chanting "Lalalalala" would absolve him from responsibility for the people she intimidated, beat up, or killed.

Gordo's younger brother, Jerry Gold (Jerry had officially changed his name from "Gould" to "Gold" because "Gold sounded richer"), was even more of a wuss. The two of them had zero qualms about killing someone if it helped their bottom line, but they treated the whole transaction like genteel ladies sipping tea.

They lived in a dreamworld.

Shaun looked at the doorway to the abandoned mining building. Jimmy was just inside, the sunlight spotting him against the deeper shadow. His clothing was streaked and clotted with blood. He was working on something, cutting away at the sun-pinked corpse.

Then he held his hand up and gave a rebel yell.

Riis's scalp.

Shaun understood the rush, the feeling of triumph with your first kill. To know that you could cross that line—and easily—made you special. She had sensed that in Jimmy when she first met him. That knowledge had ripened in the weeks after Jimmy agreed to become her son. He was impatient, but he had to be schooled first.

Today she'd finally let him experience his first kill: she let him have Riis.

She smiled at the way her boy had listened to Riis's pleas and appeared to consider them. He knew what was required, and deflected pity. Actually, Shaun suspected Jimmy didn't have pity.

To his credit, he did not toy with Riis. He did not tease him. He listened, he considered, giving great weight to Riis's pleas…and then he shot him twice, a clean shot through the eye and a follow-up shot to the chest.

Bang bang.

Look at him now, holding up the scalp!

This would be the first and last time Jimmy would be allowed to celebrate in the end zone. The whole point was to divorce yourself from emotion, good or bad. Do your job. Take pride in it, but carry out your assignment in a workman-like, efficient manner. Don't get too involved, because that is how even the good ones get tripped up. She'd learned all this, and she would teach Jimmy.

It made her proud to know she was not only a mom, but a teacher.

"OK," she called out. "Time to get rid of them."

Jimmy stared at her. He had the scalp on his head. Blood was dripping over his eyes and onto his nose.

"Don't be such a clown," she shouted.

He removed the scalp and bowed deeply, with a flourish of hair and blood. "Ta-daaaa!"

Like the magician they saw in San Francisco.

Cocky.

She could have debriefed Hogart and Riis and sent them on their way to screw up another day. But there had been pressure. Recently, Jimmy had begun to withhold his affection.

All he could think of was his first hit. Shaun had told him to wait, to be patient, hoping he would learn discipline, but now she wondered if her decision to let him kill Riis might have been too much, too soon. It worried her. *Their bond could not be broken.* Which might have been the reason she let him have his way today.

Was she an overindulgent mother?

She hoped her decision to let Jimmy kill Riis wouldn't turn out to be a big lapse in judgment.

Chapter Nine

TESS WAS DRIVING BACK TO THE SHERIFF'S OFFICE WHEN SHE saw the woman and the boy.

She'd answered a burglary call out in Two Points, a wildcat development of manufactured homes in the desert flats south of Paradox, and had come back by way of County Route 9, which turned into Third Street. When Tess rolled to a halt at the stop sign at Third and Yucca, she noticed the "For Sale" sign up at Joe's Auto-Wash.

She constantly scanned her surroundings. That was part of her job: to look for trouble. Tess was always on the alert for any kind of anomaly, anything out of place.

She spotted a woman, a boy, and a new white truck in one of the bays at Joe's.

The boy was using the spray gun to reach the top of the truck and the woman was scrubbing the wheel wells.

The woman, whose back was to Tess, stiffened. She straightened up slowly and turned to look in Tess's direction. For a moment, Tess thought she'd been mistaken—was it a man? No, a woman.

The woman gave her a long look and then turned away—a casual move that was anything but—and went back to work. But Tess could sense the woman was aware that she hadn't driven on. Tess could imagine the woman sending feelers out into the air. Silly, but she didn't dismiss it because so much of police work depended on instinct. Instinct had saved her life on more than one occasion.

The strange thing was, the woman looked like a cop. She was clothed the way a male undercover cop would dress: she wore a knit polo shirt loose over the hips, jeans, and good athletic shoes. When the woman turned away, Tess saw the outline of a weapon on her hip, under the shirt.

The truck was brand new. Tess memorized the temporary Arizona license sticker in the back window of the truck, then drove on, circling the block. She came back up the other street—Yucca. Now she could see the inside of the car wash bay from the other side. Everything was silhouetted against the hot glare of the sun, but Tess could see that the woman was standing in front of the truck now, watching as she drove past.

Tess felt a jolt to her heart. Pure adrenaline, laced with fear.

Something about that woman, the way she watched Tess drive by. It made Tess feel as if she'd dodged a bullet. When she reached the next stop sign, she realized her legs were shaking.

* * *

BACK AT THE SHERIFF'S OFFICE, TESS RAN THE WHITE TRUCK'S temporary license number. The truck was new off the lot at Talbot's Chevrolet in Clarkdale, Arizona. It had been sold to a Sedona company called "Sandstone Adventures."

Tess spent the next twenty minutes trying to run down Sandstone Adventures, but after checking several business directories, she found no such company. She called a friend of hers who ran a jeep tour out of Sedona.

"Sandstone Adventures? Never heard of them."

"Are you sure?"

"I know every company in this town. I have to—they're the competition."

"Thanks," she said.

She called the dealership that sold the truck and asked to talk to the salesman. He was reluctant to divulge any information about a customer at first, but at last, he told her that the buyer wanted the truck for a company.

"What did he look like?" Tess asked.

"It was a she."

"Did she look like a man?"

"Are you kidding? She was a real looker. Long blonde hair, pretty rich looking."

Could that be the same woman? The one who clearly enjoyed looking like a man?

Tess knew what Pat would say: nothing there.

But he hadn't seen her in the flesh.

"Anything else you can tell me about the woman?"

"She had a kid with her."

Tess's pulse quickened. "How old?"

"I dunno. Eleven, twelve, maybe? Kid had a yo-yo. About drove me nuts. A distraction, you know?"

It was her.

By now, the woman and boy were probably long gone. Why would they stay in Paradox? Tess would keep an eye out for them, sure, but she wouldn't go looking. She'd have no reason to pull them over. They had not broken any law as far as she could tell.

Tess realized she was relieved.

Chapter Ten

Ten Minutes to Midnight

THE COYOTES ON THE BAJADA WERE YIPPING AGAIN. No
matter how often Sheriff Thaddeus "Bonny" Bonneville heard
them, their manic, high-pitched shrieks set his teeth on edge.
Been that way since he was a kid.

His coon dog, Ed, was waiting for Bonny to get up and
walk down the hall to bed, but Bonny wasn't ready yet.

Bonny thought about Bajada County's one detective, Pat
Kerney, and the deputy. They worked well together. If you
didn't know any better, you'd think Bajada County had two
detectives instead of one.

Bonny was surprised that Pat actually appreciated Tess
McCrae's help. Even a year ago, that would not have been
the case. Although Pat was pugnacious as ever, Bonny had
a strong feeling that his mind wasn't on business anymore.
Bonny thought he knew why. Pat's priorities had changed.

Bonny, himself a widower, knew plenty of friends who'd
lost their wives. Most of them wanted to get married again,
and usually did so within a year. They liked being married
so much they wanted to repeat the experience. In Pat's case,
his wife didn't hadn't died. She'd left him. But damned if old

Pat wasn't desperate to get himself back into holy matrimony as soon as possible. He'd courted just about every woman in town, including the new deputy.

Tess McCrae had put paid to that in a hurry. Rare ability, to shoot a guy down and be able to work with him the next day.

Ed whined, then lay down on the floor, inconvenienced but patient.

"In a minute," Bonny said to the old dog. He punched in the home number for Harry McCrae, a sergeant with Las Cruces PD in New Mexico. Harry answered on the first ring.

"How's my niece working out?" Harry McCrae asked.

"Oh, she's fine," Bonny said. "Remind me again what happened in Albuquerque?"

"Not much to tell. She found her husband in bed with a young woman and got mad, is all."

"Way I heard it she trained her gun on them."

"That's what she testified to."

Bonny was silent.

"She's not like that," Harry said.

"I know." "Hair-trigger" wasn't a term Bonny would use for his star deputy. He didn't even know why he was bringing it up. He and Harry'd had the selfsame conversation when he'd thought about hiring her eight months ago. "She threw the gun out the window?"

"It hit the window and cracked the glass."

"Misfired, as I recall."

"Nobody was hurt."

"Still."

"What is it you're getting at, Bonny? You regretting bringing her on board?"

"No, that's not it." Might as well give it voice. "I'm thinking of making her detective tomorrow. Am I doing the right thing?"

No hesitation at all: "If you have the good sense God gave a goose, you'll do it."

Chapter Eleven

MAX AWOKE IN THE MIDDLE OF A CONVERSATION. IT TOOK him a moment to realize the conversation was not in his head, but nearby.

His head ached. He wanted to sit up but was afraid if he did, he'd vomit. So he lay there like an aching tooth, eyes squeezed shut. The conversation went on in his head, or around his head, or a few feet away.

"Look, Corey, I said we'd split it three ways. What more do you want?"

Max recognized the voice. Luther, the motel clerk. His host.

"Just sayin', it don't work out, who's gonna be takin' out the trash?"

"There's no risk. It's not like he's some bum we picked up off the street. They'll pay through the nose to get him back."

"I'm the one'd be taking the risk. More risk, more remuneration is all. I can't see you doin' it. I'm the guy who risked my ass in Tikrit."

"And I appreciate that, I really do. But we're splitting it three ways. That's only fair. Wait a minute."

Max heard a scrape, the sound of boots on concrete. The air stirred above him, vile breath in his face. "You awake, Max?"

"He's waking *up*?"

"Max, you awake, buddy?"

Play dead.

"You're not fooling me," Luther said. He dashed some cold water on Max's face.

Max opened his eyes. It hurt to open them. Luther's face loomed like a Macy's Thanksgiving Day balloon, and his breath smelled like the lining of a birdcage.

Max squeezed his eyes shut against the pain. Dizziness followed. He was in a vortex, spiraling down inside the blackness.

After what might have been minutes—or it might have been hours—he was awake again.

"Maxie, oh, *Max*ie! Wakey *up*py."

Max opened one eye.

"That Coca-Cola has one hell of a kick, doesn't it, man?" Luther said sympathetically.

"What was in it?" Max said, realizing his voice was slurred.

"Rohypnol." Luther went out of Max's line of vision and came back with a wet rag. "Look at all this puke! Can't take you anywhere, I swear." But his tone was merry.

"What's going on?"

"You've been kidnapped."

"I was, um…" Wished he could talk better. Wished he had better vision too. Something was wrong, spatially. Objects in relation to one another were larger or smaller than they appeared. Like Luther's giant moon face, floating in and out of his airspace.

"Don't worry, be happy," Luther said, squeezing the rag into a bucket on the concrete floor. "This should all be over in a wink. No harm done."

"The vomit?"

"No. The kidnapping. You'll be snug as a bug in your bed with the lovely Talia before you know it." Then he climbed up the fixed ladder on the wall, knocked on the ceiling, and disappeared through a trapdoor.

Max stared at the ceiling where Luther had disappeared, wondering if he was still dreaming. It felt like a dream—surreal.

He had to shake this. Had to get his mind back, now. If he really had been kidnapped, he should figure out a way to get out of here. He concentrated his gaze on one object after another until they began to make sense, like pieces of a jigsaw puzzle filling in.

The room was claustrophobic. Faded turquoise walls curved like the insides of a culvert. Max was lying under an army blanket on a cot. Nearby, a bottle of water and some Lunchables sat on a card table. A large pipe snaked along one wall, ending in an ancient metal box. He noticed that the trapdoor in the ceiling once had a handle, but it had been sheered clean off.

He was in a bomb shelter.

* * *

HALF AN HOUR LATER, MAX WAS STILL A LITTLE UNSTEADY on his feet, but he made it up the steel ladder to test the door.

He pushed hard, then pounded on it with a fist. Felt around to see if there was a secret catch, but the whole thing was out in the open—no frills. With the handle stripped off, there didn't appear to be a way out. They must have fixed it so it would lock from above. Even if he overpowered Luther, Luther had to have someone above to open the trapdoor.

Which meant there had to be at least two people guarding him. Luther, and the other guy, Corey.

Max wasn't worried about his own ability to overpower Luther. Flabby and uncoordinated, Luther would be no match for a man who worked out six days a week and rode a motorcycle to unwind. Max had been schooled in the martial arts, firearms, and hand-to-hand combat.

So, yes, Max could incapacitate Luther. He could hold him hostage. But would that be a game changer? What would Corey do if Max took Luther hostage? Max remembered the conversation between Corey and Luther. Corey was a former soldier. He would likely have no compunction about killing Max.

Or, he might just bolt, leaving both of them in this fallout shelter to die of thirst and starvation.

The key was to get them to take him out of here.

He was tired. He sat down on the cot and stared at his feet, willing the otherworldly feeling he'd had for so long to go away. Had to get the Rohypnol out of his system. He opened the bottle of water and downed most of it, along with half the Lunchables.

And felt better immediately. Clearer in his head. The proposition that he might be buried forever in a bomb shelter concentrated his mind.

Max needed to center himself. He went over what had happened to him in the last few weeks. He remembered the day in Jerry's office at CCM when he got the ultimatum, and the argument that followed. He'd been hustled down to the garage, bundled into an Escalade, and driven to a jet on the tarmac at LAX. Remembered the private airstrip in Arizona, the jovial kid with an Australian accent who'd greeted him. The ride in the stretch Hummer to the Desert Oasis Healing Center.

The Desert Oasis Healing Center was like 1940s Morocco. In the healing center's restaurant, *Casablanca*'s "As Time Goes By" was piped in from hidden speakers. The waiters wore fezzes, and cabana boys waved palm fans over the swim-up bar. Unfortunately, the bar didn't serve alcohol.

Great food, beautiful people, clean and courteous attendants. The Desert Oasis offered the usual rehab fare—the one-on-one counseling, the support group meetings, and seminars. The seminars lasted for hours. That was the worst, because they wouldn't let anyone leave their seats to pee. They had to wait for certain breaks, and the bathrooms had only four urinals and a lot of desperate people—he'd seen one man who hadn't made it. Ashamed and angry, the man sat down on the sidewalk and cried.

But not Max. He held it. He even joked about it. Now, he said, he knew how women felt at concerts.

The seminars were ongoing. Not rigorous, pretty much standard, except for the denied bathroom privileges.

Still.

Max had been unaffected by his previous two stints in rehab, but this one…

Something had happened to him. It was there beneath his conscious mind, like an underground stream. Moments of terror. His vision obscured by dots of light, especially when he awoke in the mornings. He suffered from vivid hallucinations. Sometimes the man in the rowboat, sometimes snarling wolves intent on ripping him to pieces, sometimes an evil knight on a big horse, swinging a mace. And sometimes just blackness and a feeling of doom. Fortunately, the hallucinations were fading. The more he walked the earth in the real world, the more they receded. But he sensed they were just around some corner of his mind, waiting to jump out at him.

It occurred to him now, imprisoned in this underground chamber, that whatever it was had been *implanted* in him. Into his brain. Hypnosis, maybe. The confusion, the holes in his memory, the unreasoning fear, the desire to climb to the highest place he could find and throw himself to his death.

And Max himself had walked right into this. He could have flown back to LA. He could have confronted Jerry. He could have divorced Talia and called off the adoption. It had all been keeping up with the Joneses, anyway, a photo op for Talia. The baby was probably better off in Africa.

If he'd done any of these things, the world wouldn't have come to an end. But instead, he'd hitchhiked down the freeway and buried his wallet somewhere in the desert.

He'd done stupid things, all to avoid his own pain. An impossible task, since whatever happened to him remained unfathomable.

At least now, he had something physical to fight. He had an opponent to outwit.

For the first time in years, Max got mad.

Really, really mad.

Chapter Twelve

A COUPLE OF HOURS LATER, THE DOOR TO THE BOMB shelter opened and Luther climbed down, his movements ponderous and timid.

Max sat up on his cot and watched him.

Once on solid ground, Luther bounded toward him. "How's it goin', bro?"

"I'm OK."

"Excellent! I see you've partaken of the repast we left you." Luther pulled up one of the folding chairs and sat in front of Max, their knees almost touching. "Thought you'd want to know how all this is going down."

"I'm all ears."

"We're going to need your wife's phone number."

Max didn't react.

"And we're going to want you to talk to her. If you could tell her we have you at an undisclosed location, and all we want is two million dollars, and we'll return you safe and sound—that would be marvelous. You think you can manage that?"

"No."

"No? Wrong answer. What if I put a gun to your head? How'd you feel about *that*?"

Max shrugged.

"Because we mean business. This is not a game. You are in a bomb shelter. We could seal it up and nobody'd ever be the wiser. You'd die alone. I hear starvation is a terrible way to die. No one would ever know where you went. Depend on that! So if you want to go back to your movie star life, your beautiful wife, you need to cooperate. You do see that, don't you?"

Max stared Luther in the eye until Luther's good eye wandered.

Luther cleared his throat. "Well?"

"Call her yourself."

"But you'd have to talk to her! She'd have to know it was you."

Max crossed his legs. "I'll give you her phone number, but I'm not talking."

"Why not?"

"That's the deal."

"All right, all right. Give me the number."

Max did.

Luther leaped to his feet—amazingly quick for a plump man. He pulled out his phone and snapped a picture. "Didn't think of that, did you?"

Max stretched out on the cot and closed his eyes. "Honestly? I would have been disappointed in you if you didn't."

* * *

TEN MINUTES LATER THE TRAPDOOR OPENED AND LUTHER came back down the steps.

"How'd it go?" Max asked.

Luther's face looked pastier than usual, and he had that thousand-yard stare screenwriters were always putting into their screen directions. He sat on the edge of Max's cot, his chest sinking into his stomach like a collapsed balloon.

"You reached her?" Max asked.

Luther nodded.

"So what did she say?"

Luther stared at his hands. "She said, and I quote, 'You can keep him.' And then she hung up."

Max pursed his lips and blew out a breath. "I was afraid of that."

"What do you mean?"

"It's a long story."

"Well *tell* me! This is a business transaction I'm trying to do here."

"It starts out like any other story. Boy meets girl. They fall in love, they marry—"

"Would you please *cut to the chase*?"

"OK. She hates me."

"That's not what I read in the tabloids. I did my homework, you know. Say, I know what you did. You have a phone I don't know about and told her what to say. Is that it? Do you think this is a game?"

"No game. She hates me."

"Look, I told you, I know the whole story. I know about your first divorce. I know you remarried—I read it in *Vanity Fair*. This time you had a new appreciation for each other, a deeper love…"

"Crap. We were both forced to go to the same wedding as friends of the bride and groom, did too much oxy, had a one-night stand, thought it would be a lark to go to Vegas and get remarried, and woke up the next day with a hangover and a marriage neither of us wanted."

"But I don't understand…why didn't you just get an annulment?"

"*V.A.M.Pyre* was coming out the following week."

"The movie?"

"Yes, the movie. Jerry suggested we wait."

"Jerry?"

"My manager."

"And you actually did?"

Max rubbed his eyes. "There never was a right time. My film release, her film release, the Golden Globes, the Academy Awards, the Haiti relief trip, *The View*. There was never a moment when we could stop. The story was too good. The mags were calling it 'a second chance at love.' Talia's built her whole career on being the fresh-faced girl next door. If we divorced, I'd get the blame. I'd be the bad guy. I'd be headed straight for Mel Gibson territory." He smiled at Luther—his patented ironic smile. He felt that smile down to the soles of his shoes. "So now you see what you did? You solved the problem for her. She'll make a beautiful widow."

"This is Talia L'Apel we're talking about. She wouldn't do that."

"Remind me what she said again?"

"Unbelievable." Luther put his head in his hands.

"Imagine how *I* feel."

"But surely she wouldn't want you to die of starvation in this hole! She's America's Sweetheart!"

"How's anyone gonna know?"

Luther hopped to his feet. "Just wait. Just you *wait*. I've got something to do, but I'll be back soon."

"I'm not going anywhere."

∗ ∗ ∗

"ARE YOU OUT OF YOUR MIND?" JERRY GOLD YELLED.

He'd been storyboarding when Talia had called him into the kitchen to tell him her news. She'd told the kidnappers to go to hell in no uncertain terms. If they were lucky, she said, Max was being executed as they spoke.

He repeated, "Are you out of your mind?"

She gave him her best innocent look, which really *was* amazing.

Talia L'Apel was the sexiest woman on the planet, did things to him in bed you couldn't even imagine. But she had the instincts of a small-potatoes con. He understood that, and accepted it, because he was madly in love with her, but her intellect…

What she lacked in innate intelligence she made up for in luck. Take her name, for instance. Talia's real name was Talia Lipowitz. That could have actually worked, in this day and age. Look at Kim Kardashian. But starting out, she'd wanted a romantic name. One day, before she was even on the radar as a star (this was during her first marriage to Max Conroy), they were in a shop looking at women's suits for a bit part in a film, and the salesgirl pointed out the lapel, saying it "really makes the garment." And Talia got that shine in her eye. "Lapel," she breathed, stroking the suit. "That's French, isn't it?"

Jerry tried to talk her out of it. He thought she'd be a laughingstock. But Talia was not only stupid, she was stubborn. (Not to mention heartbreakingly beautiful.)

And so Talia Lipowitz became Talia L'Apel, and lo and behold, people ate it up. Turned out that Talia was smarter about this kind of thing than he was. He'd overestimated the intelligence of Talia's public, and it was then he decided to take dumbing-down lessons from her at every opportunity.

Jerry balked at carrying her Yorkie, but otherwise, he deferred to her streetwise cunning and manufactured just-off-a-turnip-truck innocence.

Except for now.

This time she was flat-out wrong. "You're going to screw up everything! What about your baby from Africa? What about your reunion?"

"What about it? As far as I'm concerned, it's less work I have to do. I don't have to pretend anymore."

"Less work? Is that how you see it?"

"I don't know why you're looking at me like that. I thought you wanted something like this to happen. Now we don't have to work so hard, don't you see?"

Dammit. How in God's name had this shitstorm happened to *him*?

Chapter Thirteen

NOT LONG AFTER LUTHER LEFT MAX, THE TRAPDOOR opened again. Luther made his way down, followed by Corey, followed by Luther's uncle, Sam P., who stepped delicately for a huge man.

Corey carried a tripod and a small video camera. Black material swung from his belt—Max realized they were ski masks. The ski masks went with the scimitar in Sam P.'s hand.

"Really?" Max said. He lay on his cot, legs crossed at his feet, hands clasped behind his head.

"Get up, asshole," Corey said. "It's time for your close-up."

Max obliged. He was calm now, as if he were in the eye of a hurricane, and the hurricane was his own rage. The rage would be easy to tap, but he could control it. "Where's my mark?"

"Knock it off, jerko," Corey said. "Do what you're told and everything's going to turn out fine. Otherwise…" He made a slashing motion to his throat.

"You really think a video will change Talia's mind?"

They ignored him as they set up the tripod facing the wall. The lighting here was not the best, but Max thought it would only enhance the terror of the scene. "May I make a suggestion?"

Sam P., who was about to don his mask, said, "Certainly, sir."

"Guess he wants us to shoot his *good* side," Corey said.

Max said, "Who are you supposed to be? Rabid Islamists? Because if you're going the scary Islamist route, you're setting up a certain expectation."

"Everyone's a critic," muttered Luther.

Max shrugged. "If you're going to do this, don't you want to do it right?"

Corey grumbled, but Sam P. said, "Let's hear what the man has to say. He's been around the block a few times, after all."

"If you want to scare them, fine. But what's the endgame? They have to believe you're real kidnappers who want money, not Sharia law and death to infidels. If you pose like that and threaten to behead me, they'll think that sending you money won't buy anything, because you're extremists who will kill me anyway. See what I mean?"

Sam P. looked at Luther and Luther looked back. "He's got a point."

"This is ridiculous," said Corey. "He's snowing us, man! He's playing with our heads."

Max said, "Look. Don't you think I want to make it out of here alive? Don't you think I have a stake in this?" He looked from one to another to another. It was his sincere look, the look he had when he was about to a) go to war, b) stand up to the bad guy or c) kiss a woman who needed kissing. He let his eyes bank like coals, smoldering with meaning. With belief.

Sam P. sat down on a folding chair. Amazing it could hold him. "So what do you propose we do?" he asked.

"You go simple, no frills. Just sit me on a chair and videotape me. Ask me a couple of questions. Just straight-forward stuff—it will be chilling, trust me. Because it will be believable."

Sam P. thought about it, then slapped his thigh. "Sounds good."

Max saw Corey's face fall. Corey had wanted to wear the mask.

"Another thing," Max said. "Are you sending this just to Talia?"

Luther looked diffident. "That was the plan."

"Because here's what she'll do. She'll erase it. Just wipe it right off her phone—boom, like it never existed."

Luther looked at Sam P. and Sam P. looked at Corey. They all looked at Max.

The center of power had shifted. Max was in control now. "See, what you've got to do—when the time comes—is go viral. That way she's forced into meeting your demands. America's Sweetheart isn't going to stand by while her husband is killed by kidnappers, not with TMZ on the case. Not with *Entertainment Tonight*, and *The Huffington Post*, the cable shows, the bloggers, the tabloids, YouTube—she can't ignore you then."

Absolute silence. Then Sam P. said, "Dammit! Why didn't *I* think of that? Max, I bow to your expertise."

Corey muttered something unintelligible under his breath.

"OK, first thing we have to do is make it look like you've hit me."

"*Hit* you?" Sam P. recoiled in horror.

"You have ketchup?"

"I think so."

"Go get it. And if you have any charcoal, or something to make me look bruised up a little, get that too."

Sam P. said to Corey, without looking at him, "Do what the man said."

Corey grumbled, but went.

And so they did it. Max sitting in a chair. Dim lighting, but just the right kind of lighting to show it was, indeed, Max Conroy. Max looked stunned but brave. He had to keep in mind that he was a leading man, so he maintained that strong, manly presence, even though he was tied to a chair. He played the part of the weary hero who had fought bravely against his attackers but succumbed to overwhelming odds.

He finished up with the thousand-yard stare.

A hundred screenwriters can't be wrong.

II: ICONOCLAST

Chapter Fourteen

AFTER THE CALL, JERRY WENT INTO HIS STUDY. TALIA
followed, but he motioned her out and closed the door. He
needed to think.

Normally a showplace, the room's walls had been papered
with 8 ½" x 11" sheets of paper. Four rows of them, taped
up all the way around, even over the French doors looking
out on the pool. He could have taken them down days ago,
should have taken them down, but for some reason he liked
looking at them. They reminded him of the early years, when
he was just another spoke in the film industry's wheel, a lowly
screenwriter-turned-indie-prod, long before he became Max's
business manager.

It had been fun, getting back to basics. Planning and
scheming, working out how it would look—the tracking cam,
the extra-long shot, the two-shot, the extreme close-up. Most
of it was unnecessary—this wasn't a film project. Most of the
story would stay on the cutting room floor. But he realized
he'd gotten…lost. Lost in the work. Reminded himself what
it had been like as a young man, a starving artist. When he
was *creative*.

Another great thing about working on this project—he
could shut out Talia's whining. She'd become increasingly

strident as days went by. He understood it. The waiting had been difficult. She was worried, frightened that it wouldn't work out. But her voice had a knife's edge at times he just had to avoid. So he came in here and storyboarded.

The scenario Jerry and his brother Gordon had chosen for Max's death would have looked great on a computer, but there could be no computer. There would be no paper trail. Paper could be destroyed, but a computer's memory had a way of staying around forever.

One more week, he'd thought, and they would have been home free.

Jerry'd had rotator cuff surgery once. They'd scheduled the surgery and he had burned up daylight just waiting. Waiting to get started, waiting to go through with the damn thing, just hoping to get out fine on the other side and start *living* again. That's what it had been like, even though the stakes now were much higher. He wanted it done already.

And now, suddenly, everything was out of their hands.

A timid knock on the door—Talia. She knew she'd annoyed him. Knew he was upset.

"Come in."

Her eyes looked bruised. Had she been crying? Or faking? You could never tell with Talia.

She slipped her arms around his waist. "I'm sorry. I should have let you handle it. Is it going to be OK?"

He pulled away from her, went to stand before the fourth scenario. The one they'd planned. Now, after all the foresight, the risk-taking—they'd even killed a world-famous forensic expert—it might well be that the plan had been smothered in its crib.

"They'll call back, won't they?"

"Probably."

She said, "I still don't see why we can't just let *them* do it."

He stared at his storyboards. The forensic specialist, Dr. DePaulentis—what the man had done was spectacular! He'd kept it as simple as possible. The fourth scenario. No drug cartels, no terrorist gangs, no spectacular plane crashes, just…a lone bad guy. Jerry'd initially wanted a prison escapee but Gordon had pointed out that wouldn't work. A prison escapee would have to break out of a real prison, and it would be on the news if that happened.

So it was back to a chance encounter with a bad guy. Simple. No frills, but planned down to the exact detail.

A reconstructed crime scene, clues and all.

He stared past the sheets of paper at the glimmer of the pool, the fountain, the royal palms beyond. It had been fool-proof until Max escaped from the Desert Oasis. Elegant—a thing of beauty. He turned to Talia. "Now our fate is in the hands of strangers."

"But that's better, don't you see? Then there's no involve-ment on our part. No one could ever connect—"

"Have you ever played high-stakes poker?"

She looked at him. Clueless.

"What if they *do* kill him? What would that look like? A bruised, broken body dumped by the side of a road? Have you seen gunshot wounds? It's not a pretty picture. Maybe they leave him out somewhere to be eaten by predators. Or what if he's still alive? What if they send us a video? Can you picture it? He's beaten up, terrified, practically peeing in his pants. Max Conroy reduced to a mewling baby. They might slap him around. Tell him to say ridiculous things, plead for his life. What if it goes on YouTube?" He stepped toward her, his anger building. "How do you think *that* would look? It would look like seventy million dollars going straight down the drain!"

He walked to one wall and ripped down a piece of paper and held it up. "There goes the graphic novel!" He crumpled it and threw it down. Another piece. "The action figure!" Another. "The Max Conroy Memorial Limited Edition Vincent Black Shadow motorcycle!"

More sheets—ripped, crumpled, wadded-up balls of paper raining down on the Aubusson carpet. MacMillan's whiskey—he'd envisioned a series of ads profiling Max's bravery as a doomed, real-life hero. The suite of men's hair and body products. The T-shirts, the posters, the hats, the phone apps, the Maxphone, the movie, the book, the Wheaties box.

Any time a photographer, writer, TV personality, or news source profiled Max Conroy, *any* time his image was used, a little angel got its wings.

"Marilyn Monroe's estate is estimated at over a hundred million dollars! Michael Jackson's made over one billion dollars since he died. His estate is pulling in one hundred and seventy million dollars *this year*. Think about what it would be like to license a Michael Jackson, a James Dean, the next Elvis Presley! Do you have *any idea of the stakes*?"

Finally, he couldn't go on. Like a tired horse, he just stood there, his breath coming in ragged gasps.

Talia stared at him, shocked. He was sure, this time, she really was feeling what she looked like. Maybe he'd finally gotten through to her.

He sat down on the floor, Indian style, and stared out at the pool. "Do you realize now," he said quietly, "what you have done? What you've accomplished with your flip little remark?" He pounded his thigh. "He could have been an *icon*!"

Chapter Fifteen

"It's a wrap!" Sam P. shouted when they were done. "I always wanted to say that." He patted Max on the head. "Let's go and change the world."

"We'll do that," Max said. "But we have to do it right."

"You said we'd 'go viral.' All I have to do is upload to the phone and off we go."

"And we will, we'll get to that. But first, we have to wait."

"Wait for what?"

"For them to get nervous."

"Nervous?" Sam P. looked nonplussed. "Your wife told us to keep you. The only way to pressure her is to go viral—you said so yourself!"

"If you remember, I said we have to do it right. You want to do it right, don't you?"

"Well…yes, of course."

"This guy is scamming you!" said Corey. "He's screwing with your heads."

"Shut up, Corey."

"Look—"

"Shut up! I want to hear what the man has to say." Sam P. fixed his eyes on Max. "What *are* you saying?"

"I'm saying we give them a chance to think about it. To stew."

"And how long, do you propose, should we let them 'stew'?"

"A day or two."

"A day or two?" Sam P. shook his head. "That's too long. We want to wrap this up. The longer we keep you here as our guest, the more of a chance for something to go wrong. Frankly, we need to unload you as soon as possible."

"I say we go viral," Corey said. "Now. This guy is setting us up!"

"I think so too," Luther said.

Max said, "It all depends on Jerry."

"Jerry?"

"My manager. He and Talia are having an affair. Talia would be just fine with it if I dropped off the face of the earth, but Jerry has money—a *lot* of money—invested in me. I have to be on the set in a couple of weeks. She may want me dead, but he wants me alive and working."

Sam P. and Luther digested this.

Sam P. said, "So this, uh, Jerry. What's his last name?"

"Gold. Jerry Gold."

"He'll pay to get you back?"

Max shrugged. "He'll get Talia to pay, which is the same thing. There's no way he's going to let his meal ticket die in a bomb shelter in the middle of the desert. But he's going to need some time."

"Time?"

"To convince Talia. She's the one with the purse strings. And right now, she's picturing life without me, and she likes it that way."

"But this, ah, Jerry? He can convince her?"

"He'll convince her. You'd better believe it."

"How long, do you think?"

Max shrugged. "A day, maybe? She's pretty stubborn."

"But what about going viral?"

"That's our trump card. But I don't think we'll need it. What I suggest is we send the video to Jerry—you can upload it and send it by phone, you'll need to get a cheap throw-away—and then we wait."

"Don't you guys see what he's doing?" Corey said. "He talked you asshats into 'going viral,' and now he's changing the rules of the game in midstream."

Luther cleared his throat. "Horses."

"What are you talking about?" Corey shouted.

"Horses in midstream. You change horses in midstream, not the rules of the game."

Max looked at Sam P., and Sam P. shrugged and gave him his long-suffering look. The look that said, *Why do I have to put up with fools like this?*

"Wait a minute," Max said. "Luther, you called Talia."

Luther said, "What about it?"

"It was your personal cell phone?"

Sam P. looked at Luther. Luther blanched.

"They can trace it right to you."

"But you said your wife doesn't want you."

"Yeah, that's true, but Jerry does."

"So what do we do?"

Max pretended to think. Finally, he said, "It's going to take some time. They have to hire someone to get your phone records, and then they'll have to have someone in law enforcement come here to look for me. Should take a while."

Sam P. said, "How much time would it take?"

"Depends on how much Jerry wants me."

"And your estimate of that? If you can be truthful, please."

"Several hours, at least. Jerry would have to talk to the sheriff here. They'd have to put together a task force and get them out here—probably a SWAT team. Around here, that's going to take time."

"Yeah, it's going to take *time*," Corey said. "Like, we're all in this together."

"Shut up, Corey, I'm trying to think here," said Sam P.

"What stake's *he* got in this? He's the hostage!"

Sam P. looked at Corey. Then he looked at Max. "That's an excellent question."

Max stared into Sam P.'s eyes. Max could feel his teeth clench, as if he shook from the cold. The cold was the crust around him, but the furnace inside, the anger he felt, wasn't faked. He didn't have to act this time. Holding Sam P.'s eyes, he said, "I want to put it to her. I want this to blow up in her face."

Sam P. visibly recoiled. "I can see that."

Max saw Luther stir from the corner of his eye. He could feel a change in Luther. Max suddenly commanded his full respect. "Damn right," Luther muttered.

Corey said, "This is bullshit. I'm gone."

Sam P. said, "Corey, this is important."

"Yeah, well, a deal's a deal. If I don't show up at Benner's right now, he'll wonder what's up."

Sam P. sighed. "I suppose you have to go. He's paranoid enough as it is." He looked at Max. "Corey's got this sideline."

Corey glared at Sam. Started to say something, but thought better of it. Looked at Max. "I'll see *you* later. Something tells me you're not going to make it out of here alive."

"If you're going, Corey," Max said, "Get a prepaid phone. We'll use that from now on. We can upload the video on it." He turned to Luther. "Corey should take your phone. If the cops come, you can tell them it was stolen."

Max was thinking how sweet it would be to see the look on Talia's face when the video of her kidnapped husband, bruised and abused, went viral.

He wondered how she'd like to see that on YouTube. Especially the part where he pleaded for his life and begged Talia to do everything in her power to save him.

"But we have to have throwaway phones, so no one will trace it to us," Max added. "Right, Luther?"

Luther nodded, although he looked a tad bit confused.

"Corey," Max said, "turn off Luther's phone and dump it somewhere out in the boonies."

"I'm not taking orders from you. You're already dead, man. You just don't know it."

"Corey, don't threaten the man," Sam P. said.

"Bullshit!"

"Corey?" Sam P. said. "You want in on this or not? We're trying to do this right." He looked at Max. "But we'll keep our own phones, thank you very much. You neglected to mention that all we have to do to elude the, ah, *authorities*, is to turn them off. Max, do you think your wife will change her mind? Is it conceivable that she would pay the ransom to get you back?"

"No."

"Then it's unlikely that the authorities will be able to trace us through Luther's phone. Am I right?"

"She wouldn't go to the authorities."

"So it's a moot point. Luther can keep his phone. But our friend Max here is right about the prepaid phones. Corey, we'll want two."

"He's torquing you guys around, don't you get that?"

Sam P.'s voice got quiet. "Are you in or are you out?"

In the end, Corey was in.

Chapter Sixteen

TEN MINUTES AFTER HIS KIDNAPPERS LEFT MAX ALONE IN the bomb shelter, he heard an engine start up outside. Even fifteen feet belowground, encased in steel and concrete block walls, he could hear the reverberation. Big engine, maybe a 454—a muscle car.

The car screamed away, the engine going from sweet to angry.

A few minutes later Luther came down to see him.

"Corey take off?" Max asked.

"You heard the car? Down here? That's Corey's pride and joy. A nineteen seventy-one Chevelle SS. Frankly, I'm worried he's raising his profile too much, but you can't reason with Corey. You probably already know that."

Max said, "You and your uncle are smart guys. Why are you fooling around with a redneck like him?"

"He's got his uses," Luther said primly.

"You know what's missing here?" Max said. "A Porta-Potty."

Luther sat down on one of the folding chairs. "Hopefully, you won't be here that long. I am sure as hell not going to risk taking you upstairs to the toilet. Can't you just hold it?"

"Not for a day. I told you, it's going to take a while. Jerry's got to talk Talia out of her snit. She'll come around, but she needs a certain amount of hand-holding."

Luther ran a hand through his thinning hair. Kidnapping, it seemed, was taking a toll on him.

Max asked, "You feeling well?"

"I'm fine."

"You don't look so good. I want to ask you something. How are you going to complete the transaction?"

"We'll have your wife wire it to an offshore account."

"You know how to do that?"

"My uncle's working on it now."

He did not sound at all confident.

"So then what? They send you the money, and you kick me loose?"

"That's about the size of it. We haven't worked out all the details."

Luther sounded conflicted. His voice lacked conviction.

Max knew then that they planned to kill him.

The sudden, hard knot in his throat was hard to choke down. But he swallowed hard and concentrated on escape. He was smarter than them. And he had skills. He was a hands-on actor, a scrupulous researcher, and early on in his career he had done most of his own stunts. As a leading man, as an action-adventure actor, he'd been placed in a lot of fake situations. But he had skills and he'd thought through his actions, worked long and hard with stunt people, choreographers, directors, and other actors to simulate real-life fights. He'd rappelled down from a helicopter, learned to drive fast and defensively, learned a few aspects of the martial arts, and picked up a few tricks of hand-to-hand combat.

A pretty spotty array of talents, but Max was tough. This was real life, but it shouldn't intimidate him.

He realized he'd been so set on revenge against Talia and Jerry that he'd seen this as a game. It wasn't a game. As inept as these people were, they were deadly serious. If it was just Luther and Sam P., he'd have a chance. But Corey—he'd seen guys like that before. He had a certain cunning. He was impulsive. Quentin Tarantino could have written him—which meant he could go off like a rocket at any time.

Max felt the prickle on his scalp.

Corey wanted to kill him.

He remembered the day in July—he was working on a thriller called *Sudden Death*—the day he'd learned how to administer a chokehold. He'd learned other things too, over lunch at a taco stand later—stuff the former ATF agent had told him. How to disable, how to kill.

When Max stood up, Luther looked suddenly alarmed. "What are you doing?"

"I have to take a leak, that all right with you?"

"I guess so." Luther stood too. He had a gun in his hand.

"You going to shoot me?"

"No, it's just a precaution. No sudden moves."

"Just have to pee, is all."

"Because I tell you, we're in this to the end. You don't know what we're capable of."

Max sauntered over to the wall, unzipped his fly. "What are you capable of?" he asked. He didn't look at Luther, kept it casual—no worries, man.

"The stakes are high," said Luther. "You're not the first person who ran afoul of Corey."

"No?" He was having a hard time loosening up enough to let go.

Realized he'd been holding it a long time.

"Maybe if you knew how dangerous he is, how dangerous *we* are, you would understand," Luther said. "Corey put a guy into the hospital. Nearly killed him. Guy's in a wheelchair—Corey served time for it. And if you've noticed, he doesn't like you."

"He did that?" Still unable to summon up the ability to piss, his bladder really hurting now.

"Corey did that."

Max said nothing. Closed his eyes. The little dots were back in his vision—something that had been an on-and-off companion. Just another mystery since he'd left Desert Oasis.

"You OK?" Luther said with alarm.

"Dizzy."

And he was. His bladder had locked up on him. He'd held it too long, and now it was frozen solid shut.

Max heard Luther stand up.

Max sagged against the wall. "Jesus."

Luther took a tentative step toward him. Max realized he was in shock. The dots were obliterating his vision, but he knew there was only one chance.

Luther laid a tentative hand on Max's shoulder. Max glanced behind Luther, saw the gun sitting on the folding chair.

Luther, you're going to regret that.

Max whipped around, the dots flying around inside his eyes, his bladder screaming with pent-up pain, and he had Luther by the throat, the thumb and forefinger of his right hand pressing against the carotid. At the same time, the thumb and forefinger of his left hand, acting as pinchers, gripped the key spots below and behind each ear. Luther fell like a sack of laundry.

When he wandered into consciousness a few seconds later, Max had Luther's Smith & Wesson 9 mm, which he stuck in the back of his jeans. The success of the attack worked on Max and finally he could void his bladder. There was relief, but also a buzzing in his head. The fuzzy dots of light were back, dancing behind his eyes.

"Is the trapdoor locked?" Max said.

Luther could barely focus. Max knew how he felt.

"Luther, don't make me do it again. I nearly killed you the last time. I'm not an expert at this." Max leveled his gaze at Luther, kept eye contact. The dots just a distraction now. "Is the door above locked? Does Sam P. have to open it for you?"

"It's not locked. My uncle didn't want to have to wait by the door."

"Why didn't he come down with you?"

"It's hard for him. His weight."

"When's Corey coming back?"

"I don't know. It shouldn't take him too long to buy the phones, but if I know Corey, he's probably gone to see his marijuana source."

"He'll be back soon?"

"Very soon. You can't—"

Max clocked him. Hard, right in the mouth.

Luther sprawled on the floor, blood seeping from his mouth and nose, making a lace pattern on his chin and jaw and shirt—out cold.

Max went through Luther's pockets. Wallet, cash, keys.

He pulled the 9 mm out of his waistband and checked the magazine. Fully loaded. When he stood up, the dots behind his eyes were back. The dots Gordon White Eagle had given him as a parting gift.

He swayed a little, then his head cleared.

He remembered Gordon White Eagle telling him he would solve all his problems. He would cure him of his drugging and alcohol abuse.

"We'll see about that, Gordy," Max said. "Drugs and alcohol are the least of my problems right now."

He shoved the gun into the snug of his back. Then he went looking for Sam P.

* * *

IT WAS EASY.

Maybe it was too easy. Sam P. was watching a video. It wasn't just any video. It was a sex video.

Max had seen a lot of disgusting sex, some of it on the highest levels and in the best Jacuzzis at the best addresses with the best sluts and cabana boys and the richest jaded old farts in the world, but *this* stuff was worse. It pitted arousal against the gag reflex, but Max had a highly developed gag reflex—he could turn it on and off like a spigot. The worst thing, Sam P. liked freak shows starring the desecration of innocents—be they animal, vegetable, mineral, or altar boy.

So Max didn't mind jabbing the gun muzzle into the base of Sam P.'s testicles, even though, for one dizzying moment, he thought he'd lost the barrel in a funhouse mirror of wrinkles and folds.

Sam P. froze—not a jiggle. For a moment, the Other Max, the Max who played a Nietzsche-spouting nihilist in *Dystopia: The Second Epoch* (not his best performance; the whole thing depressed him for months afterward) took over and he felt his finger itch. He knew one squeeze would do it, blow this pathetic balloon of a man to kingdom come, send Sam P. zipping up into the atmosphere on a fart and a cry, and he stopped himself just in time.

"You'd better tell me everything," Max said. "And if you don't, I'll shoot off one part at a time."

Sam P. understood immediately.

When Max was done, he shoved Sam P. down into the dungeon with his nephew.

He kindly left them two bottles of water.

And the last of the Lunchables.

* * *

THE TRAPDOOR HAD BEEN MODIFIED—IT COULD BE LOCKED shut with a padlock. Max wondered if Luther and Sam P. had kidnapped someone else before this. The idea sent a chill up his spine. Wouldn't put it past them. He had found the key to the padlock easily enough—it hung from a hook on the wall just inside the outer door, which was unlocked. Next, Max went through the house—car keys, the video camera, Sam P.'s phone, what little cash they had, and their credit cards. He'd ditch the credit cards and use the money. He checked the video, and it looked good. He could upload it to one of the cell phones any time. Next, he needed transportation. He knew Corey would be back soon. He'd call out to his buddies, and when they didn't answer, he'd think they were in the bomb shelter with Max. If a car was missing, they wouldn't call the police. No, Corey would come looking for him.

Max had a choice: walk the three miles back to town and risk being seen, or take one of the cars, hit the freeway, and hope he had a good enough head start. From there, he could hide anywhere.

The first thing Max wanted to do was get to Gordon White Eagle. He wanted to find out exactly what White Eagle had done to him, how he'd screwed him up. He wanted the man to reverse what he'd done, if that was even possible. Then he'd settle with Jerry and Talia.

He took the gun from the small of his back and hefted it. He'd never been into weapons all that much, but had to admit this one felt good. He pictured pressing the muzzle into Gordon's handsome tanned temple. Imagined suggesting Gordon find a way to restore him to the person he was before.

And he would ask Gordon who the guy in the shower cap was.

Chapter Seventeen

Tess had the Bajada County Sheriff's Office break room to herself. No one was using the computer, so she sat down at the desk and looked up the Desert Oasis Healing Center again. The first time Tess had looked at the website, she'd seen references to "sandstone adventures" in several places. Whoever wrote the copy for the site was fond of the description. She clicked on each section and reread them.

"As you are drawn closer to the powerful force field of the magical sandstone formation known as the Flying Saucer Vortex, the most potent vortex of the area, you will discover the healing power of Celestial Vibrations. From the act of traversing the magical red rocks you will experience the feminine energy of our own unique brand of sandstone adventure."

Tess winced. She wasn't an English major, but she knew bad writing when she saw it.

So what did this mean? Nothing, by itself. But taken together with the woman and the boy, it seemed likely that they were the ones who'd purchased the truck from Talbot's Chevrolet.

Tess glanced at the tabs on the top of the healing center's website and noticed that the Desert Oasis had a gift shop.

She decided to take a look. Besides healing crystals, New Age music, shaman prayer sticks, and expensive handbags, there was a section for kids: plush toys, puzzles, expensive baby duds, and T-shirts emblazoned with "The Desert Oasis Healing Center," over a red rock vista. (Even though the red rocks of Sedona were almost twenty miles away.) Among the gifts was an official Desert Oasis yo-yo.

The boy had a yo-yo. The car salesman at Talbot's Chevrolet had told her that.

Tess was now 99-percent certain that the woman and the boy had been the ones to purchase the truck for Sandstone Adventures, and that Sandstone Adventures was a fabrication of the Desert Oasis Healing Center.

Why hide the purchase of a truck? Why did the woman dress up and wear a wig?

Something was going on.

Tess had that bad feeling—what her ex-husband, who'd worked SWAT in Albuquerque, called his "Spidey sense." She had a strong Spidey sense about the woman and the boy.

The limo Hogart was driving when he tried to pick up Max Conroy was leased by the Desert Oasis Healing Center.

She tried the Desert Oasis Healing Center again and asked the operator if she could be put through to the man at the top—Gordon White Eagle.

Of course, he was unavailable.

* * *

Tess caught Pat just as he was getting off the phone. He'd been working for months trying to get evidence on a guy suspected of battering his own father. "Yeah, what's up?" Pat was always in a bad mood when it came to that case.

"I told you about the woman I saw at the car wash."

"Yeah, you had a bad feeling about her and her kid. So?"

Tess filled him in about the woman and the boy, how they'd bought a truck for a company called "Sandstone Adventures."

"Sounds like a tour, like one of those jeep or white-water tours. Where was this, Sedona?"

"The dealership's in Clarkdale." Tess handed him the name and phone number for Talbot's Chevrolet in Clarkdale.

"You really got a thing for this gal," Pat said. "All she did was wash her truck at Joe's."

"She might be involved with those guys who tried to kidnap Max Conroy."

"Oh? And you came to this conclusion how?"

"I think she works for the Desert Oasis Healing Center. They rented the limo those two guys were in."

He looked at her skeptically. "You have anything else besides that?"

"Sandstone Adventures doesn't exist. Not as a company in Sedona. And she wore a disguise when she bought the truck."

He leaned forward. "Now *that's* interesting. What do you mean, disguise?"

She described the woman and the boy.

Pat said, "I think I've seen her around. Kind of spooky looking?"

"That's her. But when she bought the truck, she was dressed up. Dress, heels. She wore a wig. And the boy was with her."

Pat said, "Tell you what. I'll talk to my pal at Yavapai County and see what he can find out." He stood up. "Later, though. Right now I have to see a man about an assault and battery."

* * *

MAX HAD TWO CARS TO CHOOSE FROM. SAM P.'S VINTAGE Cadillac, parked out front with a "4Sale" sign in the window, or Luther's ride, an ancient Saturn. Max chose the Saturn. It wouldn't attract attention like Sam P.'s car would. He'd come out through the kitchen door, which opened out onto a carport with four bays separated by spindly posts. Across the carport, he heard a washing machine running inside the storage room attached on the opposite side. The Saturn was closest to the storeroom. He stood by the driver's side, sorting keys.

That was when he heard a car engine. Loud, muscular— Corey's Chevelle SS.

Max crouched down behind the hood of the Saturn, close to the back wall of the carport. He pulled the 9 mm from behind his back and checked it. Just in case.

The muscle car pulled into the bay closest to the kitchen door on the opposite side, engine reverberating. Max duck-walked around to the Saturn's passenger side, keeping low. He expected Corey to get out and go into the house through the kitchen door. When Corey was inside, he'd take off in the Saturn.

Corey let the Chevelle roar one more time before shutting down. Max eased up and peered through the windows of the Saturn as Corey's driver's side opened.

After that, it all went to hell.

Corey must have caught sight of him through the car windows, because he whirled and stared across the roofs of the Chevelle and Saturn. For a second Max froze (his mind screaming, move-move-move!) but everything stood still, and although he had the gun leveled across the roof in a two-handed grip, he could barely feel the trigger guard. He might have yelled "Freeze!" but he wasn't sure because his throat felt locked up and there didn't seem to be any sound. But his finger must have moved of its own volition—he realized he'd fired over the roof of the Saturn—and everything abruptly exploded in dust and noise. With the gun's kick, adrenaline took over, cascading down through his chest. He kept his finger on the trigger and shot half the magazine.

Corey ducked, then popped up and shot across the car so quickly that Max felt the bullet zip by his ear before he heard the sound. His reflexes were slower—it took him almost a second to get down, the sting to his ear a shock. He clapped his hand to his head. No blood. Still amazed at how quickly Corey reacted—was still reacting, because suddenly a hole blasted through the passenger window of the Saturn above him, glass flying.

Choices: get into the storeroom and close the door, crawl under the car, or shoot back through the window. He shot through the window. Indiscriminately.

Blind.

Corey screamed.

Max heard a bang and a thump.

Max didn't wait to see if Corey was hit or faking. He was running on pure instinct now, and that instinct was screaming for him to get away. He threw himself headfirst into the storage room and scrambled behind the wood frame. And that was when his brain hit the slow-motion button. He flashed on a hot afternoon eating Sonoran hot dogs in a Tucson eatery with a cop who had worked with him on a picture, the cop saying that if you were in a firefight you looked for three things: cover, concealment, and an escape route. The flimsy plywood of the storeroom would offer no such cover, but it would conceal him.

Close enough.

He crouched by the edge of the door. The cop had also told him always to stay low when hiding. Most people emptied their weapons at the face or the upper body.

The last thing the cop had told him: shoot first, and shoot to kill. Max followed that advice, shooting at the cars, a good three or four shots. Had to resist emptying the weapon from pure adrenaline overload.

Then he got down again.

Nothing.

Nothing since the scream.

Had he killed Corey? Was Corey lying out there dead, or injured? Max remained in place. It was unbearable in here. The washing machine ground on. Wished he could stop it, wished he could listen to the silence. For the sound of movement. But with the washing machine he could hear nothing.

Wait. Tried to get his mind to work, and finally was able to go through the possible scenarios. Corey could be wounded. Or dead. The neighbors could be calling the police even now. He listened for sirens, but heard nothing but the damn washing machine cycling on and on.

Corey could be playing dead, waiting for him. When Max was a kid, they had a cat like that. The cat would sit near a ground squirrel hole. Just sat back and waited. Eventually, the ground squirrel would get curious and pop its head out—and then, snap!

Max didn't want to be like the ground squirrel. So he waited.

The washing machine finally stopped.

The heat was unbearable.

He was dripping with sweat.

He listened.

Finally, he got down on his stomach and inched along the storeroom floor. Craned his head around the door frame.

Nothing.

The place felt empty.

The only sound was the tick of the Chevelle's cooling engine. Glass littered the carport's concrete surface.

If he moved forward, he would crunch on the glass or at least scrape on it and give himself away.

And so he withdrew, back into the storeroom.

Gun in both hands.

Shaking with adrenaline.

* * *

A HALF HOUR WENT BY, MAYBE MORE. MAX WAS BEGINNING to relax, and he knew that wasn't good. He'd been around enough cops, taken enough courses to know he shouldn't take anything for granted. He'd done the Citizen's Academy, the FBI course, a slew of them, just to get a feel for his character in *Gawker*—had been around them long enough to know that you had to remain alert and plan for trouble.

Corey might be dead. Or perhaps he'd made it inside the house. Maybe he'd found Luther and Sam and gotten them out of the bomb shelter...

No movement. No sound.

Max could call and get help; he had both Luther's and Sam P.'s phones. The sheriff's deputy—she might come. His mind stuttered again, and stuck on the vision of the deputy setting her fingers on the place mat. Something about that small movement got to him. That was the moment he thought about, not her mental gymnastics and encyclopedic memory. Not even the way she'd handled those guys in the limo.

He could call 911.

But what if Corey was dead? Max knew he'd be arrested. Even if it was self-defense, he'd still end up in jail—at least until they sorted it out. He could see the headline now.

Max sat cross-legged on the floor of the storeroom, weapon still in both hands, resting on his lap. Tried to decide. Sometimes his mind just wouldn't cooperate, and he'd be frozen, unable to do anything at all. Another parting gift from Gordon White Eagle—

The son of a bitch.

Max heard a scrape. He held tight to his gun and peered around the door.

The man in the shower cap and pink sunglasses stood back a couple of paces, close to the Saturn. He grinned. Max noticed he had few teeth. "What do you want?" Max asked him.

The man pointed to the car tires.

Max slithered out a little farther, so he was level with the floor, and stared at the tires. He could see all the way to the kitchen door.

Were those legs? They were legs, attired in jeans and desert boots, stretched out on the ground near the kitchen door. The rest of the body was hidden by the Chevelle's tires.

Max looked at the man in the shower cap. "Is that Corey? Is he dead?"

The man in the shower cap touched a finger to his lips. Then he stepped carefully into his rowboat, which had magically appeared, hovering a foot off the ground, and rowed down the driveway. He waved back, grinning, his toothless gums catching the light.

Max realized he had to know. If Corey was hurt, he'd have to help him. He made his way as carefully and quietly as he could over to the Chevelle. Trying to avoid the broken glass. Gun at the ready, clasped in both hands, pointed down in front of his body. Everything moving in slow motion— and he was at the center of the storm. His mind clear, his thoughts crystalline.

Corey lay with his head propped against the kitchen wall. There was a bloody hole in the shoulder of his black tee, but not a whole lot of blood had seeped out. Didn't look like Max had hit an artery, which was fortunate. It looked as if the bullet had gone through flesh and muscle, and very little else. The gun had fallen out of Corey's hand.

Max thought Corey must have hit his head when he fell. Otherwise, he'd still be conscious.

ICON

But Max wasn't taking any chances.

"Corey!" he shouted, aiming at the man's chest. "Corey! Look at me!"

No movement.

Was he playing dead? Was he actually dead?

"I have my gun on you. If you move at all, I will shoot you. You got that?"

He moved forward slowly, keeping dead aim on Corey's chest. He kicked Corey's gun under the Chevelle and closed the ground between them quickly. Felt for a pulse. There was one.

Corey's chest moved up and down, but he was out cold. Max went through his pockets, got his keys but left the baggie of pot on Corey's person. Ducked in through the open window of the Chevelle. On the seat was a bag with the two prepaid mobile phones, still in their boxes. Max ripped one box open, used Luther's phone to activate the prepaid mobile. It was precharged, which made things a whole hell of a lot easier.

He didn't want to use Luther's or Sam's phones too much, since they could be traced.

Max grabbed hold of Corey's boots and dragged him into the kitchen. Rested. Pulled him to the door of the pantry. Rested some more. Corey had to weigh 170, all of it dead weight. Each time he dropped Corey, Max checked his pulse. He dragged him along the pantry floor to the outer door to the bomb shelter, and then to the trapdoor. He took the key off the hook, opened the padlock, and pulled the door up. Stood back and aimed his gun into the bunker. Swept it back and forth.

– 117 –

"Either of you try anything, and I'll shoot you. You make one move toward those steps and I promise you, I *will* kill you."

Luther and Sam P. stared at him. They looked like fat, frightened rodents.

"Catch!"

Max gave Corey a push and sent him tumbling down. Corey hit Luther and Sam P. like a bowling ball hitting pins.

"You might want to hold something to the wound to make sure he doesn't bleed anymore," Max hollered down.

Sam P. said, "Max, my boy, let us reason together—"

Max closed the door and padlocked it, then put the key back on the hook.

He went through the closets in the house, looking for something he could carry the phones and the weapon in. He found a medium-sized duffel that would do just fine.

As Max headed for the Chevelle, he glanced at the driveway and saw the man in the shower cap smiling. After waving an oar in salute, Shower Cap rowed away.

* * *

MAX GOT INTO THE CHEVELLE AND STARTED HER UP. THE sound was deep-throated and beautiful—sweet. He placed the duffel holding the phones, video camera, keys, and the semiautomatic on the bucket seat beside him. The engine settled to a masculine rumble. He depressed the clutch and grabbed the Hurst shifter. Glanced at the bucket seat.

One of the other phones was sticking out of the bag, just one corner. He sat there, foot depressed on the clutch, looking at it.

You need to think about this. He grabbed the duffel and went inside the house. The air conditioner was still on full blast—it felt good against his sweating body.

Max dumped the contents of the bag on the kitchen table and uploaded the video of his capture to Luther's phone, playing it once. It looked authentic. Real.

Max felt himself drifting and pulled himself back to the present. Why didn't he take the Chevelle and hightail it out of here? Where was he going and what was he going to do?

I'm gonna break his sorry ass.

Gordon White Eagle's ass. He was going to make Gordon White Eagle put him back the way he was before. Gordon had screwed with his mind, and he could damn well *unscrew* with his mind.

At least that was his hope.

He pictured himself driving up there. Saw himself brazenly walking into Gordon White Eagle's territory, past his hired help, past the big guys—Gordon's "attendants." He pictured getting in Gordon's face, demanding Gordon fix him.

And then what?

The big guys would take him away. Back to his room, or back to the sensory deprivation tank. And they would screw him up even worse. "Isn't that right?" he asked a dwarf who was combing his beard at the kitchen table.

The dwarf shrugged.

Max was about to say something to the dwarf, that he was just a figment of Max's imagination, when the voice spoke loudly in his ear: "Freeze!"

For a second, maybe two, his muscles locked up and he couldn't move—his body was frozen in place.

Then the echo of the command faded and he went limp. He felt as if he'd run a marathon—weak, tired.

The dwarf was gone.

He closed his eyes. His temple throbbed. He didn't know what was happening—why he hallucinated, why he heard the command "Freeze," or why he obeyed it.

Max knew it was something Gordon had done to him, either by mistake or on purpose.

He had to get to Gordon. He had to get Gordon to fix him—*to put him back to the way he was before.*

And he needed to know *why.*

* * *

MAX SEARCHED FOR THE DESERT OASIS HEALING CENTER website. He knew what to do. He used Luther's phone, because he wanted Gordon to come looking for him. He found the website. Ignored the beautiful vistas, the palms, the happy people gathered in the garden—a picture-perfect support group. The beaming maître d's, the starlight dinners, the seafood bar, the pool, the stone massages. He looked past all that to the phone number and punched it into the smartphone.

Of course, he got an automated message with a series of options. He asked to be transferred to the fitness center. A young man answered.

Max gave his name and said, "Listen carefully. I have to talk to Gordon White Eagle, OK? He's going to want to talk to me."

"Oh, yes sir, I remember you. I spotted you on the bench press a couple of times, remember? I loved you in *V.A.M.Pyre.* I'll make sure he gets the message, ASAP."

"Good. Tell him I'm in trouble. Tell him I've been kidnapped, and am being held for ransom." And he gave the man the phone number.

The man repeated the number, then said, "I'll do that, sir." And the phone disconnected.

⋆ ⋆ ⋆

THE PHONE CHEEPED OUT "LIKE A VIRGIN"—AN INTERESTING, if retro, choice. Max let it ring a few times before he answered without speaking. It was Gordon.

"Is this Max? Max, are you there? Max? Whoever you are, let me talk to Max. I know we can work something out—"

Max covered his mouth and made a noise somewhere between a bleating sheep and a grunting weight lifter.

"Max? *Max?* Are you all right? Jerry told me they called Talia...Can they hear us?"

"They're holding me for ransom. You've got to help me, Gordon." Then he cried out. "*Please* don't hurt me! Please!"

"They're hurting you? Are you all right? Talk to me, Max!"

"You need to...Oh, *please*, just come and get me."

"Don't worry, Max, we'll send someone—"

"No, they want you, just you! If you don't come, they're going to kill me."

"That's outrageous! They can't kill you—you're a star. Let me talk to them!"

Max covered the phone and mumbled a few words to himself. Barked an order like a sergeant major. Screeched like a spider monkey.

And waited. Gordon never did like to wait. Finally, voice trembling, Max spoke into the phone. "They said—they said they don't want to talk to you. They're sending you the video so you know they're serious."

"Max—"

"Nooo! *Please! Oh, God. No!*"

He sent the video and hit End.

* * *

A FEW MINUTES PASSED, AND THE PHONE RANG AGAIN. MAX let it ring four times before answering.

Gordon sounded shaken. "Max? Max? Where are you?"

"You gotta come for me, Gordon. I'm in a town called Paradox. And they said come alone—no police. If there are any police they'll slit my throat. They want a million dollars by sunset."

"I can't come up with that kind of money!"

Max muffled the phone again. Begging, pleading with himself. Clapping his hands together once, twice—simulating hard slaps to the face. (He used to get high with a Foley artist. The guy was a real bore except when he was ripped, when he would perform his best sound effects.)

More barked orders. A kitchen chair thrown across the room. When Max spoke again he was almost hyperventilating from all the activity. Max was able to summon tears at the drop of a hat (even though as a leading man, he was never allowed to do so) and so he let tears seep into his voice. "They're serious about killing me, Gordon. They want one million dollars in small bills."

"But I can't—"

"If you don't bring the money…please, oh God, no, *Jesus!*"

"OK, OK, just tell them to stop. Tell them I'll be there!"

"Someone will call you in a little while and give you the address. Please, Gordon, no cops. They said they'll kill me, and they'll kill you." Max hit End. The phone rang again but this time he didn't answer.

Let Gordon stew for a while.

A half hour later, he called Gordon once again with the address. He made sure he sounded like a dork.

* * *

MAX FIGURED IT WOULD TAKE GORDON TIME TO ROUND UP the money, but he wanted to be in place early enough for his ambush to work. He had to be prepared for the possibility—the *probability*—that Gordon wouldn't come alone. He needed a place to see Gordon's approach—he should be far enough from the house that he could see who Gordon had with him, but close enough to get the jump on them. Fortunately, there was a corral across the road and halfway up the hill opposite. At the far side of the corral stood a ramada and a galvanized steel water tank, now empty. It looked like there hadn't been a horse there in years. Max positioned himself behind the tank. It was hot as hell—the shade of the ramada had not yet reached him. He watched the road to the house until he was cross-eyed. He'd see the dust long before a vehicle showed up.

Max looked at his array of phones and decided to keep the prepaid for emergencies, since he doubted it was charged for more than an hour or two. He was starting to like Luther's smartphone. He used it to call Dave Finley.

"Yo."

Max said, "It's me."

"What's going on? You OK? Damn it, bud, everyone's wondering what happened to you. Karen said you called, but I tried your phone and just got voice mail."

Max thought of the phone, buried in a plastic bag near a barbed-wire fence somewhere along the freeway north of here. Max told him about that.

"You mean you buried your phone in the desert? Why would you do that?"

"Have you heard anything?"

"Just what Karen said. She said you sounded all screwed up. Where are you, man? I could come get you."

"Come and get me?" Had he heard right? "I thought you were working."

"The Matt Damon? That was a one-week gig, it ended yesterday. What's going on?"

Max thought about it. He went in and out of being able to think clearly, and right now, his mind was buzzing like a hive of bees. Had Jerry Gold told Dave about the kidnapping?

No. Jerry knew Max and Dave were friends, but as far as Max's business manager was concerned, Dave was just the help. Somebody who palled around with Max on Max's downtime. So unless Gordon had gone to the press, which Max was pretty sure he wouldn't do, Dave didn't know what had happened.

What was about to happen.

Max looked down at the semiautomatic sitting in the dirt by his leg. Was he really thinking of holding a gun on Gordon White Eagle? Was he that crazy?

"Hey, Max! You there?"

What had he planned to do? Ambush Gordon, and put the gun to his head?

"Max, look. I know you've been under a lot of pressure, and I don't blame you for leaving that place. You need a break, man—just chill out a little, then you can get back to work."

Get back to work. That was what everybody wanted. They didn't care about him; they just wanted him to get back to work so everyone could draw a paycheck.

"I'm getting a divorce," Max said. Saying it even surprised him. But it was incredibly liberating.

"A divorce? Really?"

"Yup."

"What about the kid?"

He'd forgotten about the baby Talia was going to bring back from Africa. Funny he could forget something like that. "I don't know," he said slowly.

"Are you serious? That's going to look really cold, man. You just going to leave her with the kid? Just like that? We tried to go the adoption route, and I don't think—"

"Let her work it out. I'm sure she and Jerry will figure it out."

"Jerry?"

Max said, "It was Jerry's idea—the whole adoption thing. He said it would raise our profile—make us look selfless and responsible..."

He flashed on the day Jerry had laid it out for them. Why not adopt a baby from Africa?

It had seemed reasonable at the time.

Even thinking about it, how Jerry had presented them with the "promotional opportunity," without a thought for the child who would be brought to the United States as a prop in a publicity stunt—

Unbelievable. Had he gone that far afield?

He thought of the buried meds and booze in his backyard.

Yes, he had gone that far afield.

A stupid ploy like that, and Max had agreed to it. Talia had loved the idea, started planning all the expensive baby stuff from Petit Tresor for furnishings or a whole designed nursery by Wendy Bellisimo, and Baby Dior for clothing—he knew the names she tossed around by heart by this point. He'd sat passively by while they—Talia and Jerry—made a decision like that. Without a thought for the child who would be coming, without a thought of what the future would be like for that child or for Talia or even for himself. Anything to feed the beast. Celebrity was a state that constantly altered; it needed to be fed and watered and entertained and placated, or it could disappear any minute.

Max hated himself at that moment. How could he have been so stupid? So out of touch with reality?

"Max?" Dave was saying. "You guys are really through?"

"Talia doesn't know, and I don't want you telling her. In fact, I don't want you to tell anyone we're talking. I have to sort a few things out. I need the space. Is that OK? Will you give me that?"

"Sure…but why?"

"Because I'm asking you to, brother."

A pause. "You can count on me," Dave said solemnly.

"Good."

"Hey, where are you, man?"

Max told him.

Silence. Then Dave said, "You know what? I could come out there and pick you up."

"Come out? What are you talking about?"

"I could bring the bikes. I could drive 'em out there and you and I could ride back to LA. Like the old days, when you were just starting out."

"That's crazy."

"No it's not. I could leave now. We were filming out near Death Valley and I decided to drive over and see Seth."

"Seth?"

"The guy with the bike shop in Blythe, remember? I took a couple of Harleys for the shoot and figured I was close enough to Blythe he and I could go for a ride. But I could just as easy drive over so's you and I could ride back."

"What about your rig?"

"Seth can drive it."

"I don't know." Max was getting a headache. What Dave said didn't make much sense to him. "Have you talked to Jerry?"

"Jerry?" Dave snorted. "Why would I talk to that pissant?"

Max rubbed his forehead. The throbbing above his left temple drove him crazy. The heat was getting to him too. What was he thinking, planning to ambush Gordon? What would he do—wave the gun in his face? Could he really get Gordon to fix him?

"That sounds good," Max said. "I could use a good ride about now."

"I can be out of here in a couple of hours."

Max heard an engine—sounded like a truck. Far enough away, but going slow.

"Let me think about it," Max said. "I'll call you back, OK?"

"Max, if you—"

But Max didn't hear him. He was watching the white truck coming his way.

Chapter Eighteen

THE TRUCK WAS A NEW CHEVY. A SILVERADO 2500HD, THE same kind of truck Dave Finley hauled his bikes with. There was something stealthy about the way the truck moved, even though the engine was big. It cruised to a stop just beyond the nearest neighbor to Luther's, about an eighth of a mile away.

Max had seen it before.

His heart sped up. Something was wrong here…How could Gordon react that quickly? He rummaged through his memory bank, trying to place the truck. There were plenty of expensive new trucks and Suburbans at the Desert Oasis, but all of them had the center's logo on the side. This one was plain, no frills, the kind of truck a company would buy for a work vehicle.

The passenger door opened and a boy hopped out. The kid wasn't big—kind of weedy-looking—but he wasn't a little kid. Closer to a teenager. He held a gun down by his side but at the ready. Maybe he'd learned how to do it from cop shows.

The driver's side opened and a figure stepped out. From where Max was, the lower half of the person was blocked by the truck's hood. The person was lean and straight-backed, with hair clipped close to the skull. Max thought it was a woman, but he wasn't sure. The person was dressed like a man and moved economically. The two of them met in front of the truck.

It *was* a woman. But like none he'd ever seen. She moved like a man. He wondered if she'd had a sex-change operation.

The woman spoke to the kid. He nodded and trotted across the dirt road toward the west, ran up a desert hill and disappeared. The woman walked up the road. Casual. Glancing at her watch. A big watch—a man's watch, like his Breitling. When she reached the tall bamboo ringing Sam P.'s yard, she crouched low and followed it to the entrance, gun at the ready.

Max remembered where he'd seen the truck. It had been parked outside the Rat Motel. He remembered the truck pulling out and following the limo.

Either Jerry or his brother Gordon—probably it was both of them—had sent the guys in the limo. So why had the woman and kid followed them? Did they hope the limo would lead them to him?

Did more than one set of people want him?

He was beginning to feel like a pawn.

Max took a deep breath. He had no doubt the woman and boy would come here to the corral, once they finished with the house. Maybe they'd find his kidnappers. They would surely see the shot-up Saturn, the glass, the evidence of a gun battle in the carport.

Where was the kid? He had gone west, which meant he could be circling around the corral. Kid could have seen him from that angle, might be closing in even now. Max had no doubt the kid knew how to use his firearm. Max had spent time shooting at a range; he had been taught to shoot and shoot relatively well. He had worked with marksmen. The kid had carried his weapon as if it had grown out of his arm. Casual, but alert.

Max could easily be seen hiding behind the tank. He should move. But there was no place to go.

He had the semiautomatic. He could shoot the boy if it came to that.

But could he?

He'd almost blown Sam P. to kingdom come. But this was a boy. He didn't think he could shoot a boy.

But where to hide?

A sharp whistle rent the air.

The woman stood at the edge of the carport, among the broken glass, looking in his direction.

No, not his direction, to the right. Far to the right.

The kid yelled, "What?"

The woman stuck two fingers in her mouth and blew again.

Max sank into the ground, flat on his stomach. He hunched his shoulders like a turtle hiding in its shell. He hoped the color of his body and his clothing would look like a shadow on the earth. He heard the boy run, maybe thirty yards from him, to his right. Pelting footsteps, occasionally sliding on rock and sand, the kid yelling, "What is it?"

Max had the absurd desire to close his eyes.

Instead, he canted his head slightly, so he could see the house.

The woman and the boy stood outside the carport. The woman started around the Saturn, moving loose-limbed but alert, like a panther.

They were swallowed up by the shadows. If Max was going to escape, he'd better do it now.

Chapter Nineteen

WHENEVER JERRY GOLD WAS CONFLICTED ABOUT SOMETHING—
"conflicted" being one of Gordon's favorite expressions
(Jerry's half brother had upscale hippie psychobabble down
to a science, along with the unlimited wardrobe of Hawaiian
shirts, tai chi pants, and Birkenstocks)—he reverted to what
he'd been before he became Max Conroy's manager. Always,
he went back to the storyboard.

Better to cover all the bases.

He locked Talia out of his office, grabbed a ream of
8 ½" x 11"" copy paper and his favorite Sharpie, and set up on
the desk overlooking the pool. Talia knocked halfheartedly a
couple of times, then gave up. The woman had the attention
span of a gnat. He wondered now why he had gotten involved
with her at all. Yes, there was the secret pleasure of banging
Talia L'Apel, a big star in her own right, and he cherished
the idea of cuckolding Max Conroy, heartthrob of girls and
women from fourteen to sixty. She was terrific in bed too.
You'd be surprised how many hot-bodied actresses weren't. It
sometimes seemed the more alluring and sexy they appeared,
the more frigid they were in the boudoir. Not so with Talia,
who brought the same exuberance to the sack as she did to
the ski slopes.

Gordon had called an hour ago, telling him about the kidnappers in some hick town called Paradox and their demand for a million dollars by sunset. He was relieved that the kidnappers had called again, after Talia had turned them down. But on the minus side, there was no way Gordon could possibly come up with the money that quickly. And the idea of letting go of a million dollars...

What if the kidnappers got the million dollars and killed Max anyway? And left him to rot in the desert sun somewhere for hunters to find six months from now?

Fortunately, there was a Plan B.

"You remember Shaun?" Gordon said. "She's Mickey Barron's granddaughter. The stunt man."

"I thought she was a stunt woman."

"That's right, Jer. It runs in the family."

Jerry said, "But she's the one who—" He lowered his voice. "The one, who, you know, at Big Bear Lake?"

"Why are you whispering?"

"You know people listen in on cell phones."

"How's this? She's the one who looks like a man. You met her when she was here one time."

Jerry *did* remember meeting her. How could he ever forget? Jerry suppressed a shudder. When he had first met her, he really couldn't tell if she was a man or a woman. Not because she was ugly—she wasn't—but because of the vibe she gave off. The way she carried herself, the way she walked. Maybe it was her center of balance. Little things, all put together to create an odd, well, dissonance. But that wasn't the worst thing. What really got to Jerry was the feeling that she was sizing him up for a coffin. She spooked the hell out of him, and that was even before he learned about her résumé.

"Are you listening, Jerry?" Gordon said. "This is important. She's going to extract him from the kidnappers. And the good news? She's already there. I sent her to find him."

"In Paradox?"

"That's right."

"It's still dangerous, though. What if he gets killed in the crossfire?"

"You ever look on the bright side?"

"Just hedging my bets. That's what I wanted to tell you about—I'm in the middle of something here. I'm writing an alternate storyboard. And you know it could work, especially if we don't have the body. It might be easier too."

"Shaun's going to get him and bring him back, Jerry. Everything's going to be fine. These guys who took him sound like Grade A dildos. They're in too deep and they don't have any idea who they're dealing with. Nobody messes with Gordon White Eagle."

Jesus, Jerry thought; he really takes himself too seriously. He wondered if Gordon was using a little of his own product—the pot he supplied some of the underage counselors with. That, or all that guru happy-crappy had gone to his head. "I'll write the alternate scenario, just in case."

"It hasn't been researched, Jer. You can't just come up with something off the cuff and think you can fool the cops. Everyone these days is a forensic expert after all those years of watching *CSI*. We have to get this right the first time, because there won't be another. I worked damned hard to get Max to where I wanted him psychologically, and in my professional opinion, he's primed. I put a lot of work into him, Jerry, and I'm proud of my work. He's more than just a soon-to-be-dead movie star. He's proved my *thesis!*"

Jerry laughed out loud. "I don't think you're going to be able to patent that, Gord."

"No, but I've proved to myself I can do it," Gordon said—a little prissily, Jerry thought. "And you're not going to mess it up for me. We agreed this was the way to go."

"It sure is fucked up now, though, isn't it, Gord? How'd he get away from you? Now we've got kidnappers demanding money, and what if they hack him to little pieces? Talk about a damn clusterfuck!"

"Shaun's good. She'll get him back, and she'll get him back in one piece."

But Jerry heard a smidgen of doubt in Gordon's voice. And anyone who knew Gordon knew he never suffered from doubt.

After Jerry ended the call, he went back to his new storyboard. It was beginning to take shape—simple, elegant, with a logical explanation for the lack of a body.

He liked it.

He liked it a lot.

* * *

GORDON STARED OUT AT THE BEAUTIFUL VERDE VALLEY AND the distant red rocks of Sedona, and thought, *It'll work out.*

But in his heart of hearts, he was worried. The first time Gordon had met Shaun, he'd thought she was beautiful but unsettling. He hadn't liked the way she'd looked at him, as if he were a specimen in a petri dish. If she were an owl, he'd thought, she would eat him.

Gordon had known then that Shaun was as dangerous as nitroglycerin.

Shaun had helped him out a few times, mostly by intimidating her prey, like the socialite who claimed Gordon had fondled her while she was sleeping. Whether he had or he hadn't was immaterial. The woman was a hysteric, threatening to bring down the whole enchilada—the beautiful healing center he had built up from nothing. The Desert Oasis wasn't just a business he loved. In many ways, he *was* the Desert Oasis. He could work a Hollywood party like nobody's business, but he was at home here in the Arizona desert. He felt a spiritual call from the baking red rocks, the deep blue skies, the hawks and eagles that inspired him, and the very wealthy and fucked-up people who came to him for help.

Shaun had a talk with the woman, and that was the end of that.

Mickey Barron's granddaughter put the fear of God into people. Usually, it was no big deal. But there were a couple of times when Gordon needed a…permanent solution, distasteful as that was. Shaun was good at what she did. She'd done a spectacular job on the Russian mobster who had threatened to kill him over a debt. Gordon would be eternally grateful to her for that one.

And the DePaulentis situation had gone off without a hitch.

But Gordon couldn't help but feel that under Shaun's cold, unruffled, professional exterior beat the heart of a lunatic.

Chapter Twenty

"Maternal" was not a term Shaun would have used for herself five months ago. In fact, she had never even thought of having children. Children slowed you down. They dulled your instincts. They were something that could be held over your head. They had to go to school, or be home-schooled. They had to be fed, clothed, entertained, cajoled, raised from mewling little creatures that were, face it, ugly. She never oohed and aahed over a baby like most women did. More often than not, she ignored them. They could do nothing for her.

She'd been in a relationship once with a woman who'd had a little kid. The kid had been whiny, and worse, the woman had always put him first.

But now, watching her son creep quietly over and around broken glass, seeing the concentration on his face, his hair falling over his brow, Shaun felt her heart bloom.

From the moment she'd met him five months ago—he'd actually tried to rob her on the street one night—Shaun had felt an immediate jolt of recognition. He was like her—they were two peas in a pod. After she'd subdued him (falling just short of breaking his arm), she'd sat him down and told him the facts of life. Then she'd asked him about his family and he'd said he had none.

Turned out that was a lie. (Jimmy was a very convincing liar.) But as their relationship deepened and he came to see her as his true mother, he admitted that he'd lived with his aunt for three years. His father was in prison, and his mother died of a drug overdose.

Poor kid needed a real family.

They'd been together ever since.

The night before they left on this trip, they'd had popcorn and watched an old western. The hero stood up against the bad guys after they harassed his son, and said, "You stay away from my boy!"

My boy.

Now she asked him, "What do you think happened here?"

"There was a gunfight. But where is everybody? You checked the house, right?"

"No one there."

But it had been a cursory look around. She'd cleared every room in the main house, but hadn't had a chance to do a thorough search. Just enough to know that Max Conroy was gone. "How long ago do you think this happened?"

Jimmy screwed his eyes shut and thought about it. Looked at her. His eyes were hazel and steady. He was just like her. She experienced that quizzical bloom in her heart again.

"I can still smell nitroglycerin." He added, "When did they call Gordo?"

"Don't be disrespectful. His name is Gordon."

"*You* call him Gordo."

"I'm an adult."

"No fair."

"You need to concentrate."

He nodded. He was a serious boy, her son. He looked at the vehicles and the four bays separated by wooden posts. "He could've grabbed a car and escaped." He ticked them off on his fingers: "Three cars. The old Cadillac over by the mailbox, the Saturn. And the Chevelle SS—that one's cool. Leaves two places in the garage."

"So?"

"I don't think there was another car, though. At least not in the carport." He leveled his gaze on Shaun. "I think there was just the Chevelle and the Saturn."

"Why do you think that?"

He shrugged. "There'd be more glass. Someone would have driven over it."

"They called Gordon forty minutes ago. You see anything out there?"

"No."

Shaun stared at the blood soaked into the concrete apron near the kitchen door. She reached down and pressed her finger into it. Dry, not even sticky. She sniffed it. Copper.

She'd always loved that smell.

"You think they killed him?" Jimmy said.

Jimmy's question echoed her own thoughts. They could have killed him by accident, panicked, and taken off. Maybe there had been another car out front. There could have been a whole caravan of them. The dirt held lots of tire tracks, all of them muddled together—too much sand. Still, they would look at the tracks and see what they could see.

She stared at the silent hills bristling with saguaros, rocks, and mesquite. Noted the corral, the lean-to, the stock tank. The sun was at the top of its curve, and there was hardly a shadow anywhere. She kept her eyes on the scene, looking at it as if it were a tapestry. Looking for one thing out of place, one thread pulled. She saw the desert as a whole, as if she were taking a landscape photograph with her mind. Nothing registered. Closed her eyes to reorient herself, and looked again. This time Shaun looked at objects individually. The palo verde tree by the road. The lean-to. The water tank. The top of the hill. The sky. The house down the road. The house beyond that. A horse. Some calves. Two cars parked outside another house. All the way around, a panorama. Back to the bamboo surrounding the yard and the old Cadillac parked by the mailbox. Panned right and left again. Up and down.

Closed her eyes.

Looked at it again as a whole.

Nothing.

"We search the house again," she said. "Let's make it quick, though."

He could be dead in a closet.

But no, she was sure he was still alive.

Shaun had these feelings. They came to her almost like pronouncements. And the pronouncement she heard in her head was this: he's alive.

Not in good shape, maybe, but alive.

And still worth the price on his head.

* * *

THIS TIME, THEY FOUND THE ENTRANCE TO THE FALLOUT shelter. Hard not to notice with the nuclear symbol on the door. Shaun opened the door into the small space behind the pantry and immediately saw the padlock on the trapdoor. She glanced around and saw the key on the hook. She took down the key, squatted down beside the trapdoor, and put the key in the lock. "Cover me," she said.

Jimmy stood at her shoulder, his gun leveled.

She could feel his excitement.

The lid came up.

Two men squinted up at them.

Another man lay propped up against the far wall. He looked to be in bad shape. His shoulder and bicep were bloody. But he glared at her. A real hard-ass. She liked how defiant he was.

Defiance on its own was never enough, though.

"Hello, Miss—I am so glad you found us!" said the bigger of the two fat ones. "We might have died in here."

"What makes you think I care?"

The man stepped back. He reminded her of a big fat rabbit. A big fat terrified rabbit. Except for his long, lank hair. "Please, madam, could you point that gun in another direction? This has been a difficult time for all of us. Our…friend, here, is wounded, as you can see. He's lost a lot of blood. We're harmless—this is our home. A bad man came to rob us, injured our friend, and left us here to die."

"Can I?" Jimmy asked.

"No."

"Just one of them."

"We need them—they can tell us what happened to the movie star." She looked at the bigger, fatter, older one. "Isn't that right?"

"Yes, madam, anything you want to know. But please, can you get us out of here?"

"I think we can do our talking from here."

"But our friend…"

Shaun said to the defiant one, "Who shot you?"

"Fuck you."

"Ah," said Shaun with a smile. "We have a winner."

* * *

IT DIDN'T TAKE LONG. THEY HAULED THE HARD-ASS OUT OF the bomb shelter and tied him to a chair. He told them what they wanted to know quickly enough—how they had kidnapped Max Conroy and demanded a ransom, only to be turned down flat by Conroy's wife. "Worthless piece of shit," the hard-ass growled. "Even his wife wouldn't bail him out." Every other word was an expletive. Spittle formed on his lips like a rabid dog. But he talked. Shaun knew the right spots to deliver pain with very little leverage, and the moron wanted to talk anyway. He had a lot of bile to unload on just about everybody. He told them how Max got the drop on Luther and Sam P. He was less forthcoming about the gunfight in the carport and how he ended up in the bomb shelter with the other two. Embarrassed, Shaun thought. He should be. Thought he was such a tough guy, and some movie actor outwits him.

Max Conroy went up in Shaun's estimation. She would have to be on her toes when she found him.

When they returned him to the bomb shelter, he flipped them the bird with his good hand.

The only thing they debated was what to do with them next. Jimmy voted to shoot them.

Too much, too fast, thought Shaun. "No."

"But why not? They're the bad guys."

Shaun looked down at the three men. Two anxious faces and a rabid dog.

"Please, madam. Let us go. Please, I beg you!"

Shaun relented. "OK, you can have one."

"Why just one?"

"Discipline," she said. "There's no need to kill more than one of them."

Why couldn't she refuse this boy?

He'd had his kill. It was an important milestone, but it was only one lesson of many she had to teach him.

Maybe she just hated to deny him anything.

Jimmy looked at her with calm eyes. Adult's eyes. "OK. Which one?"

"Your choice."

"The older fat guy is a suck-up. Maybe I should do him."

"No!" cried the fat man. "Please, no! Kill Corey."

"Which one's Corey again?" Shaun asked.

The older fat man jerked his thumb toward the wall. "Our friend with the bullet wound. He might not make it anyway. It would be a mercy."

Corey shot the fat man an ugly look. "Fuck you."

"Well?" Shaun said. "Which one?"

"Please don't kill me," cried the younger fat one. He had a whiny voice, and for a moment, Shaun thought they should kill all three—just make a clean breast of it. But no, she had to stick to her principles. She'd given Jimmy permission to kill one, and that was what he'd have to be satisfied with.

Time to pluck the rat out of the cage. "Well?" she said to Jimmy.

"Can I use the forty-five?"

Shaun removed it from her paddle holster and handed it to her boy. He hefted it. Small kid, big gun.

"Who's it gonna be?" asked Shaun.

Jimmy didn't reply.

He just pulled the trigger.

Chapter Twenty-One

GORDON COULDN'T REACH SHAUN. BUT HE WAS SURE SHE was on her way back with Max in her custody.

Everything would be all right.

So they'd gone off the rails a little. Providing the kidnappers didn't broadcast it to the world—and so far they had not—he could continue on with the original plan. Although it might yet put a crimp in their schedule. Max had been gone for almost three days. Who knew who he'd talked to or what he'd done during that time?

The brainwashing techniques Gordon had used were effective, but it was not an exact science. Max had been out of Gordon's influence for a while now, interacting with other people, trying to come to grips with the breaks in his memory. Hallucinating, probably.

Gordon assumed Max would hallucinate a great deal, his mind coming back to one or two images, as often happened with sensory deprivation therapy taken to its extreme. It was fine if Max saw flying toasters or hot dogs in suits, but the important image, the one Gordon had planted so carefully during hypnosis, had to dominate: the image of a woman and a girl standing by a car broken down by the side of the road.

That would be the trigger, in combination with the audible command, "Freeze!"

If Gordon was completely honest with himself—and he always was—using the mother and the girl was gilding the lily. He didn't really need to use them. The word "Freeze" should be enough. Jerry thought it was better just to stick with the command.

Keep it simple, Gordon. That way there's no room for ambiguity.

Jerry should talk. He was rewriting the script every time Gordon turned around. Jerry's constant tinkering with the story—that was the real problem. The simpler the scenario was, the better. At least the mother and little girl would reinforce the message: just one more cue to drive the point home.

Still, Gordon was worried, which wasn't like him. Usually he let everything roll off his back. He was basically a centered person.

He took a walk out by the pool. The women were beautiful. Lots of starlets—did they even use that term now?—who had already lived twenty years in just two. They'd been big names for a time but now were drifting downward, which sent them into even deeper spirals. Some of them he'd pleasured. It had made some of them whole again.

Although one or two had threatened to call the cops.

Misunderstandings, easily smoothed over.

Fortunately, Gordon didn't have a license to lose. He was a self-made man, a true guru. He did not need a wall full of degrees and plaques to demonstrate his abilities—although he had them anyway. They might not be from the best schools, they might not be from *real* schools, but they were from the best schools money could buy.

People were drawn to him. He was—OK, he wouldn't say godlike, exactly—but he was a father figure. Someone pop singers and film stars and other celebrities and socialites and rudderless rich kids and middle-aged druggies could come to, could *trust*. That was his essence: his bigger-than-life personality, his strength, his power. His generosity.

So when Jerry asked for help, Gordon was more than willing to help him.

That's what brothers did.

Chapter Twenty-Two

TESS WAS JUST FINISHING HER SHIFT, WHICH INCLUDED cleaning up Pat Kerney's typos on his reports. The first week she'd come on board he'd gotten his bid in early for them to read each other's reports, which really meant she read *his*. He called them "typos," but Tess thought they were something else. Lately, his police reports were riddled with more typos of a specific type: "thank" instead of "think," "witch" instead of "which." In this report he'd quoted the woman as saying, the goat "wooden stop struggling."

It seemed to be getting worse.

So here she was, cleaning up his syntax while he was in the restroom. He spent a lot of time in there—his prostate.

Bonny ducked his head into the work area Tess and Pat shared. "I'd like to talk to you for a minute."

She followed him into his office.

"Close the door."

Bonny hitched his duty belt up a bit on his waist and set one haunch on the edge of his desk. "Everything OK?"

"Fine," Tess said. Thinking about Pat wanting to interview "the victim's sun."

Bonny looked at her from under his grizzled eyebrows, his eyes searching. "Something wrong?"

"Just the same old." Tess had never been a snitch.

"This sleepy county's going to get a lot worse soon, what with the prison goin' belly-up and being bought by outside interests. Things are changing around here, and there's going to be a lot more crime to go along with the building boom."

"Building boom? What building boom?"

"It's coming, don't you never mind. They're adding one thousand beds to that stinkhole across town, and the governor's making noises about all the drug cartels in this county."

"Drug cartels?"

"Yeah, I know—there aren't any. But we're talking federal money. It's all exaggeration to generate more revenue for the governor, but now all the counties are getting caught up in it. If I want to survive, I'll have to play the game. I'm too old to start a new career now, and people want me to protect 'em from things that ain't never gonna happen, at least not for many years. Which is all a roundabout way of saying that I need to make some changes around here. There are folks who aren't crazy about my detective."

Tess saw Pat's report in her mind's eye, the one he pecked out with two fingers, typing "stinkbug" instead of "stun gun."

"You come from a big city, and people—some people—are clamoring for, uh, more sophistication. Pat's retiring next year, but the election's next year too, and that'll be too late for me. So. Raise your right hand."

Tess raised her right hand.

"You're detective." He added, "I can go through the whole rigmarole, but I don't have time for that nonsense. I'm sheriff and as sheriff I can make you detective, so, tag, you're it."

"What about Pat?"

"He gets to be detective too. I figure that's what Solomon would do. But because he's still detective, you won't get a raise in pay. The good news is, you can wear regular clothes. Darrell at Watson Chevy unloaded a plain-wrap on me—you can drive that now. It's got low miles, believe it or not, so it's a step up. Only thing it doesn't have right now is a radio, and I figure we can get that put in this weekend."

Tess opened her mouth to protest.

But Bonny closed it for her with his next words: "I know about Pat's dyslexia, or whatever it is, and I know it's getting worse. It's nice of you to cover up for him but it isn't a help. Pat's making noises about going to live with his daughter and I'm not going to discourage that. What do you say?"

"He's not going to like it."

"He doesn't have a choice. I've made my decision. I hire you on to 'learn the ropes' with him, or I start looking for someone else, and Pat will be out sooner rather than later."

There was nothing else Tess could say. She had always seen herself as a detective, had been one for four years before she had to leave Albuquerque. And she was good. A part of her wanted to show just how good.

Bonny said, "Besides, you remember everyone you meet and you can tell them what they ate and prob'ly even when they had their last poop. So congratulations, go out and paint the town."

Tess permitted herself a tiny smile.

Until she realized she would have to be the one to handle Pat.

Chapter Twenty-Three

TALIA L'APEL POKED HER HEAD INTO JERRY'S STUDY.

"I'm busy here!" Jerry Gold shouted. "I don't need any distractions right now, especially since I'm trying to clean up your mess."

Talia's lips pressed together in a tight line. Talia, Queen of the Silent Treatment. Jerry could hear her moping from all the way across the room.

"Dylan's here."

"Oh, great. The one day he shows up on time. All right, I suppose I'd better see him. Give me a minute."

"Fine. He's in the foyer."

"He didn't see you, did he?"

"No, he *didn't see me.*"

"Well, for God's sake, have Delilah offer him something to drink and take him out by the pool."

He had to tell her every little thing. For a girl with such sharp instincts for garnering publicity, Talia could be awfully obtuse about some things.

Like thinking.

She had people for that.

Had people. This week, Talia was flying solo.

The last couple of weeks she'd been hiding out here whenever she could slip the paparazzi. This essentially meant she'd left behind her stylist, her publicist, her hangers-on—all of them. She'd let it be known through her publicist that she had "gone into seclusion," to prepare for her trip to Africa and her husband's homecoming. Talia had used the "I'm a private person and need my space," line, and surprisingly, people had believed it. She'd always been a convincing actress.

Everyone knew what a bad boy Max Conroy could be. Talia deserved all the sympathy in the world for helping to turn him around, and the public believed his domestication was almost complete. All he needed was the clean bill of health from the Desert Oasis Healing Center and a few happy photo ops with his loving wife and new baby.

Unfortunately for Max, that happy domestic scene would never take place.

Jerry wished he'd told Talia to stay away. Not only did they risk being caught out, but it played havoc with this thinking process. He didn't want anyone around while he was in the planning stages. Talia was a distraction. But she'd worked so hard at dodging the paparazzi, he felt he really couldn't say no.

Jerry needed more than a minute to get his mind out of the world he'd created in his storyboard.

He was serious when he told Gordon he wanted to do it his way. The other idea was too clunky, with too many moving parts—there was much more of a chance for something to go wrong. Gordon had done a beautiful job, sure—the scenario had a certain elegance. It was like a motion picture in miniature. But he didn't quite trust Gordon's ability to brainwash

Max the right way. In fact, he didn't know if brainwashing worked at all.

Jerry's plan, on the other hand, was simple.

The kidnappers could go ahead and kill Max—as long as they didn't do it on camera—but the body could never be found. That would add a new twist to the story. It would only enhance Max's legend.

Max would join the disappeared. Like Amelia Earhart. You could always count on her to make money, even though her plane disappeared over Howland Island in 1937. Sometimes ambiguity was good—look at all the Elvis sightings.

They'd have to recover his body, though, with no one in the press being the wiser. And, they'd have to dissolve him in acid.

He could never be found.

There were problems with this scenario, of course. How would they recover the body before anyone else did?

Fortunately, Gordon's go-to killer, Shaun, was in Paradox.

If Shaun could find the kidnappers—or at least find Max's body—they could deep-six him in acid.

There would be problems with the estate, but in the long run, Talia would prevail. Especially if the paparazzi pushed the story of Max's kidnapping. Fortunately, Jerry had made it his business to cultivate a few of the paps; he knew several who would do anything for an exclusive. He could leak that he was worried about Max, that Max hadn't been seen, that he'd left the Desert Oasis Healing Center and walked right off the edge of the earth.

Both scenarios had their strong points, but right now, they didn't have Max.

Jerry realized that they would have to come to a solid decision about this, sooner rather than later.

In the meantime, he needed to lay the groundwork for his new star.

* * *

"DYLAN!" JERRY BELLOWED, STRIDING OUT FROM UNDER THE ramada. "So good to see you."

Dylan Harris sat up on the diving board, looking sleepy. The young man looked like an ad in *Esquire* or *GQ*, stretched out and glistening on a white towel over chlorinated blue water.

Dylan Harris was ready for leading man status, yet still young enough to drive the tweens wild. Jerry had been cultivating him, a meeting or a lunch at a time, until Dylan began to see himself more as Jerry's adopted son than just a client.

Jerry's team had gotten Dylan some good parts, and Jerry made sure that the career arc made sense. Second to the lead, but enough breadth in some of the parts where you could begin to see Dylan taking on something weightier, like the character of Starker in *V.A.M.Pyre*. It would be a gamble, sure, but that was all part of the game—and Jerry loved the game.

Now, Jerry said, "Dyl, I'm glad you came by. I could use a sympathetic ear right now."

"Hey, anything I can do. You've been so good to me."

Jerry sat down on the end of the diving board. "It's kind of…difficult. You can't tell anyone."

"Oh, no, I won't."

Jerry sighed and stared out at the Pacific, framed by the deep pink bougainvillea on the wrought-iron railing. "Things aren't going well with *V.A.M.Pyre: The Target*. We haven't even started production yet, and I'm worried that Max won't be ready."

Dylan stared at him. His eyes reminded Jerry of a wolf's eyes, only sexier.

"I wouldn't say this to anybody else. But I need to confide in someone, and you're like a son to me."

"I'll help if I can."

"I know that. Here's the thing, Dyl: Max isn't doing very well in rehab. I'm worried he'll relapse the minute he gets out."

"That's too bad, sir."

Sir. Dylan had been raised far from Hollywood, somewhere in the south. The kid didn't even drink.

After dealing with Max's issues, Dylan Harris was manna from heaven. "Frankly, I don't think Max is up to it. All the pressure. I can't help but feel he's not going to be there on the fifteenth, when it's time to plan the production."

"Not be there? But he's under contract!"

Gee whiz.

Jerry shook his head. "Contracts are meant to be broken, and this isn't Max's first rodeo."

"So what are you going to do?"

"Hope for the best, I guess."

"Yeah."

"There are morality clauses in the contract. Terrapin Productions could let him go. But the problem is, who'd replace him? I just can't see a way out. I think of all those people, what would happen if we didn't start on time. Of course, he might be OK, but it's not like I have a Plan B."

"That's not fair," Dylan said.

"No." Jerry sighed. "Life is just not fair."

He left it there.

He figured two or three more conversations and Dylan would be envisioning himself as the new Starker.

And as Dylan's manager, Jerry would still be on top—the trifecta of the century. He'd have Max's wife, Max's estate, and manage the business affairs of the hottest new star in the business.

They just had to find Max, and make sure they buried him deep.

* * *

AFTER DYLAN LEFT, JERRY CALLED GORDON FOR A BRIEFING. Gordon told him just about what he'd expected: there was no word from the kidnappers. And no word from Shaun.

"What do you think is happening, Gord?"

"I have no idea."

Jerry could see everything going up in smoke. "You never should have trusted that crazy bitch. Anyone with half a brain can see she's stark raving nuts. How many women do you know wear a fricking fade?"

"She's done good work before. She saved my life not too long ago."

"She did? When was that?"

"Long story. A guy from the Russian Mafia was after me."

"And she killed him?"

"You don't want to know, Jer. All I can say is, the Russian Mafia left me alone after that."

Jerry absorbed this. She *must* be good. "But you said she has a kid with her."

"He's twelve, Jer. Not exactly a kid."

"Not exactly a kid? I'd say that's a kid. What's the story there?"

"I don't know."

"You don't *know*?"

"I think she adopted him."

"Adopted him. A lesbo killer like that? Can you see her going to an adoption agency and copping herself a twelve-year-old kid? What did she do? Steal him from someone?"

"Does it matter? She's good, Jerry. You don't have to worry about that."

But Jerry worried. That was what Jerry did.

Chapter Twenty-Four

MAX MADE IT OVER THE SCRUBBY HILL AND OUT OF SIGHT of the house, leaning against a boulder in the sketchy shade of a mesquite tree. He thought about Corey again. Corey was wounded and had lost some blood. Maybe a lot of blood. What if the woman and the boy found the bomb shelter? He could see Corey shooting off his mouth, maybe even trying to overpower them, and that would end badly for Corey. Not to mention Luther and Sam P.

What did he care about them? They were kidnappers.

He should put as much distance between himself and the woman and boy as possible.

Had Gordon sent the woman and the boy to get him?

That made no sense. The woman and the boy had shown up within a half hour of Max's last call to Gordon.

No way they could have made it down from Sedona.

Unless...

Unless they were already here. Unless they were already looking for him.

But who sent them?

That was easy. Gordon or Jerry or both. First, they'd sent the two guys in the limo, the ones the deputy routed.

But why that strange-looking woman? Why a boy?

Max knew he was overthinking this. *Go by your instincts.*

His instincts told him that the woman and the boy were looking for him, and that they were far more dangerous than the guys in the limo.

His instincts told him that the woman and the boy were killers. And he knew, if the woman and the boy encountered Corey, Luther, and Sam P., there would be a firefight.

And he knew who would lose that fight.

Max took one of the prepaid phones out of its cardboard box, found the number of the Bajada County Sheriff's Office by scrolling through Luther's smartphone, and punched it into the prepaid mobile.

A dispatcher answered. "Bajada Sheriff's Office, may I help you?"

"There are two people trying to break into a house on Ocotillo Road. It's the last house on the left."

"Can you describe the two people?"

"No, I'm kind of far away."

"Do they have a vehicle?"

"I'm not sure."

"Your name, sir?"

He disconnected.

"I hope they don't shoot you guys," he muttered as he started down the hill toward another settlement of houses.

They were small plots of houses, on a few acres, little ranchettes.

Everything was still and quiet.

Max knew how to hot-wire a car, but first, he looked for keys in the ignition. He knew from living in the sticks when he was a kid and, more recently, on his ranch in Montana, that people who owned ranch trucks often left them unlocked with the windows rolled down.

He got lucky on the second try. The key *was* in the ignition, and no one was around. It was an old Ford F-250. He put it in gear and drove onto the dirt road. Knew the neighbors would recognize the truck, but in this heat, everyone was probably indoors, sitting under the fans and hoping for a breath of air from their swamp box coolers.

As he reached the highway, he saw a sheriff's vehicle pull off onto Sam P.'s road ahead of him. A male deputy, not the woman who had arrested him—the woman with the memory like a steel trap.

Max turned the other way.

✳ ✳ ✳

The sound of the bullet smashing bone ricocheted in the bomb shelter like an echo chamber.

Sam P. dropped like a sack of grain, his right eye gone and the other one staring up at them in glassy dismay.

But Shaun saw Luther behind him, flailing on the floor, shrieking like a banshee.

Half his jaw was blown off. The bullet must have gone through Sam P. and hit Luther as well.

Jimmy looked down in wonder at the .45. "Cool," he said in awe.

Shaun saw Luther enmeshed in his own gore, trying to pick up the part of his jaw he'd lost, blood pouring out of him like a leaky spring.

Shaun took the .45 from Jimmy and put one through the center of Luther's forehead.

Corey was half yelling, half screaming—a string of profanities came from his filthy mouth.

Shaun aimed and shot, but there was distance and the angle—he was below them—and she missed. She shot again, hit his good shoulder, and it spun him around.

She shot him three more times, center mass. He fell forward, dead.

The stink was terrible.

Jimmy looked at her. "I thought you said just one."

She shrugged. "I changed my mind."

* * *

MAX DROVE OVER A LOW HILL AND SAW A CROSSROAD AHEAD. A car was parked about twenty feet back from the stop sign. He saw a woman and a girl standing on the far side of the car—they must be having car trouble.

"Freeze!"

Max sat bolt upright, his muscles locking, foot mashing down on the accelerator. The truck he was driving shot through the intersection.

He hit the brakes. Skidded to a halt, tires smoking.

Shaking, Max looked at the crossroad, now in his rearview mirror.

There *was* no car.

He leaned his body over the steering wheel. His mouth was dry and sweat poured down his face.

Gordon.

Gordon had done this to him.

Why, though? Because he could? Max had always thought Gordon was a pompous ass. A sociopathic pompous ass.

Max tried to picture the car he'd thought he'd seen, but couldn't.

He sat in the truck, letting his heart rate drop back to normal, and then he started up the truck and pressed on the accelerator.

But the truck didn't respond right away. There was a catch in the engine. The farm truck coughed and slowed. Max pushed the pedal to the metal, but it sank uselessly to the floor.

Out of gas.

Now what?

He was out of gas and hallucinating: just another day in the life of Max Conroy.

He checked back in the rearview mirror—no car, just empty road.

He got out and started in the direction of town. He reckoned it would be three or four miles. He listened for the sound of a truck behind him—a new Chevy truck with a big engine. He didn't know what he'd do if he heard it. There wasn't much in the way of cover here. Just the empty road and some creosote bushes and a stunted mesquite or two. He scanned the roadside, back and forth, looking for cover, just in case. He'd have a little time. There were hills here, so he might not be in their line of sight.

He didn't want to run into the woman and the boy.

After ten minutes of walking, he heard engines stressed to the breaking point.

Two sheriff's cars shot over the rise, their wigwag lights blinking back and forth.

They blasted past him. He thought he saw the deputy, Tess, driving one of the cars, but wasn't sure.

He watched them disappear over the rise. Two cars, added to the one that had driven by earlier. In a county this sparse, that could be the whole fleet. Where were they going in such a hurry?

But he knew. Something had happened back at the house. The deputy, the first one, must have encountered the woman and the boy. Maybe they'd shot him.

Whatever the cops found at the house, they would remember him walking along the shoulder of the road. *She* would remember him.

The deputy with the photographic memory would have him etched in her mind.

She would see the abandoned ranch truck too. She would wonder why the guys in the limo were after him. She would wonder what he was doing walking along the shoulder of the road in the middle of July with the sun beating down on his head, his shirt blotted with sweat and—yes—blood. She would wonder what was in the duffel he carried slung over his shoulder. The female deputy with the photographic memory would know the neighbor who owned the missing truck. The old brown Ford F-250. Of course she would.

She would see the bullet holes and Corey's blood against the carport wall, the broken glass, all evidence of a gunfight.

Max had to get out of here.

He jogged along the road, looking for a house, someplace to hide, a car, anything.

The road spanned a narrow wash ahead. The wash was overgrown with chest-high grass, green like corn—the stuff that grew up after a rain. He could hide in there. He jumped down into the dry riverbed, and that was when he saw the culvert under the road.

He crawled inside, as far as he could get.

And waited.

* * *

SHAUN FOLLOWED THE ROAD ALL THE WAY TO TOWN. THEY had closed up the bomb shelter and locked the kitchen door behind them. The place was out in the sticks. There were a couple of ranchettes farther up the road, but the bamboo hid most of the front yard from view and the carport was in shadow. It might be days before anyone came by.

Shaun and her son had both washed up at the kitchen sink and rinsed their shirts to get rid of any stray blood spatter. They'd throw their clothing away in a Dumpster somewhere on the road. They dug through their suitcases from the truck and changed hurriedly. Shaun knew they needed to get on Max Conroy's trail before it went cold.

They needed to split up. Although Max Conroy might still be nearby, Shaun thought he would head for town as soon as he escaped. She left Jimmy to scout the area while she reconnoitered ahead. He was to check the four or five houses and barns in the area and then call when he was done.

She had just made a pass through the main drag and was parking the truck so she could continue her search on foot when she heard a cop car coming, fast. No siren, but cops had a way of driving that made those big engines roar. She got back into the truck just as two sheriff's cars rounded the corner, lights flashing. She saw them turn in the direction she'd come from, and knew instantly: someone had found the bodies in the bomb shelter.

Who?

Had a neighbor come by? Or did Max Conroy have a fit of conscience?

Jimmy was on his own—for now. He would be all right. He'd hear the cop cars coming and go to ground.

She continued to canvass the town. Didn't talk to anybody, just played tourist. She knew she didn't look like a tourist, but she also knew that if she looked at anyone who regarded her with curiosity, the person would likely look uncomfortably away. They said the best assassins were nondescript and blended into a crowd, and that was true. But she'd made a living being the other kind. She knew she could be mistaken for a man, depending on what she wore and how she carried herself. People would remember her. But they usually looked away, embarrassed and guilty because they didn't want to gawk. They tried to forget her. They thought of her as a freak, not someone who might be dangerous.

She could change clothes, put on a wig, and be a different person. She'd made the transformation dozens of times.

She called Jimmy and he answered on the first ring. "Where are you?"

"I'm laying low," he said.

"They at the house?"

"Uh-huh."

"Can you get around them?"

"Sure. I'm up on the hill. They can't see me, but I can see them."

"You talk to anybody?"

"I saw one lady out with her horses. She looked smart, though, so I stayed away."

"So what do you think?"

"I don't think he's here."

"He's probably headed for town. Meet me outside the Subway, OK? Don't let anybody see you."

"It might take a while."

"That's OK. I'll keep looking for him, but now that they know what's in the bomb shelter, we've got to get out of here. So try to get there in an hour, all right?"

"Roger," Jimmy said.

* * *

MAX KNEW AT SOME POINT HE HAD TO LEAVE THE CULVERT. He could hear thunder, and if the rains came, the dry arroyo would fill up fast and funnel into the culvert—he could drown. But he was tired. After all he'd been through—the adrenaline rush—he could barely keep his eyes open. Being here, under the road, made him feel that he was not only safe, but invincible. He'd locked all three kidnappers into the prison of their own making. He'd survived a gunfight with a tough guy like Corey. He'd managed to give the woman and the boy the slip, as well as the sheriff. The only thing standing in his way now was a need for stealth and a need for transportation.

In fact, he felt better than he had in a long time.

For so long Max had been a victim of circumstances—a victim of his own making. He'd gone along to get along. He'd dutifully done what his press agent told him to do, what his manager told him what to do, what his business manager told him to do, what his CPA told him to do, what his financial advisor told him to do, what his wife told him to do. They all had their own agendas, and Max realized he'd just drifted, hating himself more and more, drinking and taking whatever prescription drug was available at the time. And, since he was a star, the drugs were always available, all the time.

Strangely, he didn't feel a craving for the drugs. How could he have lost the dependency on prescription drugs so easily? He remembered Gordon telling him that sensory deprivation therapy was the most useful tool in combating addiction, that in many cases, people just...lost the urge.

Here he was, sitting in a culvert with possibly two killers coming after him, and now Max finally felt as if he was his own man.

That feeling lasted about fifteen minutes. Then he heard footfalls.

At first, he thought he was hearing things. The footfalls were so light. Just the faintest tap on pavement, hardly enough to register. But the humming. Tuneless, barely there, like someone was thinking aloud by humming.

Then no sound at all.

He waited.

His heart rate jumped into the red zone. He eased the Smith & Wesson out of the duffel. How many people had he pointed the thing at? How many shots had he fired? It didn't seem like him, but right now he was the hunted, and he went by pure instinct.

Max felt as if he'd been melted down to the steel of his own core. He tasted it, like metal in his mouth. Determination. Anyone who poked his head into the culvert would risk getting it blown off.

He aimed at the half circle of sunshine and shadow. The white sand of the wash, the weird green cornlike grass, stalks rustling slightly in the ozone-scented breeze. The sky like a dark bruise beyond…

The click of shoes on gravel.

Was he imagining it?

Another shift of the shoe on pavement. No, he was not imagining it.

The kid.

The skinny little kid with the big gun.

We'll see whose gun is bigger.

The sound of the voice in his own head shocked him.

Whatever was in his head *wanted* the boy to come down here. Wanted to blow him to kingdom come.

Thunder grumbled.

The air seemed both electric and still. Everything stopped. He was suspended, here in this tunnel made out of corrugated tin, with the accumulated trash hooked onto the rocks, the whole world standing still…

The kid plopped down off the bank. Max saw his elbow and one sneaker-clad foot. Just the side of him. Kid had a purple yo-yo, was playing walk the dog.

Max sighted down the barrel of the Smith & Wesson.

Make my day.

Then he heard canned music—a ringtone.

Max watched the kid's legs. The knees bent. The kid sat down on the bank of the wash, his legs swinging, kicking back at the dirt. The ringtone stopped. The kid said, "What?"

Then he said, "I was just going—"

Then he said, "OK."

His knees came into the frame briefly, his elbows flapping, the tip of his head. Then he scrambled up the bank.

Max realized his hands, which had trained the gun steadily on the half circle of daylight, were beginning to shake.

Adrenaline.

He waited. He did not lower the gun.

The Smith & Wesson seemed to weigh a hundred pounds. His arms were tired. He knew it wasn't the weight of the gun. He knew it wasn't the way he held his arms out in front of him. He knew it was the weight of anger, fear, and determination.

And he knew that the weight was an acknowledgment of something else: he would have killed that kid.

Killed that kid, and rejoiced over it.

Chapter Twenty-Five

PAT ACTED AS IF TESS WERE STILL A DEPUTY. THAT WAS OK
with her. He had his pride. But she didn't like the fact that he
was phoning it in. He stared down at the three bloody corpses
in the bomb shelter and said, "This is going to be one bad
mother of a day."

Tess had met Sam P. and Luther. She'd arrested Corey
once for assault. She'd had no idea Sam had a bomb shelter,
but the house was old and built in a time when bomb shelters
were popular.

Tess knew she'd be seeing this tableau in her night-
mares—every stark detail. At will, she could see any and
all of the crime scenes she'd been called to as a detective in
Albuquerque. The familiar stink rose up, a bloated miasma,
along with the flies that had already found the dead men.
There was the overwhelming stench of death, nine parts
spoiled meat and one part the coppery odor of blood, which
lay in the membranes of her mouth. She felt her gorge rise
but willed it to back down.

"So, what do we do now, hotshot?" Pat said. He kept his
voice light, as if it were a joke.

She said, "I'm kind of new on the job."

"Right." Pat started giving instructions. Everyone out of the house, now that they'd cleared it. Crime scene tape around the house and yard, make sure to rope off the carport. One deputy to keep people from coming in—that would be Derek, who'd have the police log. Then it was just the two of them. Gloves and booties. "You wanna take the photos?" Pat asked Tess. "Or is just looking enough? You probably have it all memorized down to the fly on ol' Corey's ankle."

Tess took photos.

She kept her mind on the work, careful not to touch any blood, which was tracked all over the bomb shelter floor and bloomed on the wall like an iris where Corey had been hit. Blood spatter everywhere—plenty for an in-depth analysis.

"What do you think?" Pat asked.

Tess knew this time he was serious in his question. He often relied on her judgment. "Looks like a large caliber weapon, maybe a forty-five? They were shot from above."

"Like fish in a barrel," Pat said. "We got us a serious killer here."

It was a large crime scene. The yard out front. The kitchen leading to the pantry leading to the entrance to the bomb shelter. The carport with the shot-up cars. The flurry of footprints and tire prints outside. The investigation would extend into the night and long into the next day.

* * *

AFTER THE BAJADA COUNTY MEDICAL EXAMINER'S OFFICE removed the bodies, after Tess and Pat had measured the scene and marked the evidence to be bagged, Tess went outside to breathe some clean air.

The cumulus clouds were building up over the mountains and it looked like there might be rain. Right now, though, it was just an electric feeling in the air. The air was heavy and waterlogged from the little bit of rain left over from last night, and the creosote bushes smelled heavenly. But it was hot. She lifted her ponytail off the back of her neck.

She'd seen Max Conroy walking on the road's shoulder.

She'd seen his look of surprise when he saw them go by.

Now Tess pictured his face in the rearview, tried to peg the expression. *He knew he was in deep trouble.*

There'd been no weapon on him, but he had a duffel. The duffel looked heavy.

There was the truck too. Dan Jensen's Ford F-250. Sitting by the road, approximately an eighth of a mile beyond the spot where she'd seen Max standing on the shoulder watching the parade of sheriff's cars go by.

Max might have left the truck there.

Tess told Pat what she'd seen.

"You think he did it?"

"I think we should check him out. Even if he wasn't the shooter, he could be a witness."

"You think he stole the truck."

She shrugged. "That would be an easy conclusion to jump to."

They called the crime scene technicians, who were already on the road, and asked them to come back and process Dan Jensen's truck.

"You going to check it out?" Pat asked Tess.

"Thought I would. You all right here?"

"Why wouldn't I be?"

She nodded.

"I mean, seriously, why wouldn't I be? I've been investigating homicides for twenty-three years."

Red as a tomato, he brushed at the sweat on his face. His blue eyes angry.

Tess said, "You tell me what you want me to do."

"Just…just do your job," he said. "Whatever that is."

* * *

TESS WENT AND DID HER JOB. SHE'D NEED A WARRANT FOR the truck left abandoned on the road, since it might or might not be part of the crime scene. The judge was pretty good about these things, would OK it pretty quickly.

She peered into the truck, careful not to touch anything.

There was a Mexican serapelike throw covering the bench seat.

Tess guessed the truck had broken down or was out of gas. Or maybe just abandoned. As soon as the crime scene technicians arrived, she'd go pay Dan Jensen a visit. Just in case he had something to do with this. It was always good to surprise people.

But the dispatcher called her first, to tell her that Dan had reported his truck stolen.

Tess called Pat and asked him if he would take Dan Jensen's statement.

"Why not?" he asked. "I happened to be as free as a bird today." Then he hung up on her.

This was working out well.

It had been a couple of hours since she'd spotted Max walking along the roadside. He would have made it to town by now. Tess had the dispatcher send out an Attempt to Locate on the actor Max Conroy. In case there was a deputy or PD officer who didn't know what Max Conroy looked like, she uploaded a photo of him from the film and television site IMDb.

She called Pat again. "How's it going there?"

"About what you'd expect. Bloody and stinky."

"I need to run down the lead we were talking about—Max Conroy. I think he might have made it to town. I need a deputy here until our property and evidence unit gets here."

Bajada County's property and evidence unit consisted of one part-time crime scene technician and a volunteer who had taken a community college course on gathering evidence. They would be responsible for delivering the evidence to the Arizona Department of Public Safety crime lab.

"We need everyone we got," Pat said. "This is one massive fricking crime scene."

"I'll stay here, then."

"Yeah, that's the right call." He added, "You put out the Attempt to Locate. Don't need to go running around like you're the Lone Ranger."

"Roger," she said, and clicked off.

She sat in the shade of a mesquite, waited for property and evidence, and monitored dispatch.

And waited.

And tried to picture Max. Max getting the jump on Luther, Sam, and Corey, and killing them all.

She wondered why he'd do that. Why a movie star would go to Sam's house and get the three of them down into the bomb shelter and kill them?

She thought about the last she'd seen of him, at the diner. He'd seemed normal to her then. But what was normal?

Tess called the deputy who'd been first on the scene. "Do you know why you were dispatched to the house?"

"Somebody called it in. God, I lost my lunch. It was like something out of a horror movie. Never saw anything like it." He sounded embarrassed.

Tess said, "Somebody called it in. What did the dispatcher say?"

"An unknown person was trying to break into Sam's place."

Tess needed to hear the recording. She made a note of it. "That was what they said? They saw somebody trying to break in. Was it a man or a woman?"

"Man. The dispatcher said 'he.'"

"When you arrived, what did you see?"

"What you saw. The carport, all shot up. Broken glass everywhere. The door was open."

"What led you to the bomb shelter?" she asked.

"There were drag marks on the floor. And blood. I already gave you guys my statement."

"I know," Tess said. "I was just hoping you'd think of something new this time around."

"It was hard to *think*, after what I saw."

"I know the feeling."

She disconnected and called the dispatcher. Toni cued up the recording, which came from an anonymous source.

Tess closed her eyes and listened. "There are two people trying to break into a house on Ocotillo Road. It's the last house on the left."

Max Conroy's voice.

"Could you repeat that?"

Toni cued it up again and played it.

There are two people. Trying to break in.

"Is there any way to trace the phone?"

"No. We could spend a day or two to pin down the location, but—"

"We already know the location." Tess disconnected and stared out at the middle distance. The clouds were amassing; the air was hot and humid. But so far, no rain.

If Max killed those three people, why did he call it in?

Unbidden, the image of the woman and the boy at Joe's Auto-Wash came to her. The woman who'd bought a truck for Sandstone Adventures and dressed up to do it.

The woman who had stared right through her. Whose presence made the hair stand up on Tess's arms.

Tess knew it was never a good idea to jump to conclusions. But as she set the phone down, the voice in her mind said, *There's your killer.*

* * *

GORDON WAS GETTING WORRIED—STILL NO WORD FROM Shaun, and she wasn't answering her phone. *What was she doing?* Paradox wasn't that far away—she should be pulling into the healing center any minute with Max in tow. But he had not heard word one from her.

Then he turned on the news, and that was when he realized she'd gone too far. *Three people* slaughtered in a bomb shelter in Paradox, Arizona. Of course there were no names. But already on CNN he could see the deputies traipsing around the sunbaked property. Saw a gurney with a body bag strapped to it being rolled out the door.

Could one of those bodies belong to Max? God, no.

His phone chirped—Jerry.

Gordon didn't want to answer now.

This was one mother-loving mess, and if Max turned up a bloody pulp—and the paparazzi were able to get a photo—his legendary status would be a thing of the past.

In this day of instant gratification and overt bribery, Gordon had no doubt that if one of the corpses was Max, someone had already gotten a candid shot of him with a cell phone.

And that photo would quickly make its way to the Internet. No question about that.

In which case, Max's value would plummet, and they'd be left holding a very unappetizing bag. And knowing Jerry, Gordon knew he'd hear about it for the rest of his life.

The desk phone rang. He didn't bother to look at the readout. "All right, Jerry. What now?"

"No, sir, this is Drew," Gordon's assistant said. "There's a call for you."

"I don't want to talk now."

"You might want to talk to this one, sir. She's with the Bajada County Sheriff's Office. Detective Tess McCrae."

* * *

JERRY LISTENED AS GORDON'S PHONE WENT TO VOICE MAIL. He waited for the tone and yelled, "Gordon, will you tell me what the *hell* is going on? I'm going *out* there!" He slammed the phone on the granite kitchen island and a piece of plastic flew off, almost hitting him in the eye. This made him angrier, so he took the phone and beat it against the edge of the island until it disintegrated.

Talia stood in the doorway, her eyes wide. "What happened?"

"Turn on the TV and see for yourself!"

She grabbed the remote from the desk and turned on the television. *Horny Housewives* was on. Jerry grabbed the remote from her and muttered, "The *news*, dammit."

Three men had been shot to death in a home outside Paradox, Arizona. Their names had not been released yet, pending notification to their families.

"So what now?" Talia asked, her voice calm. Too calm. Had she taken another Xanax?

"So what now?" he repeated, parroting her "poor little me" voice. "We have to find out if Max was one of them. It's probably best not to panic *yet*." He stared at his broken smartphone. "Maybe there's a way out. If they didn't destroy his face. But you know it will come out. All the details. There will be at least one blurry corpse picture." He stared at his new wall of storyboard scenes. Not worth the cheap paper they were drawn on, now.

He needed to calm down. For all he knew, Max wasn't involved in the killing at all.

But his gut told him there was no way he wasn't.

Chapter Twenty-Six

When Jimmy met up with Shaun at the Subway, they had lunch. Jimmy had a spectacular appetite, and Shaun enjoyed watching her boy eat. Her heart filled with love as she watched him. He was always intent on his food, like a wolf or a mountain lion, and she liked that she could see the predator in him.

He looked up at her, his mouth ringed with grease from the sub. "What?"

"Nothing," she said, knowing she sounded like an over-indulgent mother.

Jimmy said, "So what do we do now?"

"We keep looking for him."

"Yeah, but where?" He stretched his arm out, as if to encompass the Subway and the whole northern part of the state.

"We'll find him. I've never lost a patient yet," she joked.

He stared at her skeptically. The lock of hair falling over one eye. He looked frail, small for his age, but he was strong. He was like a cable that would not bend. "He's probably on a plane back to LA by now."

"He's around here," Shaun said. "Somewhere. I can feel it."

"You and your feelings again."

"I've done this for a long time. I know what I'm talking about."

"Bet you didn't figure on him locking those idiots in the bomb shelter!"

She didn't like his smirk. "Don't talk to your mother like that," she said.

"You're not my mother."

Shaun said, "What are you talking about? I'm your mother and you're my son. I thought we already talked about this."

He looked away and mumbled something.

"What?" She leaned forward, her elbows on the table. "What did you say?"

"You're not my mother. I have a mother."

"Then where is she? How come I found you living on the streets?"

He ducked his head and rubbed one eye. That lock of hair, falling over his face. "My mother's dead."

"No, she's not. She's right here, looking at you, young man." A red mist lowered over her eyes. No—not a mist. A stain. She could see everything clearly, in better detail than normal—every grain on the Subway bun, every one of Jimmy's fine eyelashes, the ring of dark around his accusing eyes.

"I am your mother."

He stared at her through the red stain. Everything hyper-delineated and clear. Sound rushing in, magnified. She could hear the lowered voice of the other diners, hear the crackle of waxed paper as the kid at the counter wrapped a sub. Everything a deep, blood red.

The anger building, coming up through her throat like Mt. Vesuvius.

She repeated, "I am your mother!"

And realized she was shouting.

Everything stopped. The place went quiet.

People were looking at them.

She grabbed his hand. "We've got to go. Now."

He pulled away. "I don't want to go. You're going to get us in trouble. We're both going to end up in prison."

"Keep your voice down."

He stood up. "Screw you! You go do what you want, but I'm outta here." And he dodged past her and trotted to the men's room.

* * *

IN THE CULVERT, MAX WAITED, THEN WAITED SOME MORE. It could still be a trap. The kid could be right outside, like a cat at a mouse hole. Waiting…

But the thunder was grumbling, and he could smell moisture in the air. If it rained, he'd be washed out like everything else in this culvert.

He'd been trained by cops. He knew how to at least act like one. He duckwalked over to the edge of the culvert. Got on his stomach. Looked left first—the kid might go for the element of surprise—then right. Sweeping his gun as he did so. Crawled out a little more. On his back, gun trained at the road above. Sweeping again. Then he jumped to his feet.

No one here. No sound of cars. No skinny little kid with the heart of a killer.

Relief rolled off him along with his sweat.

He'd wiped his nose on his sleeve. Realized he'd never smelled so rank.

Fear smelled rank. And the desire to kill, that smelled rank too.

He felt it. The strength flowing into him. He felt exalted. He wanted to crow to the skies. He wanted to hunt down that kid and hunt down that woman and see it in their eyes when he drew down on them. Wanted to smash, to kill.

"What is wrong with me?" he muttered as he climbed the bank. He started in the direction of town, but his goal was the Desert Oasis Healing Center. And Gordon White Eagle would be in for a world of hurt when he got there.

* * *

TESS STARTED UP THE NEW CAR—IT SOUNDED POWERFUL and didn't miss like her last unit—and waited for a big truck to pull off the road and into the Subway parking lot. The words "Sunline Traders" were written on the side.

Back at the office, she called the Desert Oasis Healing Center. She was immediately put on hold. The canned music was Sinatra tunes without Sinatra's voice. The young man who'd answered had said, "I'll try and see if he's in. No promises."

She should just drive up there. But it was her first day as detective and they had three people dead of gunshot wounds and at least two crime scenes. They were understaffed and even though Pat was not as helpful as she would like, he was doing his job. She needed to stick around and work with him.

"Hello." The voice was deep and brisk. "This is Mr. White Eagle."

Tess thought once again, *What kind of name is that?* "My name is Tess McCrae. I work for—"

"I know who you are." Silence—did he mean to intimidate her?

"This is in regard to one of your patients, Mr. White Eagle…" She decided to be straightforward. "There has been a serious crime and—"

"Is he dead?" White Eagle blurted out.

"Excuse me, sir?"

The man took a deep breath.

"Sir? Do you have any knowledge of a crime?"

Nothing but breathing on the other end. Deep breathing. Hyperventilating.

"Sir?" she repeated. "Do you have any knowledge of this crime? Here in Paradox, in Bajada County? Have you heard anything?" Wishing now she *had* done what her instincts told her to do and had driven up to see him in person. "Sir?"

White Eagle said, "Is he…" She heard him swallow. "Is he dead?"

"Is who dead?" Tess asked.

He didn't reply. Silence stretched out. Tess said, "From where I'm sitting, it sounds to me like you have knowledge of this crime. Is that correct, Mr. White Eagle? Do you know what transpired here in Paradox?"

"No! Look. I'm just trying to understand. If there's a problem…"

"You keep saying 'he,' Mr. White Eagle. Who are you referring to?"

Silence.

"Are you referring to the actor, Max Conroy?"

Another pause. Then Gordon White Eagle said, "Why would you think that?"

"Sir, was he at your facility last night?"

"I haven't talked to the attendants today. They'd certainly alert me if he was missing…" His voice drifted off.

Fudging.

Max had left the reservation. But why did White Eagle think he was dead?

"Sir, I want you to listen to me and listen carefully. I am going to ask you a question. I want you to answer me truthfully. This is a criminal investigation, and as such I need the absolute truth." Tess was a little rusty, but she thought she struck the right tone between official business and offering a little bit of wiggle room—if he cooperated. She added, "I am counting on your cooperation."

The subtext was: remember the guru down the road with the sweat lodge? The one whose negligence led to the deaths of three people?

He was quiet on his end.

"Do you understand me? I need you to be truthful. Is Max Conroy at the Desert Oasis Healing Center or isn't he?"

"Of course he is!"

So much for her bluff. Dammit, she wished she was in a room with him. "I need to speak to him."

"I'm afraid that's impossible."

"This is a homicide investigation, sir. If he is there, I need to speak to him."

"It can't be done."

"Why, sir?"

"He's in an isolation tank. He cannot be disturbed."

"Why did you ask me if he was dead?"

Silence.

"Sir, did you think he was dead?"

"No, no. Not at all. For just a moment there I thought maybe someone might have gotten into the chamber with intent to do him harm, maybe some sicko—you know how that could happen, like that freak who shot John Lennon... but Max is checked on the hour. If there were anything, er, *untoward*, I'd know about it."

Tess had had enough of his slippery answers. Time to bring the hammer down. "Are you aware that obstructing a criminal investigation is a crime?"

She could almost hear him puff up. "I am a doctor, Ms.... I'm sorry, I forget your name. Removing Mr. Conroy from the sensory deprivation tank at this juncture could result in *grievous psychological harm*, and I will not do it!"

"Mr. White Eagle—"

"*Doctor* White Eagle," he said primly.

"Doctor White Eagle." Tess spoke quietly and concisely. "I'd like to read my notes from the beginning of our conversation. In reply to my statement that a serious crime had been perpetrated here in Bajada County, you stated as follows: 'Is he dead?' You asked me this not once, but twice."

Silence on the line.

"Do you have knowledge of what transpired—"

The phone disconnected, and all she got was a dial tone.

Chapter Twenty-Seven

ON THE JET, JERRY TRIED TO RELAX. HE RELAXED THE OLD-fashioned way: by drinking. No designer drugs for him. Macallan scotch did just fine. He planned to drink all the way to Arizona.

Talia was moping in the jet's bedroom, which was good, because he didn't have to listen to her whine. He could see why Max dumped her the first time. No doubt, Max was happy that Jerry and Talia were sleeping together. If this was a game of hot potato, Jerry was the loser.

He'd tried to reach Gordon, but Gordon wasn't answering. It could be Gordon was putting out fires, but it could also be he was in his suite taking mescaline. Peyote was a fallback position he'd used for years.

We all have our ways of coping, Gordon was fond of saying.

Gordon White Eagle was Jerry's older brother by four years. A Jew, of course, but in the seventies he'd morphed from metal band lead singer to counselor at a hippie retreat in Mendocino, and, after a couple of correspondence courses and a quickie trip to Tortuga for a diploma in "Psychology," he graduated to guru. For some reason, Gordon got the looks in the family. Jerry liked to think that *he'd* gotten the smarts. Gordon was big. Gordon was athletic. Gordon got the girls in high school. All his life Jerry had to follow in his wake.

But Jerry was richer.

Still, it was tough in high school.

They didn't look like brothers at all.

When Gordon first started the Desert Oasis Healing Center fifteen years ago, he'd had a mane that would put Fabio to shame. His hair was slightly graying at the temples, which only made him look wise. The hair went with the tan deer hide jacket embossed with Native American symbols. But time had taken its toll and like Jerry, genes were genes, and by forty, Gordon was prematurely balding. For a while, he held onto the long locks, adopting a ponytail to go with his Guayabera shirts and wire-rimmed glasses. This made him look wise and professorial. The nineties came and went, and good ol' Gord realized he needed to evolve again. He had grown more famous, more powerful, and he chose to show that power. Now he shaved his head twice a day, his gleaming tanned dome a wonder to behold. He wore a diamond earring in one ear, and kept the deer hide jacket.

But Jerry was richer.

* * *

TESS CALLED BACK AND ASKED TO SPEAK TO MR. WHITE Eagle. The administrative assistant told her that Dr. White Eagle was unavailable.

First, White Eagle had stonewalled her, and now he was unavailable.

His story about Max and the sensory deprivation tank made no sense. In Tess's interactions with powerful people—and that included the second-in-command of a New Mexico drug cartel and a corrupt mayor—this was not at all unusual. She'd seen it many times. The tactic was almost universal among high-octane public figures—men, mostly—who felt they could get away with it precisely *because* they were wealthy and powerful. The object was simple: stick to the lie, no matter how ridiculous it sounded. Tess never ceased to be amazed by the sheer audacity of it. These guys seriously thought if they just stuck to their stories, they could get away with anything. And many times, they did. It didn't surprise her that Gordon White Eagle had tried it on her; she would have been surprised if he hadn't.

One thing was clear: the guru of the Desert Oasis Healing Center didn't know what had happened to Max Conroy, but he assumed Max was dead.

Why would he think that?

She called Pat. "I know we won't release the names of the victims until next of kin are notified, but I'd like to make sure no information leaks out in the next few hours. OK?"

"You think I'm a rookie?"

"No."

"Then don't ask me crap like that. We're not releasing the names until the last dog dies. And one of those dogs is not answering his phone."

"Good. I need to go to Sedona."

"Sedona? Now?"

"It's a lead."

He gave her the silent treatment. She was pissing off a lot of people today. "It's a lead, Pat."

"Bonny know this?" Pat growled.

"No, I'm going to call him now."

"And I get to do the dirty work."

"Are the bodies gone?"

"On their way to Phoenix as we speak. But I'm going to be here a long time. I thought you would be joining me—it's a real joyride, *Detective*."

Pat had always been good at making her feel guilty. "I'll get back to you when I know what's up," she said.

She knocked on Bonny's open door. He looked up. "Something up, Detective?"

She told him about her conversation with Gordon White Eagle.

"He sounds slippery. But is that any reason to suspect him of anything?"

"I don't know, sir. I think it's important, though."

Bonny sighed. "Pat's gonna give me fits over this. Still, if it's a lead, you'd better follow it."

* * *

When Bajada County sheriff's deputy Luke Jump cleared his throat, Pat Kerney looked up. He was still down in the bomb shelter, trying unsuccessfully to negotiate his way around all the blood. His blue booties were turning purple.

"Yeah? What?" Pat asked.

"We went through the guesthouse."

"And?" Luke Jump talked slower than anyone he'd ever met. "Anything interesting?"

"Well, uh, as a matter of fact, I think there's something you should see."

"I'm in the middle of something, not so's you'd notice."

"It, uh, might be important."

Pat climbed up out of the slaughter pen, as he was beginning to think of the bomb shelter, and followed Jump out past the pool to a smaller version of the main house. They went through the postage-stamp living room and into the hallway. The guesthouse had old blue-gray carpet of a tromped-down pile that reminded him of a nest of caterpillars. The air was on and it was cold.

Luke, gloved in latex, gently pushed on the door at the end of the hallway.

It was a small room. The curtains were pulled partway across the floor-to-ceiling glass window overlooking the pool. A lozenge of sunlight fell on the dingy carpet.

Pat noted the laptop on a cheap veneer desk—some kind of picture on it. The image jittered slightly.

But the object that dominated the room was a 60-inch, flat-screen, high-def LED TV, backlit by the window and the bright sunlight.

An image from a homemade video frozen in the frame.

A man sat in the murky turquoise gloom of what Pat knew instantly to be the bomb shelter. He sat on a chair, trussed up like a Thanksgiving Day turkey. His head hung low but he stared upward, into the camera. Blood clotted his forehead and dripped into his eyes.

It took a moment for Pat to recognize the man.

When he did, he felt the thrill of a job well done.

When a case came together, it came together with the solid thunk of a car door closing. Final, like that.

Now Pat knew who had killed the three men in the bomb shelter.

He knew, because he'd met him yesterday at the Round Up Diner.

The actor, Max Conroy.

* * *

MAX MADE IT INTO TOWN WITHOUT BEING SEEN. IT HELPED that he went cross-country through the desert. No water, in July, the humidity pulling any juices he had out of him. He stopped outside a little homestead, another small ramada, this one occupied by two horses. There were algae in their tank, but he wasn't particular; he drank. Waited for the water to sink in, and drank again. He didn't want to drink too quickly, or he'd get a stomachache and possibly eject the water. He'd learned that when he had done the remake of *Hondo* a few years ago.

He encountered no one on the couple of occasions he had to cross a road. He guessed the sheriff's office had sent everyone they had to the scene of the crime.

His mind kept returning to the house, to the bomb shelter.

The first deputy must have come across the woman and the boy.

Either that, or the woman and the boy had found the bomb shelter, which meant they'd found Luther, Sam, and Corey.

But they wouldn't call anyone. He knew that in his bones. They would continue doing what they were doing. They were looking for him. And they'd almost found him.

He could see it: the deputy pulling up to check out the house, seeing the shattered glass, the shot-out windows, and he would investigate.

And the woman and the boy would shoot him. Max pictured him falling, talking into his radio. And they would... what? Finish him off.

Yes, if he could identify them.

He was glad the deputy who showed up wasn't Tess. He was very glad about that. But he needed to find out what happened. He needed a TV, or at least a radio.

Max formulated a loose plan as he skirted the main section of town. He'd go to the Subway by the freeway and see if he could get a trucker to drive him to Sedona.

But then he saw the white truck in the parking lot—the new Chevy truck.

They were here.

He went into the convenience store inside the Pizza Hut across from the Subway instead. Glanced around and saw a couple of men eating lunch, who might be truckers. He thought about approaching them when they finished. And so he kept a low profile, looking through the magazines. Fortunately, his face wasn't on any of the tabloid or celebrity mag covers, and neither was Talia's. Lindsay Lohan was in trouble again. *Thanks, Lindsay.* He blended in, with his cheap shorts and Arizona tee. With the sunglasses, people didn't give him a second look. He kept one eye on the plate glass window, until he saw the woman and the boy come out, get into the truck, and drive away.

They headed down the road he'd come in on—maybe they were retracing their steps, looking for him.

Max walked over to the tables in back where the truckers were. He chose the black guy. He wasn't sure why.

He approached the black trucker and asked him if he was heading north on 17. The guy gave him a weird look, then shook his head.

OK, it was the white guy.

He went up to him and asked the same question. The guy nodded.

"Would you take a passenger? I've got money."

The guy eyed him. He looked mildly suspicious but not overly so. "I'm not supposed to carry passengers," he said at last.

Max pulled the money out of his jeans. "Here's a hundred-dollar bill. All I want is to get to the Verde Valley. That's not very far, is it?"

"That's a good way."

"A dollar a mile," Max said. "Can't do better than that."

"I don't think so, buddy."

Max said, "I just need to get to Clarkdale. My ride broke down."

"You're a little ripe, you want to know the truth."

"OK," Max said. He laid down another hundred. "Does that make me smell any sweeter?"

He hoped it did, because after that he had a ten, a five, and three ones.

The guy took the money and stuck it in his jeans. "I guess I can put up with it for a while."

"Good."

"See that rig out there, the third one, parked at the edge of the lot? The blue cab? That's mine. You go sit out there and wait till I finish my pizza."

Max did.

The guy called out behind him, "You look familiar. I seen you before?"

"Not around here," Max said, and went out to wait by the truck.

* * *

IT WAS HOT AND MUGGY AND HIS HAIR DRIPPED WITH SWEAT. He sat in the shade of the semi truck, hands clasped around his knees, the asphalt burning through his cheap, thin shorts. About ten minutes in, he heard another big truck start up and cruise out of the parking lot, changing through the gears as it drove onto the on-ramp.

Twenty minutes went by. The guy had to be finished with his pizza by now. How long did it take to wash his hands and clean up a little bit, if he had to?

Max opened the glass door into the convenience store and almost bumped heads with the black trucker. He scanned the booths—his trucker was gone. "Hey," he said. "You know that trucker who was sitting with me?"

"Uh-uh."

Max went into the bathroom. Nobody there. He came back out and found himself watching the black trucker walk to his rig and get in.

His rig with the blue cab.

Max knew he'd been conned. Max realized that having everything taken care of for him all this time, he'd lost his street smarts.

He was left with eighteen dollars, no credit card, a couple of cheap prepaid phones, and a stolen semiautomatic pistol.

Then it occurred to him: Dave.

Dave Finley, his buddy. Dave said he was coming. Sometimes it was hard to know if he was serious. Dave was a fountain of ideas—he put words to any stray thought that drifted through his transom—but he wasn't big on follow-through. Max hadn't taken Dave seriously when he'd suggested they meet and then ride back. More than likely, Dave had forgotten all about it.

Still…

Max went over his other options. He could go to the sheriff's office and tell them the whole story. About how he was kidnapped by Sam, Luther, and Corey. About the woman and the boy. He doubted they'd believe him, though. They'd see him with blood on his shirt and jeans, and ask to look in his duffel bag. The guns, the phones…

By the time he'd explained everything—if he was able to convince them of his innocence—he would have lost half a day. He wanted to get to Gordon and he wanted to get to him now.

Max recalled seeing a TV set hanging from the ceiling at the Subway. It would be good to know just what he was up against. The deputy had spotted him and his fingerprints were all over the stolen truck. He needed to know what had happened in that house.

Head lowered, looking downtrodden and homeless, he shambled over to the Subway. He certainly was ripe enough now. No one looked at him; as a matter of fact, they looked at anything but him. He went to stand in front of the TV set. A game show was on. He waited. No one came up to ask him to get out of the way. He looked at a family sitting in one of the booths, and caught the eye of the mother. Her gaze slid away immediately, and she concentrated on her sandwich.

He was the next best thing to invisible.

Max knew the two kids manning the counter were talking about him behind his back. They wanted to tell him to leave. You do it. No, *you* do it.

Here he was, Max Conroy, whose face was on every newsstand in every grocery store in the country, and people couldn't see past his grimy clothes, dirty complexion, and body odor.

Finally, there was the local announcer, breaking in with news.

Max watched the announcer's lips move. The sound was turned on low. There was a shot of Sam's house. Max watched as two people pushed a gurney holding a black body bag out of the carport toward a waiting white van.

He didn't feel anything—he realized he'd been expecting it.

He swallowed on a dry throat.

He felt as if everyone was watching him, but of course they weren't. His ears burned anyway. And then it hit home.

He knew all three men were dead. And he'd been the one responsible. He'd left them there—

Like fish in a barrel.

He shut his eyes, but it didn't shut out the bad feeling.

Nothing he could do about it now. Except *run*.

He called Dave. "You mean what you said about coming out here?"

"I said I was. I'm on my way, man."

"Seriously?"

"Yeah, I said I would."

"Where are you?"

"About two-and-a-half, three hours from Paradox."

Max said, "When you get here, I'll be…" He glanced over at the tamarisk tree on the corner across the street from the truck stop. He described it. The abandoned adobe house right behind it, the empty lot, the tree with shade as black as ink. You could hide a baseball team in there.

Chapter Twenty-Eight

MAX SAT UNDER THE TREE FOR APPROXIMATELY TWENTY minutes before deciding to go back to the Subway and get himself a bottle of water and something to eat—at least a candy bar. He'd be waiting under the tree for a long time. And Max wanted to find out what was happening at the house on Ocotillo Road. He knew his fingerprints were all over the crime scene.

Once again, he was able to walk into the crowded sub shop and nobody recognized him. He shouldn't be surprised.

Max and Dave used to go for long rides, stopping in at biker bars all over Southern California. Dave wasn't his exact double, but he looked a lot like him and acted like him too. When they went to biker bars, Dave would wear Max's Breitling watch, the diamond stud in his ear, and dress better. Max would look scruffy, cheaper. He even had a clip-on ponytail. And the bikers would buy drinks for "Max Conroy"—Dave—because they knew he rode. They'd buy drinks for Max too.

Max had learned to turn it on and off. At a certain point, Dave would be outside checking his bike, and Max would go off to the bathroom. When he came out, people in the bar would suddenly see him as Max Conroy, not the guy

ICON

they'd been hanging out with playing pool. It was like a light switch—just a change in the way he saw himself, his attitude.

He also knew how to give the paparazzi the slip.

But he used them too. He went to certain parties and clubs, attended events like golf tournaments and rock concerts, and let them snap away. He did it because an actor could not just stand still. Part of the job was actively courting publicity. You had to get your name splashed across the tabloids, your photos on sites like TMZ. The constant speculation about his marriage, about the coming baby, about his potential breakups, his drug use—he fed the fire. He had to. If he didn't keep running, the parade would pass him by. He didn't like it, but that was the game.

There were certain paps he tipped off. Certain photo ops he went for. He would have liked to fit a narrative, but because he used and he drank, that didn't always work out. The narrative chose him. So much of it, if not manufactured outright, was blown out of proportion. Jerry Gold was a master at this. So was his publicist, Diane.

Diane must be going nuts right about now.

So he walked into the Subway and nobody noticed him.

Then he glanced up at the TV. And saw his face.

He knew the photo—it was an arrest photo for a public drunk charge five years ago. He looked one hell of a lot better than Nick Nolte.

Max was still wearing his Arizona cap. He tilted his face downward, but looked up under the brim.

The announcer was saying that Max Conroy was a "person of interest" in the killings at the house on Ocotillo.

Panic surged, but abated quickly. He was Max Conroy. No one would believe this—it was impossible.

But still. *Person of interest.*

Max decided he'd err on the side of caution and get out of here. He couldn't wait for Dave. He wanted to get to the Desert Oasis, wanted Gordon to tell him the *truth*. He needed to go and he needed to go now.

He walked to the door. Calm. Anonymous. He pushed the door open, held it for a girl with a stroller and a little boy. She didn't say thank you, didn't even look at him.

Good.

Out in the blaring sunlight, he looked around. Turned right and started for the side of the building, thinking about the long wait ahead of him.

Then he saw them—the woman and the boy. They appeared to be killing time outside the Pizza Hut. The boy looked resentful, but the woman seemed to have an air of satisfaction about her, as if she'd won a round or two. But he knew the woman's eyes were roving behind her sunglasses, like a spotlight moving back and forth across the landscape. Restless, always probing.

Just looking at her chilled him to the bone.

He ducked back from the corner of the building.

Did they see him?

He knew—*knew*—they were looking for him.

Everyone was looking for him. He was a *person of interest*. But if the woman and the boy got him, God only knew what would happen. Look what they had done to the men in the house.

He pictured a scene out in the desert—saw it cinematically—and they were walking him to his execution. He saw his death: two to the back of the head, left for the coyotes to clean up.

A car cruised by. It was the deputy in an unmarked cop car. The car slowed to a stop. He could reach her in three strides.

He thought of the woman and the boy and came to a conclusion.

Crazy.

But so was he.

Chapter Twenty-Nine

TESS WAS ALMOST TO THE FREEWAY ENTRANCE WHEN SHE saw the big truck blocking the on-ramp—Sunline Traders. Both of Paradox's PD cars were parked behind it, and a Paradox PD officer was placing reflective triangles out on the road.

Tess circled the parking lot around the Subway, thinking she could use something cold to drink. Mostly she was thinking about how she'd approach Gordon White Eagle. She put the car in park, and that was when the passenger door wrenched open and she found herself staring at the famous movie star, Max Conroy. He slid into the car. "Don't try anything. I have a gun."

Tess looked down. He did have a gun in the waistband of his jeans, and his hand hovered near it.

She had no idea of his abilities, but he *could* draw the weapon and shoot her, or shoot himself, or shoot wild. Guns were unpredictable that way.

Cursing the fact that her new ride had a broken locking mechanism, Tess raised her hands. *Don't antagonize him. Play for time.* All those bromides that had been scrupulously inculcated into her. Because of her "ability," she remembered every single moment of every lesson. The problem was, Tess not only got the lesson, but every subfile of the lesson.

Don't antagonize. Play for time. De-escalate the situation.

As if reading her mind, he said again, "Don't try anything."

"I won't."

He saw her phone on the seat between them at the same time she did. He grabbed it, buzzed his window down, and threw it out. "I don't want to kill you, but I will if I have to."

That was a cliché she'd heard in at least fifteen movies. Those exact words.

"I'm good," she said. "What do you want me to do?"

"Drive."

"Drive where?"

"Up I-17."

"OK," she said. "Do you see that truck over there? Sunline Traders?"

He said nothing. She glanced out the corner of her eye and saw that although Conroy was nervous, he was also in control. She wondered what he had to lose. The impression she got was: nothing.

"The truck?" she said again. "It's blocking the freeway entrance."

"Then take the access road."

No choice. She did.

* * *

THEY DROVE. MAX COULDN'T BELIEVE HE HAD THREATENED the deputy with a weapon. It was unreal. He knew what he was doing would change everything. It would end badly. He knew that, but he didn't see that he had a choice.

"You don't have a radio," he said.

"No."

"Why is that?"

"The car's new."

"Oh."

The guy in the pink granny glasses and the shower cap materialized between them. Shoved his bony elbow into Max's side. Max could see his own hand, still hovering over the semiautomatic pistol's butt sticking out of his waistband, with Shower Cap superimposed over it. Max could see right through him.

Shower Cap said, "Tell her what happened."

"Why should I? She won't believe me."

The deputy glanced at him, her eyes sharp. "What did you say?"

"Nothing. Just keep your eyes on the road and drive."

"You need her help," Shower Cap said.

"Fuck off, I'm doing this my way!"

This time the deputy didn't glance at him. She glanced at his gun. Her voice was calm—soothing but in charge. "Do what 'your way'?" she asked him.

He didn't answer. What could he say? He was hallucinating? He was the one with the gun—he didn't owe her any explanations. He just wanted to get to Gordon White Eagle.

"Gordon White Eagle," the deputy said. "That's where we're going? The Desert Oasis Healing Center?"

How had she heard him? He must have spoken out loud.

Shower Cap grinned, started to fade. Max fished around for a thought—any thought. The image that cropped up was a silly one, but he gave it voice. "Why aren't you wearing a uniform?"

She said, "I'm not a deputy anymore."

"They fired you?"

"No. They made me detective."

"Detective? You were promoted."

"You could say that."

"I played a detective in three films. Worked with a homicide dick."

"We don't call ourselves 'dicks.'"

"Sorry."

They lapsed into silence. The heavy Caprice ate up the road. They must be going eighty.

Tess. That was her name. The woman who'd saved him from Gordon's thugs. The woman who had a perfect, photographic memory.

He wanted to trust her, but she might take exception to the fact he'd threatened her with a firearm...

The land whizzed by, the color of a dusty lion, studded with prickly pear and yucca, scrub bushes and trees. Mountains off to the left. Mountains off to the right. The two-lane unspooling before him, leading him to Gordon White Eagle. Finally, he would get relief. Finally, he would make Gordon fix him. The deputy—the *detective*—might even be a help. He wanted to be put back together, better than Humpty. But more than that, he wanted the answer to a simple question. Why? Why had Gordon messed him up like that?

Why send a killer like the woman after him?

Why?

And now he was on the run, a "person of interest" in three killings. And somewhere out there, looking for him, were the woman and the boy.

Finally, he couldn't stand it anymore. "I didn't do it."

Tess kept her eyes steady on the road. At least he thought she did; he couldn't see past her sunglasses.

"Didn't do what?" she asked.

"Kill those guys." His throat was dry. He licked his lips. She seemed so damn *calm*. "Everyone thinks I killed those guys in the bomb shelter. Why else would I be a 'person of interest'?"

She said nothing.

"You don't believe me."

"Why don't you tell me what happened?"

He did. He described everything, how Luther had lured him to the house. How they'd kept him in the bomb shelter. The ransom demand, the kidnap video. "You know what my wife said?"

"Talia L'Apel?"

"Yeah, Talia. She said, 'You can have him.' What do you think of that?"

She shrugged.

"So now they think I killed them. Do you believe I have superhuman powers? How would I get the drop on three guys? Especially Corey. That's one mean son of a bitch." Stopped himself. "*Was* a mean son of a bitch," he amended. "But I didn't kill him."

"Who did?"

"I'm pretty sure I know."

"Oh?"

First time there was an inflection in her voice. Interest. Could he be making headway with her?

"I think Gordon sent somebody." He paused, realizing how paranoid he sounded.

"Who?"

He couldn't tell if she was just humoring him, waiting for her chance to get at the weapon in the holster on her side. He should have grabbed it and tossed it out of the car when he'd had a chance, but he hadn't been thinking straight.

His window was still open, the air buffeting him. "I'm going to take your gun. Don't try anything." He leaned sideways, reaching for the butt of her weapon.

And at that moment, quick as a snake, she knocked his hand aside and whipped out her gun.

The car started to slow.

"Nobody will believe me," Max said. Staring at the gun muzzle. Mesmerized by it.

"Not after this they won't," she said.

"Listen, I—"

He didn't get a chance to finish his sentence. He felt the thud, rather than heard it. He did hear the squeal of tires. The car lurched sideways—Max had plenty of time to think about it, because everything slowed to a glacial pace. It was like one of those motion simulator NASCAR rides you find at amusement parks, only much slower: sunglasses floating through the air, Tess's weapon joining his like an animated Disney movie, the one with the waltzing fork and spoon, the rear window taken up with a black and silver grille, an *enormous* grille with a giant Chevy logo, the squarish titan-sized white hood above; and then the view shifted and went topsy-turvy as their car left the pavement and soared-rolled-shuddered down the embankment in a fountain of dust.

Chapter Thirty

Gus Stenholm, who worked part time for Belvedere Mining as security, had not been to the Rosasite Mine for a couple of days, due to a bad cold. Usually, he drove around there once a day to check the outbuildings for vandalism, but the main reason he had this job was to make sure no hiker or bunch of pot-smoking kids breeched the old adit on the property. That was pretty much his whole job, which would go away once Belvedere filled the mine up as required by law. He slowed for the Frying Pan Road exit, glad for the four-wheel drive SUV. Used to be hell driving around in the first car they gave him—a Mercury Marquis that had been run into the ground by Bajada County sheriffs. Got hung up on a hump of dirt on one of those two-tracks and dinged the oil pan. That was the end of the Merc.

The sun was low enough now for every stunted little bush to cast a long shadow. The graded dirt road wound through hills up onto the bajada. He turned off onto what was little more than a two-track out to the old mining buildings. The last time there had been a real road out to them had to be in the twenties. Now it was just twin paths that hunters used through the ocotillo and prickly pear cactus. But Jack Godin, who liked to fly his Piper Cub all over God's green acre, said he'd spotted a wrecked car over by the slag heap.

A newly wrecked car, since a few people had dumped cars there over the years.

Jack was a teller of tall tales, but Gus knew he wouldn't flat-out lie.

As he approached the old buildings from Belvedere Mining Company, the smell of burning came through the air vents.

He stopped outside the building. The many-paned windows at the front had been shot out by kids or by hunters or both, and the place was strewn with junk. He drove on past the mining building, up the steep road to the slag pile. He rounded the hill and parked on the little turnout and walked out to the edge, looking down the slag heap. The shadows slanting down in the red glare, the brown, black, and purple slag glittering here and there where the sun hit it. Down below he saw the long rectangular shape of a car lying on its side.

He called it in.

Couldn't get down there—not with his knees.

Gus stepped out of the SUV and, gun drawn, walked along the edge of the slag heap, looking for movement. The light getting dimmer by the minute. He almost tripped over a rock, and looked down. The rock had been painted crimson, looked like. Kind of resembled a man's head.

Vomit shot out of him like a projectile missile when he realized it *was* a head.

* * *

The Bajada Sheriff's Department had access to the automated fingerprint system. Marge, a ranch woman turned part-time deputy, was the go-to person for fingerprints. Marge rescued dogs and always had one of the smaller ones with her. You always knew when she was coming your way because the doggy smell preceded her.

Pat didn't have to smell her, though; he was still at the slaughterhouse on Ocotillo Road. Marge told him the fingerprints on Jensen's truck came back to one Max Conroy. Apparently, before Conroy became the world's biggest dreamboat, he'd spent three semesters teaching auto mechanics at a community college in Fullerton—the system required every teacher be fingerprinted. A lucky break.

So Max Conroy stole the truck, which, along with the kidnap video, put him right here on the stretch of road running right by the house on Ocotillo. Turned out his fingerprints were also all over the crime scene in the bomb shelter, as well as the carport and inside the Chevelle and the Saturn.

Amazing how that happened.

But he'd been acting strange at the cafe yesterday morning. Pat thought at the time that Conroy had been disconnected from the proceedings. In his own little world. Pat remembered Tess McCrae's recounting of the men in the limo giving Max a hard time.

And now this: Gus Stenholm's photos of the car wreck at the Rosasite Mine slag heap, sent via his cell phone. The car was a stretch limo. Gus had also sent a picture of a man's head on the ground—it looked like a misshapen beet.

Jesus.

Pat didn't know if the head belonged to Hogart or Riis—
or if the head belonged to either one of them—but he was
pretty sure that both Hogart and Riis were dead. Unless they'd
pushed their own limo off the slag heap, which defied logic.

The body count was rising. Three dead in the house, and
probably two at the mine. Max Conroy had been busy.

Pat knew Conroy was unstable—and that was a polite
word for it. He'd sensed that from the moment he'd sat down
with Tess and Max. No surprise that Max thought he could
do anything he wanted, even kill. Hollywood was a cesspool.
All those hijinks, everybody sleeping with everybody else,
out-of-wedlock babies—and they were *proud* of it—the drugs,
the alcohol, the silly liberal causes—they thought they were
entitled.

He called Bonny. "I'm gonna need more help, now there's
a secondary crime scene. Where's Tess?"

"She's been advised of the secondary crime scene at the
slag heap. But right now she's working the case from another
angle," Bonny said.

At that moment, Pat could have thrown his phone against
the wall.

It wasn't right. Here he was, with two bloody scenes and
no help. They were both detectives. He was still a detective.
Bonny should tell him where Tess had gone. But he wasn't
about to ask. No way he'd give Bonny the satisfaction.

All he said was, "I could use her here."

"I'm sure you could," Bonny said. He sounded sympathetic but unmovable. "As soon as she's available, she'll meet
you at the scene."

As soon as she's available.

To hell with him.

To hell with them all.

For a moment Pat was temped quit right then and there. But he was six months away from retirement. His mother always told him, "Don't cut your nose off to spite your face." He swallowed his bile. "Anything else?"

"You measured the scene and collected evidence?"

No, I've been lunching at the Casbah. "You mean doing my job? Yeah."

"Sorry," Bonny said. "I was just thinking out loud. When do you think you can get to the mine?"

"Soon. I'm gonna need some help, though."

"I can send another deputy, but we're running out of them," Bonny said. "Never saw anything like this—five homicides that we know of. It's a good thing I have you both working this."

Pat swallowed again. He had to take it. He had no choice. And meanwhile, Tess McCrae was out doing God knew what, following "leads," looking for the bad guys with that X-ray vision of hers.

Sometimes, X-ray vision wasn't enough. Sometimes it took years of working as a detective, years of putting in the time, the late nights, the long days, to know what you were doing. To be a real detective.

Four years in Albuquerque didn't quite do it, Pat thought. No matter how talented you were.

Chapter Thirty-One

Jerry followed Talia off the jet and into the silver Range Rover with the Desert Oasis insignia on the side. The Desert Oasis Healing Center logo was the proud but Roman-nosed profile of a Plains Indian, maybe a Sioux warrior, against a background of what he could only guess were the concentric circles of an open-pit mine. The guy driving the Range Rover was dressed like an Australian and had an annoying fake Australian accent. But Talia liked him. Jerry could tell because Talia was all over Jerry, doing it for the fake Australian's benefit. She'd been on strike sexually, but now feathered kisses along his neck and reached down between his legs. Fortunately, the leather man purse she'd bought for him for Christmas and insisted he take everywhere was between her long lacquered nails and his genitalia.

You can take the actress out of the trailer park… "You have to excuse our friend here," Jerry said. "She was so upset over Max's disappearance, she took one Xanax too many."

"That's all roight—I've seen it all before, mighty," the fake Aussie said. "We'll be there in two shikes of a lamb's tile!"

Gordon met them in his usual regalia. The fringed deer hide jacket was white this time. But Gordon looked pale under his tan and seemed distracted. Normally, his gaze was a laser. His voice was a laser. His personality was a laser. But now he looked…stunned.

"What's up?" Jerry asked, not expecting a real answer. Gordon wasn't into sharing. He liked to deliver his tablets from on high.

But Gordon said, "We've run into a snag."

"What?"

"Max is gone."

"Gone? You said Shaun had him."

"I can't raise her."

"I thought Shaun would have him by now."

Gordon shrugged.

"What? You're shrugging? You don't know where he is? You don't have a clue?"

"No, and so far, we're OK. I've done damage control with the press and the cops. As far as they're concerned, I've made it clear I'm safeguarding his privacy. But there've been so many sightings—the rumors are flying. I've put it out that he has a stunt double who looks a lot like him, which is true, one of the paps ran with it. There are all sorts of stories going around, which can only help us. As long as nobody knows anything, and we stick to the script, we should be fine."

But Gordon didn't sound fine. Jerry couldn't believe what he was hearing. His brother—the stonewaller of the century—was having a major meltdown.

For a moment—a brief moment—Jerry savored this.

Then he decided it was time to get down to work. "Gordon, you'd better tell me everything. You said you fucked him up. What did you do? Did you plant anything in him that would turn him into a killer? Like *The Manchurian Candidate*?"

Gordon stared at him. His eyes were like fixed blue marbles in his tanned totem of a face. "No way. All I did was make him impressionable, so we could herd him the right direction."

"You mean the stuff about freezing on command, right?"

"What do you *think* I mean?"

"Sarcasm isn't going to help this situation, Gordon. You've been known to improvise."

"Improvise."

"Yes, improvise. You've really screwed it up this time."

"Fuck you."

"Well, fuck you."

Gordon pinched the spot between his eyes and his nose. "Look, this isn't doing us any good. I have to think."

"Ha! You're finally getting it that Shaun might not be the goddess you think she is. She snowed you, Gordon. Maybe she was good with the Russian mob, but why can't she handle one drunk and stoned actor? Master criminal my foot! She's barely sane."

"I've seen her sharpshooter medals. She's legendary."

"Yeah, so?"

"She's killed a lot of people, Jerry. And never went down for any of them."

Gordon loved to use terms like "went down." Like it made him sound tough. "OK, so she's good," Jerry said. "But maybe motherhood's changed her."

Gordon waved Jerry's theory away. "That's ridiculous. I'm sure she's secured him by now and is on her way. We've got to have a little faith."

"Faith, huh? We're down to *praying*, now?"

"This is no time to switch horses. She's the only one I know who can drill a man from ten feet away in the heart with a twenty-two. And kill him dead. That's what I hired her for. Because she can shoot like that, and she can kill without conscience."

"There are plenty of people like that, Gordon. You should have dug deeper."

"Actually, there aren't. In fact, there are very few with her particular skill set."

"So where is she now, Gordon? Can you tell me that?"

"I don't know."

Chapter Thirty-Two

THE CAR CAME TO REST UPRIGHT—AMAZING. THE CAPRICE
had turned around, 180 degrees, and slid backward down the
steep embankment.

Max thought: a big, heavy car. It had saved them. He
looked at Tess McCrae. She was trying to get the seat belt off.
Her movements were slow, but everything else was slow too,
and when he moved his fingers it felt as if he were trying to
pull taffy—everything seemed to slip out of his grasp. The gun
was on the seat and he needed to pick it up, get some control
here. His mind was so scattered he didn't even think about
the truck that had run them off the road until he heard the
click of feet on rock.

Max glanced around—there seemed to be all the time in
the world. Everything was quiet. He felt weightless, under
water. But he could see the kid scrambling down the embankment, balancing a gun and his yo-yo. The kid shucked the
yo-yo loop from his finger so he could hold the gun in
both hands.

Max pawed at the gun on the seat again.

Tess was almost out of her harness.

They were in an amphitheater. No, that wasn't right. But
there were a lot of rocks—boulders. Big, round, vanilla-colored

boulders and spears of yucca. There was a place in California where they used to shoot otters—he and his dad had gone out there once; most of it was long gone, but the area looked somewhat like this…Why was he thinking about that?

Pick up the gun.

He did.

Magically, his fingers came alive, wrapped around the butt.

Fire a warning shot at the kid. Scare him off.

He aimed through the window, shot to the right of the kid and down. Didn't want to hurt him. He'd wanted to once, when he was in the culvert, but now he realized that he'd been wrong. You don't hurt a kid.

Just scare him.

Both hands holding the gun, he shot. The gun kicked. He thought the butt hit his jaw.

Funny thing—the kid reacted. He fell over like a rag doll. Flopped for a second and was still.

Tess, who was still struggling with her harness, turned her head in the kid's direction. Her face was pale. She said, "Did you shoot him?"

"No, no, I was aiming away from him!"

"Ricochet," she said.

He looked at the surrounding rocks. The kid lay still, blood seeping out underneath him. He was dead. No question about it.

"Help me with this," Tess said. "You may have to cut me out."

He reached over, still in shock. He had a jackknife and he sawed on the shoulder harness belt's heavy material. His thoughts were slow, but he knew he was missing something.

"Where is the woman?" Tess said.

The woman.

He squinted past the kid. Everything surreal. "I don't see her."

"Maybe she's still in the truck. Maybe she's hurt. Get me out of this and I'll go look."

He cut her loose and she shoved at the door. It creaked open. She slipped out. She ran from boulder to boulder, just like they did in the movies, and all Max could do was watch.

He stared at the kid. Thinking: *get up.*

The kid lay there. The blood soaking into the ground. It was a reddish stain, diluted by the dirt.

"Get up," he mumbled.

Time floated.

Shower Cap peered in through the window and grinned.

"Where's your boat?" Max asked.

He heard the Caprice door grate open. Tess leaned in. "You OK?"

"I think so."

"The woman's in the truck. She's not moving—has a big bruise on her forehead. There's a place up the road—I'm going to call it in. You should stay still. I don't like that cut on your leg."

He wished he hadn't thrown her phone out the window. But it had seemed like a good idea at the time…He glanced down and saw blood. Moved his foot and heard the squishing sound of blood.

"Wait! I'll go with you." Realized he was shivering.

It was the wind. The temperature was dropping, the sky dark. The car must be facing west, because he saw the sun near the horizon like a baleful red eye, narrowing against the onslaught of the clouds.

She stared back up the embankment at the truck. Nodded. "OK, let's go."

They left the car and started walking along the highway. Max felt himself shivering. Thunder grumbled and the wind picked up even more. Rain spotted the highway with drops the size of quarters.

Then came the onslaught.

He looked back in the growing twilight of rain. One last ray of sun gleamed off the windshield. He squinted. Did he see movement? Or was the woman inside unconscious, or even dead?

He was so tired. He didn't want to think about the boy. Put one foot in front of the other. He held the gun, though. He wasn't going to give up the gun. But he stayed with the cop. She was the leader.

Did that mean he would be turning himself in?

He cleared his throat. "I didn't kill anybody." Amended it. "Except for the boy, and that was an accident."

She said nothing.

"You believe me, right? Those guys that died in the house—I saw the woman and the boy searching the house. They were there. I could put them there. I'm a witness."

"What about the two men at the mine?"

"What two men? What mine?"

The detective said nothing.

He reached for her arm, but stopped short of grabbing her. It was as if she were protected by a force field. "What's going on? They killed someone else?"

She looked at him, her face inscrutable in the gloom and the rain. "Are you just being a good actor?"

He stepped back. "Actor? No! I didn't kill the guys in the house. I did *not*! Why should I? Why would I? I have everything I want in the world. I have a career. I'm well paid—*very* well paid. I have a wife and…"

He faltered. He knew she could read through him. He knew the question that was coming.

She said it. "Then why are you in rehab if your life's so good?"

"You don't believe me?"

She started walking again. "It's not what I believe. It's what the county attorney will believe."

"Then I'm under arrest?"

"Look at it this way: you've got a chance to tell your story."

He laughed. "It's a moot point, isn't it? You can't hold me if I don't want to stay. What are you going to do? Shoot me? If I try to escape, are you going to shoot me?" He glanced at her holstered weapon. "You might need those bullets, if that woman wakes up and comes after us."

Silence.

"Who else did she kill?" he asked. "Who else is dead?"

"Ah, the right question at last." She looked up at him. Those steady eyes, so calm. Calm and in control. "We think she killed a man named Hogart and a man named Riis. They were the men who kidnapped you in the limo."

And that was when he knew he was well and truly fucked.

* * *

Dave Finley checked his watch for the hundredth time. He'd been parked on the street by the tamarisk tree for almost an hour, had walked over to check out the Subway twice and the Pizza Hut once. He'd driven around the parking lot and up and down the main drag of Paradox and onto the patchwork of intersecting streets, which petered out quickly into desert. Not much of a town, that was for sure.

Now he just sat in his truck, waiting.

He'd tried the number Max had called him from, but it just kept ringing. Max wasn't answering his cell either.

"Where the hell are you, buddy?"

Dave took a drag off his cigarette (his fifth—he always smoked more when he was nervous). He had the radio on, but so far all he was hearing was country music.

For all he knew, Max was on a nice cushy jet heading back to LA. While *he* sat out here waiting.

But he doubted it.

Max had always attracted trouble. Look at that wife of his, Talia. Now ol' Max had painted himself into a corner with that baby from Africa and no matter what he did, he was screwed.

Dave flicked the cigarette out into the street and watched the cherry bounce. He needed to quit. In fact, he needed to do a lot of things. Dave stared into the rain and darkness, watching the light show over the mountains. Still keeping an eagle eye out for Max, but he had the feeling Max was gone. Had no idea where he was, or what he should do now.

He'd already done that little favor for Jerry—Dave had found a woman and her daughter who fit the bill. The mother and daughter had been ahead of him in line at the Safeway, believe it or not, and he had seen the mother using a food stamp card. He'd struck up a conversation with the mom and handed her a line of bullshit about an audition for a small part in a film, that it would mean good money—"union scale." She was starstruck, all right. He told her not to tell anyone because they were behind schedule and didn't want to audition too many people—they wanted to cast the film as soon as possible.

He got her number and told her he'd call her with the where and when.

Dave didn't know why Jerry had asked him to go looking for a woman and a girl. Jerry was always scheming over something, and Dave figured anything that could hurt Max was fine with him. When he brought Max back—*if* he could bring Max back—he'd get the whole story later tonight.

Revenge was a dish best served cold.

And so he waited for Max. After all, he was Max's buddy, his wingman, the guy who could always be counted on to look the other way while his best friend boffed his wife.

* * *

Up ahead Max saw an old gas station by the side of the road. The pumps had been torn out. The place was now an antiques and curios store. Just beyond it was a ramp up to the freeway. The building had a colorful sign that said "Jeepers Creepers." All sorts of weird stuff had been stuck to the outside wall: dolls, farming implements, serapes, small appliances. Max walked with the cop, only because he didn't know what else to do. He was an American. He was innocent. He hadn't killed anybody—except for the boy. (And that was an accident.) He could take off and hitch his way out of here, but then what would he do?

He would be a fugitive.

He had to think about this.

When he'd escaped the Desert Oasis, he'd wanted to be a sort of everyman. Live out of the spotlight, do a good day's work. Be normal. But what was normal? Because he knew that even though he lived in America, even if he was innocent, there were plenty of people on death row all over this country who were innocent. Plenty who had been executed. He'd been on the mailing list to save Cameron Todd Willingham in Texas. And look what happened there.

No, he didn't want to be everyman. Everyman had the odds stacked against him. Max had power. He had fame. He had influence. All the things he'd disdained recently.

Now he needed them.

So he would go with the female cop. He would act like an innocent man because he was an innocent man. And he would get the *best fucking defense lawyer in the business.*

Once Gordon fixed him.

And so he walked with her, an innocent man, and relied on her strength, her presence. Her straight back, the way she moved.

He knew and she knew that he had a gun. He could take her any time. But of course he wouldn't. Because he was innocent.

But she didn't seem to mind that the man who'd held a gun on her before was now walking alongside. Maybe because of his condition.

He looked back at the truck again. Dim in the dark and the lashing rain. Smaller and smaller. The truck didn't move. Nothing moved. Maybe the woman was dead.

He hoped so.

They were on the porch of Jeepers Creepers. The old door rattled in its frame as the cop knocked on the door. The clock in the door was turned to 5:00 p.m. He glanced at his watch. It was going on five-thirty.

It was good to be out of the rain.

I killed that kid.

He couldn't get away from it. It kept coming back. In the culvert he'd wanted to kill the kid, and now he had. And here he was in the gloom and the rain coming down like a water-fall around them, completely untethered from the world, everything still going in slow motion, and his only thread to reality was the cop.

* * *

TESS TOLD HIM TO STAY ON THE PORCH. THERE WAS A HOUSE out back. She said she didn't know the people well, but knew their names and whatever she'd picked up from driving around the county. So she went looking for the Olsens.

Max stared down the highway. He could barely see the truck. It was far away.

Max was shivering. He rubbed his arms to warm himself and looked at the artifacts stuck to the wall.

Then he heard it. A howl.

And everything he'd just thought went out the window.

* * *

Tess heard it too. The house behind Jeepers Creepers was dark. There was no vehicle in the carport, which surprised her. She knew they had come from Wisconsin in 1984, that they owned a 2009 Ford-350 truck with a matching camper shell and a "Choose Life" license plate on the back bumper (she knew the plate number too, of course). She knew they had an Australian sheepdog named Pearl with one blue eye and one brown. She knew they kept to themselves except for their regular attendance at the Streams of the Desert Pentecostal Church in Paradox. She assumed they did their shopping in one of the suburbs north of Phoenix. She'd been 99-percent certain that the Olsens would be home.

But she was wrong.

The car was gone.

The dog looked out at her through the curtains.

No help here. But they were close to the on-ramp to the freeway, so they could go up there and flag someone down…

Then, the unearthly cry. It wasn't a wolf. It wasn't a coyote. It was human, but there was something feral about it too. Like she imagined the damned in hell would sound.

The hairs on the back of her neck rose.

The howling went on and on. It gave her goose bumps.

She looked in the direction of the howl. A light arrowed along the road, then flared. Headlights passed over the store in front. She heard the car slow, stop. The woman? Had the woman been able to start up the truck? It didn't sound like a big truck, though. She started back around the house and headed for the porch of the antiques/general store.

She heard a car door slam, and the sound of a car accelerating.

She reached the porch.

Max Conroy was gone.

She watched the taillights wink as the car turned onto the on-ramp to the freeway.

Max had hitched himself a ride. Should've known he would take off.

The howl again. She looked down the road and saw a figure in the darkness. The figure held something in its arms. As Tess's eyes adjusted to the light, she saw it was the woman who had chased them. The woman held the boy, lifeless, against her chest. And she howled.

Max had not been lying when he'd told her about the woman and the boy. Tess sensed that if the woman saw her, it would be all over. She could feel the woman's anger, the hatred. It scared her. Tess had been a cop for a long time. She was very rarely scared, even a little. Adrenaline would come to her aid, and she would act. But the screaming of this woman, and the sight of the woman *herself*, made Tess want to slink away. To shrink into the shadows and become anonymous.

This was a mother bear who had lost her cub. There was despair, but overriding it was rage. It was palpable in the air, in the rain, and there was a raw edge that seemed to pry into Tess's internal organs. Danger. High-voltage danger.

And so Tess did slink. She hid. She hid because she could not stand the raw grief of the woman who had killed at least five people.

Tess waited.

The howling stopped.

The rain continued. Incessant, but softer now, whispering.

She heard a truck start up—a big engine. She heard it accelerate. Saw the pinpoint lights coming. Saw the truck flash by, slow, and turn with a squeal of tires onto the on-ramp, headed north.

She'd seen the truck. Only a glimpse, but it was huge, gargantuan. She'd seen the damaged front end. And the light was dim but she thought she saw two figures. One taller, on the driver's side. And one smallish, slumped against the seat.

The woman and the boy.

The rain lessened. Tess could smell alfalfa hay, creosote bushes, and ozone. It was full dark now. She needed to flag down someone and reach dispatch.

Chapter Thirty-Three

MAX LET THE OLDER COUPLE DRIVE HIM THROUGH Cottonwood as far as the turnoff for Clarkdale. There, he told the man to pull over on the side of the road. He regretted hijacking the car, regretted letting them see the gun stuck in the waistband of his pants. He could see the interview now. "He seemed like a nice enough guy, but then he told me to pull over and turned us out of our own car."

The couple stood by the side of the road, looking scared. The man was staring at him. "You look familiar. Aren't you the guy in those movies? The ones with the vampires?" His face lit up and he snapped his fingers. "Max Conroy, that's it! Lou, it's Max Conroy." He turned to Max and said, "Didn't I read you were staying around here somewhere? I could swear I read something about it. So what is this? Part of a movie? Are we going to be in the final cut?"

Max said, "No, no. I'm not Max Conroy. But I get that a lot."

The wife looked at her husband, then glanced around the empty parking lot. She touched his arm. "Bob, I don't see any cameras."

But Bob shook her hand away. "Are you certain you're not Max Conroy? You sure look like him…Can I have your autograph? I'll give you my address and you can let us know where we can pick up the car."

His wife glared at him as he reached in, rummaged through his glove compartment, and came up with an owner's manual for the car. "Just put the old John Hancock anywhere," he said, fishing around for a pen.

Max said, "I'm just his stunt double. We don't even look that much alike."

"That's good too. I never met a stunt double before. What's Max like?"

"He's OK. Made some bad choices with women. You know...movie stars."

The husband said, "Yeah, not a whole lot of brains there, you know? What a way to make a living."

Max signed the manual, "Best wishes—Dave Finley, stunt double for Max Conroy."

As he drove away, they stood there in the rain. Both of them waved, although Lou's wave was less enthusiastic.

Max vowed that when he was done with Gordon, he'd leave the car, a late '80s Chrysler LeBaron, where they'd find it.

He drove on 260 past the little airport and took 89A toward the mining-turned-tourist town of Jerome. The road laddered up the mountain, full of switchbacks and hairpin turns. The Desert Oasis was on the same road. Jerry had told Max that Gordon had bought the land cheap, since the property prices in the nearby upscale resort town of Sedona were sky-high. A Sedona address was a necessity for a holistic-themed celebrity dry-out center. But apparently, the Verde Valley was close enough.

Mine tailings notwithstanding.

Max was holding it together, but only barely. His clothes were wet and he was shivering in them. The old car's heater didn't help much. He thought about Tess McCrae, left in the lurch at Jeepers Creepers, but knew she'd get back on track soon enough. And he had no doubt she'd look for him. But by then he would have concluded his business with Gordon, and Gordon would have fixed him.

Fix him. Did he really believe that?

Max guessed that, given the choice of dying on his Two Red Hills Navajo carpet, Gordon might choose to fix him.

If he could.

The rain had turned to a steady drizzle. It was dark. Max could see the lights up ahead, knew they belonged to the ramshackle houses of Jerome clinging to the mountain.

The Desert Oasis was three or four miles from the first switchback to Jerome, hidden by a stand of aleppo pines and a bushlike tree that grew like a weed around here. Max peered past the slashing windshield wipers, trying to make out pines in the darkness. Gordon had wanted the place to look and feel exclusive, so there was no sign, just a rolling gate behind the pines and a tall fence to keep the inmates inside. The good old DO.

He turned off and drove up to the rolling gate. He'd managed to get the touchpad number from the laundry truck guy, but when he punched in the numbers, the gate didn't roll back. He tried combinations of the numbers, but he hadn't written down the information and now it was lost.

There *was* an intercom. He thought about talking into the speaker, but then Gordon would know he was coming and would prepare for him. He sized up the fence and the gate.

The fence was tall chain link. He could scale it easily. Or he could go over the gate, which was solid and lower. He backed up and drove the LeBaron under the pines to the right of the gate so he wouldn't block access.

Behind him a car flashed by on the road, followed by a motorcycle.

He got out of the LeBaron and walked toward the gate.

Max stared at the gate. Should he climb the fence, or go over the gate? Two cars flashed by on the road behind him. It occurred to him how vulnerable he was out here—he'd left his gun in the car. He heard the crunch of tires on dirt. A truck turned in behind him, its big diesel engine sounding rough. In the moment it took for him to look around, the massive truck was right there. He squinted into the blinding light, the needles of hard rain like a shiny curtain. He was pinned to the gate by headlights under a gleaming, crimped-up hood.

The truck revved, growling like a mad pit bull, then launched forward, as if it had thrust itself from massive hind legs, hurtling toward him. It accelerated at an unbelievable rate, the engine switching from a roar to a catamount shriek. For all of a second, he couldn't move. The headlights bloomed yellow behind his eyelids, and the square grille seemed to grin at him, the gleaming Chevy logo askew, filling his vision as fear buzzed in his ears.

He hit the ground hard and rolled just as the truck rammed the iron slats of the gate with a clang that shook his teeth. The smell of burning rubber, hot oil, and exhaust told him how close he was to being squashed like a bug. He rolled more, thinking if he could just get to the fence, if he could get over—

Impossible.

It was her. The killer.

Max didn't stick around to look. He scaled the chain-link fence and launched himself over just as the truck backed up for another run. Behind him, he heard the truck bull through, flipping the chain link up. Max didn't have time to get to his feet so he wriggled away, just as the tires bit into the wet ground near his face. The truck's momentum carried it past him, the chain link enmeshed in the grille like a hockey mask. Max skittered down into the gully. The truck had come to a halt thirty yards away. *Stuck.* Tires spun in the dirt. The engine screamed. Max thought about flagging down someone on the road, but he would only endanger someone else. The rain was coming down, hard, as he ran for cover. The truck's big engine shrieked. Max ran along the gully, aiming for the LeBaron. The gully was already filling up with water. He kept to the path along the gully, which was overgrown with weedy trees and some kind of vine that grabbed at him.

He heard a snap above him, slashing through the trees.

Realized it was a bullet. He dove to the dirt, half in the churning water.

Had to get up and run. If he could make it through the hole in the fence and get to the LeBaron—it seemed impossible to do.

He wished he had a gun. He'd shoot her, no question. And he wouldn't wait for her to start shooting at him.

He squinted back at the truck, amazed at how much ground he'd put between himself and the vehicle. The truck idled, exhaust burbling out of its tailpipe. The taillights were bright red. But she was after him. He couldn't see her, but she was following in the rain. He heard another snap, and a twig shattered near his head.

He had to make a break for it. He couldn't just hunker down here and wait for her to reach him. He was maybe ten yards from the car now, and it was his only chance.

He dashed, zigzagging, which made the yards he had to cover longer but made him less of a target. Dirt kicked up at his feet, and a bullet clipped his ear. His heart was bursting. Adrenaline shoved him forward; he stepped onto the flattened chain-link fence lying on the ground, snagging his boot on a sheared-off corner of the mesh. He managed to extricate himself and reached the car, fumbling for the door latch. His fingers slipped in the rain.

She was coming for him. He could see her dark shape, walking deliberately. But no shots.

Did she have to reload?

He didn't wait to find out. He was dead anyway. He scrambled into the car. Turned the key and nothing happened, turned it again too quickly. The start made the hideous metal-on-metal sound. He tried one more time, and this time it caught. Another slingshot sound and a loud bang against metal, but he got the car going and hit the accelerator. It lurched forward toward the fence. *Put it in reverse!* He did, and floored it.

She was almost to him. He entertained a thought of running her down, killing the monster once and for all, but he was going too fast. The LeBaron slewed out onto the road in a cloud of smoke and burning rubber. He was already facing one way, so he hit the gas and drove, heading up into the mountains toward Jerome.

Chapter Thirty-Four

THE GLOOM AND THE FALLING RAIN ALMOST RENDERED TESS invisible. Cars sped by on I-17, catching her in their head-lights, but they were going too fast. She held up her badge, but the drivers were by her in a flash and it was doubtful they'd register what the badge meant anyway.

And so she trudged north, holding up her badge. The Verde Valley was a long way from here.

It was probably thirty, forty miles away.

Finally a DPS vehicle flashed by, slowed, and pulled over way up ahead. The reverse lights came on and the car backed down the verge toward her.

"Bajada Sheriff's," she said to the highway patrol officer. "Tess McCrae."

"What happened to you?" the officer asked, once she was in the car and they'd pulled back out on the road.

"Long story." She told him about the wreck, being run off the road by a white Chevy truck. She gave him the license number.

He nodded. "I just came from there now. Your car is part of a crime scene."

One of the many crime scenes, she thought.

They turned off at Cottonwood and drove to the DPS office on Encanto. Once in the office, the DPS officer introduced her to their detective in this sector, an older man named Glazer. Tess went through it with him, gritting her teeth in some parts. Shamed that a movie star like Max had gotten the jump on her.

Embarrassing. She wasn't going to lie, though.

"He produced a firearm?"

"No, he just showed it to me. It was in the waistband of his jeans."

"It was an implied threat, though."

"Yes." She felt it was important to add, "He was scared of someone. He was trying to get away."

"And you're sure it was the actor, Max Conroy?"

"Yes."

The interview was painstaking, emphasis on pain. She felt like a first-day rookie. Tess gave him just the facts, though, although they were damning enough.

She recalled her conversation with Max. He could have been snowing her. She admitted that. But she didn't think so. And there was proof. He was right about the white truck, and the woman and the boy.

Glazer wanted to hear all about Max Conroy. Tess told him what she knew, not what was conjecture, that the woman and boy were after him for some reason. "They tried to kill us."

"And you have no idea why."

"No."

"And you say the boy is dead."

"Yes, but she took him with her."

"Took him with her. You mean, put him in the vehicle and drove away?"

"That's what I'm saying." She felt defensive. The man looked at her with skeptical eyes. He didn't think much of a cop who let someone get the jump on her.

His lips tightened into a line. Tess knew what it was like to sit on the other side of the table, knee to knee with a suspect. All the mental games you played to get the upper hand. There was a whole toolbox of them, and she knew all of them. She'd been considered the best interrogator in her department in Albuquerque. And now here she was, feeling that they were halfway humoring her and halfway pegging her as Bonnie to Max Conroy's Clyde. How'd she lose her phone? Why didn't the car have a radio? How did she team up with Conroy?

When she'd finished, Glazer nodded. He stared at her, skeptical.

She stared back at him. *Stay calm.* It helped to know that she'd been in his shoes hundreds of times. She knew the drill. "Are we done here?"

He grunted, stood up, gathered the papers together. "Wait here," he said.

Forty minutes later, he returned.

"I talked to Sheriff Bonneville. He asserts that everything you said was true." His distaste was clear. "Bonny's always been eccentric, but it's his agency and I guess he runs his ship his own way."

Underneath, he was saying, *It sure isn't a tight ship.*

He added, "We want you to go to the hospital for observation."

"I don't plan to do that."

He shrugged. "Your call. But you're beat up. You could do yourself some damage."

"Is one of my people coming?"

"He's on the way. You can wait in here."

"Thanks."

"Soda?"

"No, thanks."

He ducked out. She had a feeling he was watching her through the one-way mirror.

Let him. All she had to do was wait.

Chapter Thirty-Five

TWO MILES LATER, THE TRUCK LOOMED IN MAX'S REARVIEW mirror. It roared up behind him and almost connected. He hit the gas and spurted away.

No match, though—and he knew it.

They were quickly coming up on the first hairpin turn. He could not go too fast. And yet the freight train on his tail was moving up, closer and closer. Ready to project him into space.

Doubtful this thing had airbags.

The rain had lessened to a drizzle, but it was almost completely dark.

He kept hitting the gas, gaining a few feet. The truck behind him seemed to have steering problems—he saw it overcorrect a couple of times as they made the hairpin.

Max thought through his options. He tried to remember this road—but he'd only been on it twice. Knew the streets were narrow and one section was one-way. If he could slow it down without getting pushed by the truck, he could jump out and run for one of the houses. But the truck hugged his bumper, and he couldn't stop.

Max could almost feel the hatred coming at him. He glanced in the rearview mirror. Although it was dark he could see her sitting like a mannequin, high up in the truck.

And a smaller figure, strapped into the passenger's side. The *kid*? Could it be the kid? Was he dead, or just wounded? He only saw the silhouettes. He heard the truck throttle up, the loud, big engine—and felt the thud as she hit him. Tires screeched—his. He felt the back end slide a little, then catch, and he hit the gas. The truck came up and bumped him again, a glancing blow. He kept his hands steady on the wheel—*don't overcorrect*. He'd had training, a lot of training, but most of it flew out the window now. He spurted ahead again, looking through the mist and the rain for an offshoot road, or an empty parking lot, but all the lots were full. The cars must belong to tourists, kept on the mountain by the thunderstorm. He could go left, onto a side street, but by the time he thought it, the street was gone.

"You remember when you were in *Brickyard Dreams*?"

Max turned his head in the direction of the LeBaron's passenger seat. Shower Cap was belted in beside him.

Jesus! The woman behind him had the dead boy belted in the car, and *he* had a goddamn hallucination sitting in his front seat. "What?"

"Rinaldo—remember? You remember Rinaldo Anisetti? He liked Grey Goose vodka and plump women. He and his crew worked with you for a week."

"Yeah, yeah, I know." And suddenly he *did* know. Anisetti had taught him how to drive an Indy car. They'd worked on turns. Max had learned to hit the brakes hard before the turn, ease off when he hit the curve, and accelerate out of the turn. Something about the wheels. The more the car's wheels turned, the less you used the steering wheel. The words came back to him: *apex, turn-in point, exit*. It was his instinct, anyway—he knew about centrifugal force—it came naturally to him. With turns like these, you tried to bend the turn rather than kink it—make as flat an arc from point A to point B to point C as possible.

In a town like this, where turns were tight, it could buy him a few yards. He hoped.

They followed the crooked street past mining shacks and old brick structures, the buildings sweeping by in the night like pickets on a fence, the mist coming off the pavement. The rain had stopped. It was a Saturday night, and the revelers were out in force, wandering down the uneven sidewalks and off high curbs, stepping back in horror as the two vehicles, like coupled rail cars, hurtled past.

He saw another offshoot ahead, just before a hard right-angle turn, and made for it. At the last minute, three people broke from the curb and started across it, and this time Max overcorrected, and he hit the brakes, the tail end fishtailing, the truck behind him hitting him another glancing blow. But the smack in the back fender actually helped him make the corner, and he hit the gas coming out of the turn. He glanced in his rearview and saw the truck stopped in the middle of the road. Saw it back and fill, and start back after him. By that time, he was coming up on another right-angle turn and a stop sign. He rolled through it, looking for a place to hide.

Keep going. He pressed on, cataloging every possible escape, even though he knew he was going too fast. Looking for a garage or another side road or…

As he rounded a curve, he saw a building in the middle of the road. It took him a moment to remember this was the split he'd encountered before—the road was a one-way street to the right of the narrow building, and ran the other way to the left.

Instinctively, he hit the gas and went left. No place to turn in—it was all town buildings close together. A car came at him, horn blaring. He missed it. Some people started to cross, saw him, horror on their faces, and jumped backward, the spray of his passing soaking them.

Shower Cap was banging his arm on the side of the car, the spray and wet air blowing through the open window of the LeBaron at him.

Max made it to the next bend. *Turn left.* Most people turn right, so you turn left. He did. *Flatten the arc.* He did, and realized he was now almost out of town. He could find some place to go to ground.

Suddenly, he felt headlights pin him from behind. The woman had come the same way down the wrong-way street. He looked in his rearview mirror and there she was, coming up and coming fast. She'd be up his tailpipe in a minute.

Another tight turn ahead. He barely made it.

He saw her overshoot into a small side street diagonal to the road. She'd have to back up to get turned around.

Max hit the gas, for the first time feeling joy. He felt exhilarated. Free.

No place to turn around, but he kept looking. Glancing in the rearview mirror. Only darkness behind him in the road, and lights from the houses on either side. She seemed to be gone. It gave him a breather, a small relief.

But he didn't trust it. She was like a nightmare. She would be back.

He peered into the rearview mirror, into the side mirrors, and saw he'd been wrong—she was still there. He saw a streetlight's reflection slide over a big vehicle, white light bouncing off it. She must be going sixty miles an hour.

And then he saw flames.

They licked up between the slats of the monster Silverado's grille.

He could almost hear the water hiss as spray from the puddles hit.

Reflections scrolled off the windshield. She was almost to him now, her face like a Halloween mask, the rictus of her teeth and the crazy glint in her eyes. And now, in the wavering orange reflection of the flames, he could see the kid's corpse as it lolled in the shoulder harness, arms jiggling, head flopping. Madness.

More curves coming up. It was terrifying, this bat out of hell on his tail, screeching around corners, moving up, bumper pushing into the old Chrysler LeBaron, but Max knew what the flames meant, and he permitted himself a tight smile.

He mostly worked on motorcycles, but he was a pretty good car mechanic too.

"I can wait you out, bitch," he muttered at the rearview mirror as he avoided another group of pedestrians.

Then they really were out of town. The road straightened out a little, and she was speeding up on him again. Her grille on fire, her face likewise alight with obsession and hatred and *need*.

The LeBaron's tires reeled the road in. The burning truck remained on his bumper. Max muttered, "Now, now, *now*!"

But nothing happened; the truck remained pinned to his tail.

It had to blow sometime.

Didn't it?

Had to.

But the damn thing kept coming.

He drove through a series of serpentine curves, knowing he could make them, even though the rain had started up again and made the road slick.

The land dropped precipitously to his left. If he went over, he'd be dead. The LeBaron's tires screeched as he braked slightly going into the corners, hit the accelerator coming out, the truck right *on* him. Up ahead he saw a hairpin turn. Mine tailings loomed up across the broken riverbed on the left. Weedy trees whipping by like snakes. *Too fast!* The gorge was less steep on the left, but he guessed it was at least a one hundred feet down.

Then he heard it.

A terrible grinding noise, the loud bang-bang-bang in rapid succession, like a washing machine full of rocks.

She'd thrown a rod.

The engine block had cracked, and now everything was going to hell—including the steering and the brakes. He watched with deep satisfaction as the truck missed the curve and hit the guardrail, launching out over the canyon below, the fire still streaking behind it like a *Starsky & Hutch* rerun.

Chapter Thirty-Six

MAX TURNED AROUND AND DROVE BACK TO A SCENIC pullout. Cut the engine and rolled in. Just sat there, shaking with adrenaline and fear. And satisfaction.

He could hear a muted whump—fire. The bright light flared in his side mirror.

But the fire went out almost as quickly as it had started—doused by the rain.

Not long after that, the rain lessened to a soft patter, then stopped altogether. Typical of thunderstorm cells in the desert.

A few wisps of gray smoke floated into the sky.

Max turned the car around, drove back, and parked above the wreck.

The truck lay far down the steep embankment, partially hidden behind a big juniper bush. Nothing moved.

She had to be dead.

No way she could live through that.

He got out of the car and sat on the guardrail—the part that was still intact. Weedy trees and a snarl of bushes along the roadside and running down the slope concealed much of the land on his side. He just sat and stared at the wreck, watching for movement. But he saw nothing. An hour, watching. Two hours. Nobody on the road, nobody coming by.

He stared at the portion of the burned-out hulk he could see. Stared a hole through it.

Waited some more.

He had to be sure.

* * *

WHEN MAX FINALLY RETURNED TO HIS CAR, HE WONDERED if the cops were looking for him. He'd sped through town, the truck glued to his tailpipe, nearly running down pedestrians—it was possible someone would be able to identify a 1987 Chrysler LeBaron. (Unlikely, since the car was old and obscure and it had been dark and pouring rain, but you never knew.) Max had not heard any sirens. He'd been out in the open for at least two hours, looking down at a truck lying in the gorge. The wreck was a long way from town, and there were plenty of twists and turns to hide it from view.

Max figured if he kept to the back streets of Jerome—if he kept to the speed limit—no one would notice.

He was right.

He glanced at his watch and was surprised to see that it was only eight o'clock at night. There were only a few people and cars on the streets. But Max didn't see one cop car. He took the back streets. Here he'd left a litter trail of the hijacked and the dead, and yet nothing in this town had changed.

Hard to believe.

He drove back to the Desert Oasis Healing Center and piloted the LeBaron across the flattened section of chain-link fence, careful to stay out of the gully.

Why tell them he was coming?

Lucky for him, the guardhouse a half mile up the road was empty. No rent-a-cop was going to sit out there on a night like this.

* * *

THERE WERE PLENTY OF EXPENSIVE CARS IN THE LOT. THE richest of the rich. The fucked-uppest of the fucked-up. Max reached the glass front doors to the main wing and walked in. Nobody in the foyer—a long glass tunnel between the front entrance with its cactus garden and the pool and cabanas on the other side. A massive, generic chandelier, the kind you'd find at Marriotts everywhere, cast a dim orange light. He walked in the direction of Gordon's office. His footsteps echoed on the Saltillo tile.

Everyone locked up for the night.

He got to the door to Gord's office. What now? Knock? No.

He aimed a kick under the doorknob, and to his surprise, the door flew open.

No one there.

The anticlimax almost buried him. He'd been planning so long for the confrontation, now he felt lost.

"Sir?"

He spun around. It was Gordon's assistant, Drew.

"Good to see you, uh, Max," the assistant said. "You look like you could use freshening up. Would you like to go to your room?"

"So you can lock me in?"

"That wasn't my intention, sir. I thought you might want a hot shower and some fresh clothes."

Max pictured the clothes. The trademark white drawstring yoga pants and blousy white pirate shirt. Add Birkenstocks, and you could join an ashram.

"Your leg, sir. You're bleeding. I could call the nurse."

"Just, let's..." He felt a little dizzy. "I want to talk to Gordon. You get me? He's gonna want to hear what I have to say."

"Of course, sir."

And Max was ushered through the right wing to his room.

Right back where he'd started. He thought about fighting, but you couldn't fight all the time. He was tired, wounded. The adrenaline that had fueled him was beginning to dissipate.

He still believed that Gordon needed him more than he needed Gordon. He was still Max Conroy, the star of the *V.A.M.Pyre* series. The golden goose, for want of a better term. He truly believed they needed him more than he needed *them*.

And so he took a shower. A nurse practitioner dressed his wound and gave him antibiotics. He felt better. When she was gone, he looked out at his reflection, mirrored against the lighted pool. Trying to nail down what he would say to Gordon, but unable to hold onto his thoughts.

A light knock.

"Come in."

It was Shower Cap.

Max thought: I'm hallucinating again.

Shower Cap put his finger to his lips and crept into the room, his movements exaggerated and low, like Groucho

Marx. It helped that he wore a doctor's white smock and a doctor's head mirror instead of the shower cap.

Am I hallucinating again?

Max closed the door behind them.

Shower Cap drew the curtains closed.

"I'm glad you're back," he said.

"It's like I never left." Max was beginning to remember now. How could he have forgotten Shower Cap? Only Shower Cap's real name was Darren. Darren Fitch-Wender.

Shower Cap was the mascot here. Max knew that Gordon's silent partner in the DO was Darren's father, Thaddeus B. Fitch-Wender.

Yes, *that* Thaddeus B. Fitch-Wender.

How could he have *forgotten*?

Max had holes in his memory, but how could he have forgotten Darren?

Darren was in his midforties and had lived here for at least fifteen years—since shortly after the place was built. Darren was a drummer in a semifamous heavy metal band twenty years ago. He'd done a lot of drugs, and eventually they'd taken their toll. Max had heard the story of Darren's life from Serena, his masseuse, after Darren had popped in one day and sat cross-legged on the table opposite. He'd worn only a sari and his shower cap.

Max stared at Darren, who was checking the bathroom for intruders. He crabbed around, checking the windows and doors, then looked at Max and put his finger to his lips. "Checking for bugs," he whispered.

Max assumed there were bugs. Whether or not this nutcase could find them, he didn't know.

"What's going on?" Max asked.

"I brought your script back. Remember?"

Max didn't remember.

He didn't remember much at all.

"I thought you'd want it, now that you're back."

"What script?"

"*The* script. Shhhh! The walls have ears."

"How'd you find out I was here?"

"Everybody knows you're here. The Maxter is *back*!" he hooted.

Suddenly Max knew why he always saw Shower Cap in a boat. "Man in the Boat," he said.

Darren turned around. "Shhhhhhhhh!"

"Sorry," Max whispered. "That was the name of your hit record: *Man in the Boat*. Wasn't it?"

Darren nodded. "I did the drums!" He started with a flurry of hands, and Max remembered that too. Shower Cap—Darren—was always playing drums in the air.

Darren's band, Phonetic, had had the one mildly dirty hit, "Man in the Boat," which had inspired Max's hallucination. Max associated Darren with a boat because of the song. Max said, "What script?"

"*Your* script, of course. It has your name on it. I found it one time when I was waiting for my dad in the office. It's a secret."

Finally, someone crazier than he was.

"Should I check your pulse and respiration?" Darren asked.

"I don't think that's necessary. But I could use your help."

"I'm all ears."

Max whispered, "Where's Gordon?"

"Gordon's waiting."

"Waiting?"

"He said something about cooling your heels."

"You heard him say that?"

"I used my stethoscope."

OK.

"On the door."

Max wondered how much he could rely on any information he got from Darren. But he guessed that Darren had overheard Gordon talking about cooling his heels. That sounded like Gordon. It sounded like a trick Gordon would pull. Gordon loved to play psychological games. So this was why the wait.

Let Max stew.

Max had built himself up for this confrontation. He was ready to roll. But now here he was, *cooling his heels*, waiting for Gordon to make his grand entrance.

Two could play at that game. "So you have the script?"

Darren pulled it out from under his doctor's jacket. "Ta-daaaa!"

Max sat down on the bed and looked at the title page.

There was nothing on it except a stamp that said, "Final Draft."

Darren said, "I'd better go."

"Yes," Max said. "Thanks. Thanks a lot for finding my script."

Darren beamed. "I *thought* you would like it. Don't let the bedbugs bite—if you know what I mean." And he pointed at the ceiling tiles. Then he danced over to the door, wriggled his fingers good-bye, and was gone.

Chapter Thirty-Seven

JERRY LOOKED OUT THE PLATE GLASS WINDOWS OF GORDON'S suite at the pool. "So he walked right in?"

Gordon said, "When you think about it, that was his only choice. He needs me. I'm the only one who can bring him back to full mental health."

Pompous ass, Jerry thought.

Talia spoke for all of them: "So now what?"

"All the world is a stage, and all the players are…on it," Gordon finished. Shakespeare had never been his subject of choice.

"Oh, puleeese." Talia crossed her legs sexily.

Gordon ignored her. "Of course, as far as the cops and media know, he was right here all along. And no one can prove different. He was in rehab, in the sensory deprivation flotation tank, and we protected his privacy. Because that is what we *do*."

Jerry laughed. "Good luck selling that, Gord. Just turn on the news. Seems to me a lot of people saw him."

"Or saw somebody like him," Gordon murmured. "Like his stunt double."

"So what now, Gordon?" Talia said, that mosquito whine to her voice. Once this was over, once Jerry got control of

Max's estate, he was going to sever his relationship once and for all.

"I want him primed. If you think he's messed up now, you should see him in a while."

Jerry said, "We've got to talk about what we're going to do next."

"Oh, we will, Jer. But I, for one, am savoring the moment. I've been vindicated. From where I'm sitting, it's 'move along folks, nothing to see here.' I made the right call."

"The right call? What right call?"

"All along I've stood firm and told the media I've been protecting his privacy. The media, the cops, I told them the same thing. He's here, he's undergoing life-affirming therapy. Confidential therapy. I did not waver."

Talia examined her nails. "Does this mean we're not going to dissolve him in acid?"

* * *

Sheriff Bonny Bonneville made sure the door to his office was closed, then said to Tess. "You telling me you'd stake your career on that? Max Conroy is innocent in the killing of five people?"

It was just the two of them, although Bonny knew there were a few deputies crowded around the door, listening. Bonny lowered his voice. "He took you hostage. At gunpoint. At the very least, he's in deep for that."

"I know."

Bonny stared out the window. Not that he could see anything. Just raindrops sliding down the glass and darkness behind it and a few street and porch lights, mostly glare. He tried to concentrate on everything his newly minted detective had told him, but it was hard to make sense of it.

Bonny knew what his mentor, the long-dead Sheriff Walt McKinney, who had been sheriff of Bajada County for forty years, would have said.

What does your gut tell you?

"Tell me again about the woman and the boy."

Tess described them. "The boy is dead, though."

"I'll put out an Attempt to Locate for them both. Phrase it this way, 'one or both.' And the truck is operable?"

Tess said, "She drove right by. With the boy strapped into the seat."

"You're sure he's dead?"

She looked at him. Her honest hazel eyes, smooth face, neat hair. Nothing spectacular—she wouldn't stop traffic—but there was something about her. Something that couldn't be summed up in words. *Reliable*, maybe. Although that didn't do her justice.

Besides, she had that weird ability—what did they call it? Superior autobiographical memory.

He swiveled back in his chair and propped his lizard-skin boots up on the desk. "Tell me everything you remember."

* * *

IT WAS QUITE A LONG LIST. BONNY PUT OUT AN ATTEMPT TO Locate for a white Chevy Silverado 2500HD with a black bed liner. Tess had given him the license plate number. It was a new truck, this year's model. Of course, Tess remembered the woman too. She described her down to her New Balance athletic shoes. The woman sounded like something out of a horror movie. Half man, half woman, and all mean. The fade haircut. The man's clothes. The strange boy. Tess said she'd seen the woman with a .45 and a .22.

The .22 was an assassin's gun. Tess was sure she was a hired assassin.

But would a hired assassin scalp one of the men at the mine site? "That doesn't sound like an efficient killer to me," Bonny said.

"It was the boy," Tess said.

"The boy?"

Tess licked her lips. She was rarely unsure of herself, so he was taken aback by it. "I think," she said, "it was a blooding."

Her voice was soft.

"What did you say?"

"I think it was a blooding. She let him have the kill, and he went overboard."

"You mean, like an animal?"

Tess looked at him with those disturbingly calm eyes. He noticed for the first time she had a sprinkling of freckles on her nose.

"She was training him to be like her. To be a killer. I think..." Tess paused. "She doesn't see the boy as her son. I think she sees him as her cub."

* * *

BONNY KNEW HE'D FACE A FIRESTORM OF CRITICISM. HE'D be called every name in the book. But he sent out the Attempt to Locate for the man-woman and her cub (who might be dead or, for all he knew, regenerated like you saw in those god-awful horror movies his kid liked). He sent it out to every other agency in a five-hundred-mile radius. He fielded a dozen calls personally. He did not talk to the press, although the phone rang off the hook. He wondered if he should call a press conference. This was too much. He was in his late fifties, and it might be time to retire anyway. He could see himself on a lake in the White Mountains, fishing. In this state, in this day and age, this was no job for an old man.

Pat Kerney demanded to see him. Tess remained seated in Bonny's office, and she said nothing during Pat's tirade. Pat ended with, "We're the laughingstock of the country!"

Tess just looked at Pat with those calm, reliable eyes.

After ten minutes, Bonny said to Pat, "Are you done?"

"Yes, I'm done!"

"Then follow my directive."

Pat slammed out the door without another word.

Bonny sighed. "I've probably sunk my reelection bid, no matter what happens," he murmured to no one in particular.

He glanced at her, looking for a sliver of doubt in those hazel eyes.

And found none.

Chapter Thirty-Eight

MAX LAY ATOP THE BEDSPREAD, TRYING TO REMEMBER. DID Jerry or Gordon ever show him a script? He didn't think so. In fact, he was pretty sure they hadn't. But Gordon had mentioned something about it.

He tried to remember. Something about a scene…one more scene for the film he'd just wrapped. The director had said something about it. That was his impression. But maybe the director hadn't said anything at all. Hard for Max to remember. Everything got mixed up for Max these days. It was as if someone had been pouring stuff into his brain like veggies into a SaladShooter, and what came out was chopped into little pieces.

Desert God was the name of the film.

But the film had already wrapped, except for a few leftover scenes that didn't involve him.

Would they really want him to do a scene now, while he was in rehab?

No. They wouldn't.

He turned to the first the page of the script and started reading.

The scenario was all too familiar.

The scene opened with a long shot of a car on a lonely road in the middle of nowhere.

The room's temperature seemed to drop fifty degrees. He could practically feel his organs shrink inside him.

There was a woman and a girl.

In the script, there was also a mother and a girl.

A mother and a little girl.

His face grew hot and his heart rate sped up.

A mother and a little girl and a car in the middle of nowhere.

The logical part of his mind told him there *was* no car, there *was* no mother with a little girl, not in *Desert God*. None of them belonged in the story. Whatever this was, it wasn't *Desert God*. The scene had been tacked on.

Gordon had planted this—the girl, the car, the command telling Max to freeze. He'd planted it in Max's subconscious. Gordon had plenty of tools available—hypnosis, drugs, therapy sessions. Therapies that seemed normal on the surface, but who knew how his psyche could be manipulated? He thought about the people who went to self-help seminars and ended up jumping to their deaths.

And those were just *self-help* seminars.

What could Gordon do if he had an uninterrupted three weeks?

But the question was: why? Why try to *Gaslight* him like this? What was the point?

He couldn't think of a reason, but there had to be one.

The answers might be in the screenplay.

He turned the page.

And then he knew.

A knock came on the door.

"Come in," Max said.

It was Gordon White Eagle's assistant. "Gordon will see you now."

Chapter Thirty-Nine

Max was led to a room off the spa.

Gordon lay on his stomach, naked to the waist, the rest of him wrapped in a fluffy white towel. A masseuse hammered his back with swift, lethal-looking hands.

It was difficult talking to a prone, half-naked guru being tenderized by a large black man in a Speedo. Max knew that Gordon had thought this through, that he wanted to keep Max off balance and, if possible, uncomfortable and even subjugated.

Max thought about telling Gordon it wasn't working, but instead said, "We need to talk."

"So talk."

Max slid his semiautomatic out of the waistband of his jeans and glared at the masseuse. The masseuse ducked out. Max put the gun muzzle to Gordon's head. "Sit up. Now."

Gordon sat up.

Max noticed the smattering of gray hair on Gordon's sagging breasts. The man was crying out for a fitness regimen.

"Max," Gordon said warmly. "It's so good to see you, but if you'll forgive me, I don't particularly like having a gun to my head. What say we talk this out like the friends we are?"

"Fine," Max said, pulling back. "Take the towel off."

"What? Don't you think it's a little undignified—"

"Off!"

Gordon did as he was told.

"Now, I'm going to lock the door, and we'll have a nice little talk."

"You're not going to—?"

"How can you ask that, Gordo? I've slept with the most beautiful women in the world. Why the hell would I want to fuck you?"

He made sure the doors were locked, then said, "Smile." He took a couple of candid shots of Gordon with his phone. "A few pics to remember you by."

"Have you been watching the news? Every law enforcement agency in the country is on your tail."

"Really?" Max looked around. "I don't see any."

"You will—I've already called the police. They should be here with a SWAT team any minute.

"Right. It's been, what? Almost two hours since I got here? I don't think any SWAT teams are on their way."

Gordon was silent. Fuming. Max enjoyed the fuming part. "Gordon, I wouldn't bother you, except I'm going to need your help."

"I'm not interested in helping you."

Max jammed the gun muzzle against Gordon's jugular. "Are you interested now?"

Gordon mumbled something. Max took it as a yes. But he kept the muzzle firmly against Gordon's neck anyway. "You know what I want, don't you, Gordon? I want you to fix me. I think they call it the Pottery Barn Rule. You breakie, you fixie."

"Fmmoo."

"'Fuck you?' Gordon, that's not a nice thing to say. Especially since I'm the wronged party." He jammed the muzzle harder into Gordon White Eagle's neck, denting the flesh. "Here's the deal. You put me back the way I was, and I'll go away and never bother you again. And I'll definitely leave your carotid intact. How's that?"

"Mmmffffooer."

"Yes, I know what I am. But that doesn't change anything."

A beat. Then: "Mmmkay."

"Good." Max withdrew the Smith & Wesson. "Now, fix me."

"I'll have to hypnotize you to do it. And even then, I can't promise anything."

"I'm worried," Max said. "I get the feeling you aren't taking me seriously. You think you can snow me, don't you, Gordon?" Max looked at the ring on Gordon's finger. "Is that Zuni?"

"Zuni? What are you *talking* about?"

"The ring. Is it Zuni?"

"Yes, it's Zuni. You've got a good eye."

Max lifted Gordon's hand, admiring the Zuni ring on the stubby fingers, the Navajo sand-cast bracelets, and the Rolex watch. "Take off the jewelry, Gord."

"Why?"

Max motioned with the gun. "Take it off."

Gordon did as he was told and set them on the massage table. Max lifted Gordon's hand again and placed it on the cushioned leather surface by Gordon's thigh. Not optimal. The table had a little give, but what the hell—he smashed the gun butt down hard on Gordon's Zuni bracelet.

The scream would have put a banshee to shame. You'd think Max had brought the hammer down on Gordon's knuckles instead of the bracelet. Which, believe it or not, bounced back without a scratch. But Gordon was whimpering.

"OK, Gord, we now understand each other. First, we're going to have a sit-down and you're going to tell me exactly what you did to me. Everything you did to me. Then we're going to scroll through your virtual Rolodex for a psychologist who's good. The best. Someone who can unscrew me as good as you screwed me. And you're going to get me to him and he's going to fix me. When we get to where we're going, the paparazzi will be there, and you're going to escort me in and they're going to see you. And if this guy isn't as good as he should be, if it doesn't work out, I will come back here and smash every single finger on both your hands. Do you hear me?" Gordon opened his mouth, but nothing came out. He seemed to be in shock.

"OK, here's what we're going to do. I don't care how you do it. You must know somebody who's good. Are you going to find me the right person? Are you?"

Gordon nodded.

"Are you *sure* you're going to find the right person? Because if you aren't going to try, you might as well tell me now."

He nodded again. For a minute Max was worried the man's head might fall off his neck.

There were tears in White Eagle's eyes. But there was also a light in them—he knew Gordon was trying to figure out how to get the upper hand.

"Don't say another word, Gord. You're going to tell me *exactly* what you did to me, how you did it, and you're not gonna leave anything out. Then we go find the right guy to fix me. We're going to your office now, where it will be nice and private. If that's OK with you, nod, OK?"

Gordon nodded. For the first time since Max had met him, Gordon looked cowed.

The fastest way to Gordon's office was across the parking lot. Max pushed open the fire door to the outside. "Let's go."

"Just let me put some clothes on—I'll go with you. You don't have to point that gun at me."

Max ignored him. "And when your pal has me all straightened out," he said, "We're going to have a conversation about why you want me dead."

Gordon stopped in his tracks. For a second, he was as immobile as a giant redwood. "Dear God, Max. *Kill* you? You can't mean that! I wouldn't—"

"Shut up. I read the script. All I want to know—"

Gordon glanced to the side just as Max heard the scrape of a shoe on pavement.

Gordon said, "Freeze!"

Max froze, although he recovered quickly.

Not quickly enough—a giant, hairy forearm and elbow came up around his throat, and he was pulled backward through the side door of the Desert Oasis Healing Center.

"No drugs!" Gordon called after him. "We don't want anything in his system."

"Put him in the submersion tank?"

Gordon said, "Yes, put him in the submersion tank. When he comes out, I want him one step away from a blithering idiot."

Chapter Forty

"So now what?" Jerry asked Gordon. Max Conroy was out of commission in the flotation tank, and Jerry and Gordon were outside by the pool, enjoying the coolness after the rain. Talia had chosen to stay in her room watching *America's Kids Got Talent*.

Gordon had never answered his question.

"What do you mean?" Gordon, clothed once more, this time in drawstring yoga pants and a white tunic top, stretched out his huarache-clad feet and lit a cigar.

"Which way are we going to go?"

"You mean, which one of your harebrained storyboards are we following? I don't know yet."

Jerry stifled his anger. He knew that they were in this together. "It's important, Gord. It could mean millions—no, *billions* of dollars. All I'm trying to do is—"

"All you're trying to do is muddy the waters with seven or eight scenarios." Gordon leaned forward in his lounge chair and pointed his cigar at him. "This isn't a writers' workshop, Jerry. This isn't about storyboards or screenplays or rolling *credits*, it's about taking care of a problem. What part of that don't you understand? We wait until it's dark and dump him somewhere where no one will find him."

"You're kidding, right? Just dump him in the desert? What if he's found? Do you know what the coyotes and God-knows-what could do to a body? Not to mention the heat! If he's found…" Jerry shuddered. "Let's get this right. Let's save something."

"How? Your suggestion was to dissolve him in acid. If we do that, no one will ever find the body, sure, but there are the legal issues. Probate. I liked the original idea better."

"Look, I'm not tied to it." Jerry wriggled forward in his seat. "Let me see what else I can come up with. All options on the table."

Gordon nodded. "Seriously, Jer. What about the DePaulentis plan? Maybe we should just go with the original—the way we planned it in the first place."

"It *could* work."

"But what about the sightings? There have been some. And that woman cop?"

"I don't know, but I'm going to go work on it." He'd always been a good screenwriter—he was fast and he was good—and this was the ultimate challenge. If he just thought of it from that standpoint, as a mental exercise, as *fiction*, he could do it. His fingers almost itched. When the creative urge hit him, his fingers tingled and his gut roiled. He was primed. He stood up.

"Where are you going?"

"No time like the present."

* * *

But as the night went on, Jerry realized that you couldn't make a silk purse out of a sow's ear. And was this ever a sow's ear. Talia huffed around the room, in between long-suffering silences. The room was plastered with Storyboard #1 through Storyboard #7, and none of them worked. The bed was covered with Storyboard #8. Talia now sat cross-legged in the doorway to the bathroom alcove, steaming.

"Just what the hell do you think you're doing, Jerry? All these stupid scenarios—it's ridiculous. Do you think this is a *game*?"

"There's a story in here somewhere."

She grabbed an 8 ½" x 11" sheet of paper taped to the minifridge and crumpled it up. "What's *this*? There's a secret cult that set him up to make him look like a killer because they didn't agree with his politics? What kind of crap is that?"

"It's just one in my chain of ideas."

"Your chain of ideas."

"Yes. When I start a project like this, nothing is off the table. I toss in every idea I can think of, because that stimulates creativity. It gets me thinking outside the box. Then I narrow it down to—"

"Oh, shut up." She pressed the button for room service. "Can I get a massage at this hour?"

Before she left, she told him in no uncertain terms that he was never going to get laid again—not unless they *fixed* this. "I don't care how you fix this. But I want him *dead* and I want his estate *intact*!" And she slammed out of the room.

* * *

AROUND 10:00 P.M., FRUSTRATED, STYMIED, *DEPRESSED*, Jerry turned on CNN. And there it was, an apparent re-airing of a press conference from earlier this evening. Sheriff

Bonneville of Paradox, Arizona, speaking into the flashing cameras. Jerry didn't want to hear it. Didn't want to hear about Max's rampage all over Arizona, or how many people they thought he'd killed now.

"The woman may be with a young boy, about ten to twelve years of age. The boy may be wounded."

Jerry sat up, transfixed, listening to every word.

When the press conference was over, he rang Gordon's line. Gordon sounded as if he'd been asleep. And he'd definitely been drinking, or maybe popping those peyote buttons again. "Wass?" he asked.

"Gordon, it's our lucky day," Jerry said.

"What're you talking about?"

"We *can* do it, Gord. Plan A. We can get our money's worth out of the DePaulentis thing after all."

"What do you mean?"

"Max isn't wanted by the law. Near as I can tell, they're after Shaun and the kid."

Gordon's voice changed: he was all business. "Get up here now, Jerry. We need to plan this."

"See you in five."

* * *

TESS MCCRAE WAS REISSUED HER PREVIOUS VEHICLE, THE battered old unit with high mileage and an oil leak. Bonny sent her home because he wanted her "fresh in the morning." And she was tired. Banged up from the crash, and worse, shaken by the sight of the woman walking on the highway, holding the boy. But instead of heading home, she drove onto I-17, going north. When she arrived, the crime scene was lit up like a night football game. The Department of Public Safety was hard at work, measuring the scene. Tess's car sat on a flatbed tow truck, which pulled out as she arrived.

A detective detached from the roped-off scene, approached Tess's radio car, and introduced herself as DPS Detective Laura Cardinal.

"Did you find it?" Tess asked.

"Yes." Cardinal held up the evidence bag containing the purple yo-yo.

The Desert Oasis logo on the yo-yo was clear in the bright-white light that eerily lit the scene.

"It was right where you said it would be, although it was hard to find—it fell into a crevice between those rocks." The detective nodded toward the rocks close to the road. She looked tired from the long night, but her eyes were probing. Tess wouldn't want to be on the wrong side of the detective. "How'd you know?"

"I saw him throw it."

"The boy."

Tess nodded. She didn't say that she must have been too tired and shaken up after the crash to think about it until now. Her memory was her best asset, and yet it had taken awhile for her to realize the significance. "It was on a string around his finger. He was juggling that and the gun. So he pulled it off and threw it."

Cardinal stared at her. "That's quite some memory of yours," she said.

"Some days are better than others," Tess said.

Chapter Forty-One

In Gordon's palatial suite, Jerry and Gordon went over their plan. Fortunately for Jerry, Talia had decided to take a bubble bath. He'd sneaked out without telling her.

They went over the scenario the way it would look to the cops:

Max drives out into the Verde Valley to look at some property he's interested in. On his way back, he sees a man and woman struggling at a roadside pullout. Max heroically intervenes. The bad guy shoots him and finishes off the woman and the girl. In a panic, the man dumps the woman's car with the woman and girl inside. He does this by rolling it down an embankment—a half-assed attempt to hide his criminal act. He takes off in his own car, leaving Max dead by the side of the road.

"That's what the investigators will think," Jerry said. "Max dies a hero, trying to save the woman and the little girl."

"I know all that."

"When he doesn't show up the next morning, you go looking for him and are shocked to find him dead at the rest area."

"It still seems a little elaborate to me," Gordon said. "Especially the part where we have to drive all those bodies to the scene of the crime. Anyone could see us."

Jerry punched up Google Maps on his smartphone and chose the satellite option. "See? There're a couple of trees back from the road, and some brush. Besides, we'll only be there just long enough to arrange everything so it looks right for the cops."

"Pretty convoluted," Gordon said. "No wonder your screenplays never sold."

Jerry said, "Are we going to stop now, Gord? I thought we agreed on this scenario. I thought you were with me on this!"

"I am."

"You just have to be convincing when you discover him. You can do that, can't you?"

"In my sleep." Gordon paused. "You *do* know this isn't just a screenplay, right? We're playing for keeps. What we're doing is *real*."

"I know that."

"We can't have any witnesses."

"I know that."

"I'm talking about the actors—the woman and the girl."

"I'm good with that," Jerry said, and he was. He thought of them as collateral damage when he thought about them at all. It was unfortunate—no doubt about it—but he chose to block his feelings on that score, one reason he had a glass of Macallan scotch at his elbow right this minute. Max had to die a hero. His death had to be bigger than life, important— there had to be self-sacrifice. When you considered what Max's estate would be worth, at least a billion dollars in the next ten years, there was no margin for error.

And so he concentrated on the plot points. "The main thing we have to do is make sure we get Max's body there in a timely manner. According to Dr. DePaulentis's paper, lividity becomes apparent within a half hour to two hours after death, which you will admit, is a pretty short time frame when we have to move him. So we've got to do everything we can to make it appear he died at the scene."

"You're sure there'll be no blood?" Gordon said. "You can guarantee that."

"There are no guarantees, Gord, but a twenty-two straight to the heart isn't going to go anywhere. It might bounce around a little inside, but there's not enough firepower to go through. That's why we have to have a trained shooter."

He didn't say it, but there was a word for a killer who specialized in executions with the .22. *Assassin.*

However Max fell when he was shot on the soundstage, they would have to be careful to transport him in the same position. Jerry had timed the drive from the soundstage to the pullout, which was only twenty minutes away. The timing would be tight, but the likelihood that Max would be in full livor mortis was actually pretty slight. When the heart stopped pumping, the blood would settle into the organs and sink to the lowest points, but the whole process could take up to twelve hours to be complete. Any changes within that time frame, Jerry thought (he *hoped*—DePaulentis hadn't been entirely clear on this point) would likely not be remarkable enough to puzzle a forensic pathologist.

But to be on the safe side, Jerry had driven out to the pullout and removed all the rocks and debris from a ten-foot-by-ten-foot area of dirt, the place where Max might conceivably fall.

They'd just have to deliver Max there in a timely manner.

Jerry took another sip of scotch. "As far as livor mortis goes—"

"Livor mortis?"

"It's another word for *lividity*. How the blood sinks to the bottom of a person when he dies. Remember? Anyway, we don't have to worry about the woman and the girl, especially if we just shove them in the backseat of their car like the bad guy would do. Any way they land is fine. Especially after we roll the car down that hill."

They went back to the beginning. When the woman and her daughter arrived at the mall, they would be ushered onto the soundstage. Max would be there, hopefully still disoriented from over twenty-four hours in the isolation tank, and easy to manipulate.

They'd shoot him first, two to the heart with a .22. The mother would be next, and the little girl last, since she would be easiest to kill.

"How far do we go with the mother?" Gordon asked.

"Pants off—I told her they can wear casual clothes, so I'm guessing it'll be pants. And maybe her underwear. Maybe tear something, but we have to make sure to use gloves. We don't want to leave any hair follicles or microscopic bits of skin, dander, anything like that. And jumpsuits. Whoever places them where they need to be has to wear a jumpsuit and a shower cap over a hairnet. Use the precautions in the DePaulentis plan."

"And where are we going to hide whoever's going to do it, do you think, Jerry? If the mom and the kid see some guy in a jumpsuit, rubber gloves, and a shower cap over a hairnet, alarm bells could go off. People have a sixth sense about things.

We're no different from animals, when you come right down to it. We can sense danger. We don't want this to be a mess, Jerry."

They would put the mother and daughter in the car and drive them out to the pullout, then a half mile farther on, push the car over the embankment. They would transport Max to the site in the box truck.

"Careful to keep him in the same position," Jerry stressed.

"Agreed." Gordon got himself a drink and sat down again. "I'm worried about that twelve miles to the pullout. That's a lot of time on the road."

"No it's not."

"Two cars? Transporting three bodies? Any time on the road is dangerous. Someone could see us."

"What are they going to see, Gord? Someone driving by. It'll be dark by then. All they'll see is headlights, and who notices what kind of cars are on the road anyway? Do you know that the least reliable evidence of guilt comes from eyewitnesses? Eyewitnesses, generally speaking, suck. Part of that time they'll be on the road, they have to go past the RV park…Don't look at me like that, Gord, it's no big deal. *Night*, remember? And Max's car will go about a half hour later, so they're not even seen together on the road. Trust me. Nobody's going to notice a thing. The mother and daughter will be covered up, and Max will be in the cargo truck."

Jerry added, "The main objective is to make sure Max is laid out just the way he hit the floor on the soundstage. That could be a dangerous window of time—but it's a short one. And we'll be doing it when it's dark. We straight on this?"

"We're straight."

"Good."

Chapter Forty-Two

Concentrate.

Max knew how easily he could lose all sense of time and space, and worse, his own identity. It wasn't just disorientation. The word disorientation was nothing compared to what he knew would happen to him. He couldn't feel his hands, his feet, he couldn't smell anything, he couldn't hear anything, he couldn't see anything. He felt nothing against his body, no pressure at all, as if he'd been wrapped in cotton wool. There was no point of reference. He knew he'd lose all sense of time, he knew he would lie suspended in the darkness, lost, desperate, unable to hear his own cries for help. And he knew it would come on him fast. The hallucinations would take over and he would be completely lost. He needed to concentrate. He bit his lip so he could feel something. The sharp pain, the taste of blood. It helped. He needed to think about one thing. One word, one mantra—a chant that would keep him sane. He flailed around for a word, any word, for that one clear thought, but panic began to consume him.

Think!

He couldn't.

Think think think think think.

But nothing came. Nothing.

Amazing to think he'd once used drugs and alcohol to blur his senses, to disorient himself.

And then, from somewhere, it came to him, one tiny word. Freeze.

Freeze. The word Gordon had used against him. Programmed into him: Freeze.

What was the opposite of "Freeze"? Don't Freeze. He backed it up with another thought. If they tell you to freeze, don't. Don't freeze. Move. And move fast.

His lips formed the words. "Freeze, Move." He made no sound, but he could feel his lips moving. They still belonged to him. He kept moving his lips: *Freeze, Move.* Over and over. *Freeze, Move. Freeze, Move. Freeze, Move!*

He started to drift, lassitude spreading to his arms, his legs, his whole body. Had to fight against it, hold on to those two words by the most tenuous thread, as if he were tethered to a balloon.

When they came for him, when they got him out of here, he knew what he would do.

MOVE.

III: THE LAST PICTURE SHOW

Chapter Forty-Three

JERRY WAS HAVING A LATE LUNCH OUTSIDE ON THE DECK when Gordon walked up, pulled out a chair, and sat down.

Breaking the mood completely.

"I was thinking," Jerry said. "There's that ramp down to the loading dock at the outlet mall, where the big trucks go in. With the high wall? That's where we can hide the truck, the woman's car, and Max's—"

"Shaun's a no-show."

"What?"

"She's still missing. Which *means*, we don't have a shooter."

"Missing? Maybe she's embarrassed because she couldn't find Max. I sure hope you're not going to pay her anything. Some assassin she turned out to be. Hell, I'll do it," Jerry added. Right now he felt as if he could do anything.

"You're not a real assassin."

"She wasn't much of one either. What do you think, she decided to go on vacation in the middle of a job?"

"We don't know what happened."

"No, we don't."

Gordon said, "We need a real shooter. Someone who can drill him from a couple of feet away with a .22, straight through the heart. It sounds easy, but it's only a .22. You can't do that. I can't do that. Most people can't."

Jerry understood what Gordon was saying. The .22 was a deal-breaker. They wanted a small, clean wound, not only to avoid copious amounts of blood that would impede their ability to stage the body elsewhere, but also in case the paparazzi managed to pay their way into the morgue and snap photos. A big, bloody hole would ding Max's market value. "What about Dave Finley?" Jerry said.

"Can he shoot?"

"He's a stunt man. He can do all that kind of stuff. He certainly would do a better job than we would."

There was a commotion by the pool.

Jerry shaded his eyes. "What's going on?"

"Dave's putting on a show as we speak. We're keeping the paparazzi back, but they've got the telephotos out in force. They think they're getting some good shots. If I do say so myself, he looks good in that white Speedo. Hale and hearty—healed of his addiction and ready to reunite with his wife."

"And baby."

Gordon said, "Don't remind me."

"He look different to you?" Jerry asked.

"Max?"

"No, Dave. He looks…I dunno. Almost like he's had some work done."

Gordon stared at him. "Work done?"

"You know, a tuck here, a snip there. *Work.* He looks, I know this is going to sound crazy, but the more I see him, the more he seems to look like Max."

"He's his stunt double. Of course he looks like Max."

"I suppose…" It wasn't important. "So what happens next?"

"Dave's going to climb into the Cadillac Max rented and drive off into the sunset."

Jerry pictured grainy shots of Max behind the wheel of the car, maybe hiding his face a little, not willing to give the paps a good shot.

Perfect. "You think he can pull it off?" he asked.

"I don't know."

Jerry said, "You know Max screwed Dave's wife."

"Yeah. That's what I'm counting on."

Chapter Forty-Four

SHAUN HAD BAILED FROM THE TRUCK JUST AS IT HIT THE guardrail. This had been more luck than anything else—she'd shoved the door open, and before it had a chance to slam back on her, managed to dive for the asphalt. She'd caught it exactly right, the guardrail slowing the truck for just an instant.

Luck.

In her stuntwoman days, Shaun had jumped from cars at least ten times, but she'd had a lot of help—wires and such—and most of it was illusion. But she knew to tuck her shoulder in, curl into a ball, and roll. Easier said than done, but the trees and bushes on the edge had caught her fall. She'd kept rolling until she hit something hard and it all went black.

Shaun had been out for hours. Her bloody face had stuck to the rock she'd run into.

Take stock. She moved each leg. Moved each arm. Moved her neck. She was OK. Felt her face and head with her fingers. There were lacerations on her forehead, her cheeks, her lips, her eyelids. A copious scalp wound. Her leg felt as if it had been slashed in two by a razor blade—she guessed it had caught the edge of the guardrail. Heat radiated from the bone, feverish. Possibly there were internal injuries. She felt like glass had broken inside, somewhere in her pelvic region, but ignored it.

Her boy.

It took her two hours to get down to the truck, and it would take her half a day to get back up. She slid down the hill on her cheeks. Turned over and crawled through the dirt and dry, cutting grass. She staggered to her feet, then crawled again.

There had been no police cars. No sirens. No rescue workers. No helicopters. The truck had come to rest against a big juniper. It looked like part of the juniper's shadow.

Her boy was in there.

Her boy.

He'd been incinerated.

She didn't recognize the thing strapped into the passenger side. It was mostly soot. If she touched it, it would crumble and flake off on her hands. Tendons in the arms curled up like a boxer's; there was some red gleam of muscle and the smell of cooked meat.

"My boy," she whispered. Her voice was harsh; her vocal cords could barely grab purchase.

She reached in to touch what was left of his face. Jellied eyes stared out at her, resentful. "You should have listened to me," she said. "I tried to look after you."

She'd told him not to go after Conroy. But he was a boy. Boys were risk-takers. They died.

But this was her son.

And now she couldn't take him with her anymore. She pressed her fingertip into his chin, the grinning bone, the finger skating through something that might have been soot or might have been flesh. The residue clung to her index finger. Part of her son. Part of him. She streaked it on her lacerated forehead and on her cheeks like war paint. She inhaled him.

Shaun couldn't take the rest of him with her, so she started back up the slope.

* * *

MAX CONCENTRATED ON THE ONE SINGLE WORD, "MOVE," while he waited for the hallucinations, the paranoia, the blind *fear* to take hold. He would lose all sense of time and space. Of *self*. He knew he would lose touch with reality, but more than that, he would lose touch with his core, the thing that made him Max Conroy. He would be reduced to a thin, terrified voice crying in the wilderness.

Max expected this. He kept chanting the word "move" to himself, all the while gearing himself up. Be prepared, he thought. Just try to remember the word "move."

But nothing happened.

He continued to be Max.

And pretty soon, his thoughts branched out from the word "move." He began to think, to plan. How would he get out of this situation, what could he do? He thought about the script Darren had given him to read, his one or two lines. The girl, the mother, the car. And a strange thing happened. He was becoming *stronger*, not weaker.

Max lay in the tank, touching nothing. No sensation on his skin, no sense of smell, no taste, nothing to hear, no one to reach out to. But he felt a presence. Realized with surprise who it was. The deputy-turned-detective. Her calm eyes, her *proximity*. Bide your time, she seemed to say. The idea that he was not alone, that she was somehow here with him, perhaps even looking for him, bolstered his courage. Plan for every contingency, she told him. Be ready. He held onto that—an inner flame that glowed inside him, like a bright green fire.

Be ready.

Chapter Forty-Five

DAVE FINLEY SLID INTO THE SEAT OF THE CADILLAC CTS-V sports coupe, careful to stare straight ahead. A profile was easier to fake than a full-on shot. The paps were kept out by the barred fence surrounding the healing center. He couldn't hear their cameras clicking, but he could see the long tele-photos pushed through the bars. Plenty of other people had snapped photos of him today—everybody had a cell phone—but he knew from experience how people accepted him at face value. No one had ever questioned that Dave was Max when they went on their little adventures. Not in all the years they had switched places.

A couple of paps followed—one on a motorcycle and two in cars.

Dave was good at evasive driving and knew all the tricks. He and Max had ditched a lot of paparazzi in their time.

Once he'd shed the paps, he drove down into the Verde Valley.

He was supposed to take Argos Road, a two-lane that headed out into the wilderness to the west. But as he drove, he thought, *Maybe I should just take the Cadillac and keep on going.*

What was he thinking when he told Gordon he'd have no problem shooting Max? He would be happy if *they* did it, but no way would he get himself into the middle of that. *He'd* never killed anybody.

Dave checked his watch. He was supposed to drive out to the property (there actually was a place for sale way out there in the boondocks, although he would not stop) and then, later today, meet up with them at the outlet mall soundstage and they would go from there.

That was before they had asked him to kill Max.

Did *that* ever come out of left field.

But hadn't he pictured himself shooting Max a dozen times? Confronting Max over that time in the canyon with Karen, and watching Max beg for his life?

He felt the familiar rage build again. How they'd betrayed him, thinking he'd gone off ahead down the canyon. And yes, he had gone on ahead, but decided to go back for them. And that was when he saw them:

His wife and his best friend.

He should have confronted them then. But he didn't. Instead, he'd swallowed his anger.

His resentment only grew. Good ol' Dave, Max's best buddy since they were kids. What a joke.

Dave had always known, *if* he were ever to go through with it, he'd hire a hit man.

It had been easier just to go along with Jerry and Gordon's plan, once he knew what they were doing. Let them take the risks. And then, this morning, when they'd met in Jerry's suite—

They told him that not only did they expect him to shoot Max, they wanted him to shoot an unarmed woman and her kid!

The woman he'd solicited at the Safeway.

Their killer, the crazy woman Shaun, turned out to be a no-show.

And they expected *him* to do it? To shoot a woman and a child?

Dave knew when something was doomed to fail. As much as he'd like to see Max dead, he wanted someone else to do it.

Plus, he had his doubts he could even do it. Drill Max with two shots to the heart with a .22?

Crazy. You had to be a stone-cold killer to do that. Even an expert marksman would be affected by executing a guy. It was bound to affect his aim.

Jerry'd told him why they wanted Max to be shot in the chest with a .22. They wanted him to look good. "If somebody got into the morgue and got pictures of him, at least the wounds would be small and neat."

Small and neat.

Jerry was in his own little world. The asshole spent too much of his time coming up with crazy schemes.

It wasn't going to work. Not when you dragged a woman and a kid into it. How do you keep a lid on *that*?

As much as Dave hated his so-called best friend, he'd have to put his money on Max.

At least he could save the woman and her daughter. He'd called earlier to tell her what time she should be at the outlet mall, giving clear directions to go to the back of the largest store in the middle of the mall. She didn't answer her phone this time either. He waited for the tone and left a message, telling her the shoot was off and they didn't need her after all.

He hoped she got the message.

Dave turned onto the main drag in Cottonwood, where he'd parked his truck and cargo trailer behind a Pep Boys store. He left the Cadillac in the parking lot of the Pep Boys, careful to wipe down the steering wheel, dash, car door handles, seats, and everything else he'd touched. He left the window rolled down and the keys in the ignition. With luck, somebody would steal the thing.

Chapter Forty-Six

Tess didn't get on the road until midafternoon, driving up I-17 in the direction of the Desert Oasis Healing Center. She'd had a lot to do, what with two crime scenes in Bajada County and Pat being shorthanded. Fortunately, they'd had some help from DPS, which had enlarged its investigation beyond the accident on the I-17 access road.

Earlier today, Tess had caught the local news on TV. The story had shifted from Max Conroy sightings to a warning to watch out for a woman who had been involved in a car accident with a Bajada County sheriff's detective the day before. Tess had sat down with a police artist earlier today. The woman's face was indelible in Tess's mind, and that transferred to the artist's likeness of her. The resemblance was chilling.

The woman was a person of interest in six deaths. She was considered armed and dangerous, and citizens were cautioned not to approach her under any circumstances.

Tess was halfway through the two-hour drive to Jerome when she spotted a vehicle flashing past on the freeway coming from the other direction, a truck pulling a cargo trailer—the kind you'd haul motorcycles with. She saw it for only a moment, but knew immediately who it belonged to.

The logos on the trailer and on the truck door were identical to the logo above the door of a fabricated metal shop in LA: Luna Vintage Motorcycles. Tess had seen the sign in the *People* article on Max Conroy. Max and his best friend from boyhood, Dave Finley, had posed before the building. Max wore a white undershirt, and Dave wore a black one. Their arms had been crossed—just a couple of toughs. The photo had been taken at an angle so they seemed to tower over the viewer in grainy black and white. Max was shorter and leaner than Dave. Dave's face was fuller and he wore sideburns. They could almost be twins. They could definitely be brothers.

The truck and trailer hurtled down the freeway in the opposite direction. The same sign: Luna Vintage Motorcycles. A Ouija board sun on one side and a Ouija board moon on the other, and underneath the name of the shop, the word "good-bye." Silver letters on black.

Was Max in that truck?

Tess turned off at the next exit and got back on the freeway going the other direction. She roared up on him, toggled her wigwag lights, and hit the siren.

Chapter Forty-Seven

MAX KEPT THAT BURNING GREEN FIRE IN HIS MIND AND IN his heart until he was fished out of the isolation tank. For a moment, as he hit the air, terror gripped him. It was a nightmarish feeling. He felt lost. Familiar, after his days in the isolation tank the last time. Everything was gray, unrelentingly uniform, opaque—except for the freak show of horror puppets that had jumped out at him suddenly—birds of prey screeching in to pick him up in their talons; holes opening up in the earth; dogs eating him alive. He knew they weren't real, so he tried, mentally, to stave them off. He lay on his back, immobile. The sharp burst of adrenaline left him weak, his extremities cold. He was aware of being shoved onto something and tried to figure out what it was. It jerked him forward, and then he knew what it was: a golf cart. From there, he was carried like a duffel and dumped on some kind of soft surface, laid out on his back and strapped in. Whatever he was strapped onto jiggled. It seemed to collapse under him, and he was shoved across an expanse—maybe a floor, maybe something else, his head and upper body leading the way.

He still couldn't hear—he must still be in earmuffs—and he was blindfolded. Still insulated in the cocoon, except he was moving.

Fear kited up inside. He tried to speak. Maybe he was speaking.

Hold onto the green fire, he thought. Hold onto the deputy-turned-detective with the calm eyes.

Bide your time.

If I can, he thought, *if I ever get the chance—they're not gonna know what hit them.*

Chapter Forty-Eight

By the time Shaun made it back up to the road, the sun was low in the sky. She took stock of her surroundings. It would be a long walk into town.

Shaun heard the car coming before she saw it. She flagged down an older green sedan. Just the one man. Good.

Her appearance clearly shocked him.

"There's been an accident," she said.

The man got out of the car, shoving his keys into his pocket. He followed her around the guardrail and looked down.

"Good Lord—"

Two to the back of the head: *phut-phut*. He crumpled to the dirt. Shaun fished out the keys to the sedan and pocketed them. She pushed the man down the embankment until he took over from her and rolled. He came to rest about fifteen yards down the slope. She went down and rolled him a little more, into the trees that looked like bushes.

The car was old but OK. She opened the glove compartment. A Glock 9 mm sat atop the driver's manual. She checked the magazine—it was full. Good. Somewhere along the way, in one of the two car accidents, she'd lost her .45, and she needed more firepower than the .22.

The bad news: the bullets were full metal jackets. Shaun didn't like FMJs. Many times FMJs resulted in through-and-through shots, which lessened the chance of killing someone with the first round.

But, she thought, the Lord provides.

Shaun didn't believe in God, but she believed in coincidence, and finding this gun was a good sign. And she liked the words, "the Lord provides."

She cruised through Jerome and took Highway 89A to the Desert Oasis Healing Center. She drove up to the gate and spoke into the speaker. The gate rolled open and she drove through.

* * *

ON THE FREEWAY, TESS UNSNAPPED HER HOLSTER AND approached the truck from behind and to the left, outside the range of the side-view mirror. The driver buzzed down his window.

"Keep your hands on the wheel where I can see them," she said.

"What did I—"

"Hands on the wheel," she repeated.

The man peered into the side-view mirror. Max Conroy.

No. Not Max. The other guy. Dave Finley, who owned the motorcycle shop. She had him hand her his license.

Tess cuffed him, settled him in the back of her car, and leaned in to talk to him.

It didn't take long.

Finley told her he didn't know where Max Conroy was now, but he knew where he would be later this evening.

"What time?" she asked.

"I think they said six o'clock."

"Where?"

"The Conquistador Outlet Mall."

Tess remembered seeing that mall, but it was a way out of her territory. "Is it outside Cottonwood?" She found the mall on her phone, Google Earth view. "You said Diane von Furstenberg?" she asked.

"The middle store. But the back entrance."

"What are they doing there? Who else is with him?"

He hesitated. He'd been cooperative until now, although he'd tried to sound clueless. Clearly, he knew a lot more than he was saying.

"Sir?"

"They're shooting a scene for a movie."

"Can you tell me who else will be there?"

"Gordon White Eagle of the Desert Oasis Healing Center. His brother, Jerry Gold. A woman and her daughter."

"Do you know the names of the woman and her daughter?"

"No."

"Do you know the nature of the movie they're shooting?"

"Nope."

"Can you describe whatever vehicles they might be driving?"

He shrugged.

"You don't know what vehicles they might have?"

"I have nothing to do with it. What I'm telling you is just what I heard."

She tried to get more out of him, but he shifted to mono-syllables.

In the end, she let him go on his way with a warning that the right brake light on his trailer was out. She said if he called anyone to warn them, she would nail him for obstruction of justice.

He seemed to believe her.

* * *

SHAUN PARKED THE CAR AND WALKED INTO THE DESERT Oasis Healing Center. There were few people, but she registered their shocked faces. The guy at the desk half-rose from his chair. "Ma'am?"

"Where is Gordon White Eagle?" she said.

"Uh…" She saw his right shoulder dip. Shaun knew there was a button, an alarm. She knew because she'd overseen the installation of it.

"Where's Gordon?" she asked again.

"I don't know. Let me see if I can ring through."

"Where's Gordon?"

"He asked not to be disturbed, he—" The young man stared into the barrel of Shaun's .22. "He's at the outlet mall in Verde Valley."

"Is Max Conroy with him?"

"Pardon?"

"Max Conroy—the actor. Is he with him?"

"I believe so, yes."

She kept the .22 concealed from any passersby with her body. "Are you *sure* Conroy's with him?"

"Yes. Yes!"

"Thanks."

Two to the forehead:

Phut-phut.

Chapter Forty-Nine

GORDON, JERRY, AND TALIA ARRIVED AT THE OUTLET MALL a half hour early. The tall wall behind the defunct Diane von Furstenberg store hid the box truck, which had first been driven up to the loading dock to deposit its contents (Max Conroy).

As Gordon emerged from his car, he glanced around. "Where's the Cadillac?" he asked.

"Dave must still be on the road," Jerry said.

Gordon placed a call to Dave's number and got his voice mail.

They went in through the back. The soundstage looked pretty convincing. There was a green screen along one wall, a couple of cameras, lights, a boom, and a few other pieces of equipment. The equipment cases littered the edge of the set, and Gordon almost tripped over one. He told Jerry to move them.

Just window dressing, obviously, but enough, Gordon hoped, to confuse Max and fool the mother and the daughter. "There's no car," he said to Jerry.

"That's OK. It's all illusion."

"But the mother and kid might think something's up."

"There was no way to get a car in here," Jerry said, in that annoyingly patient voice he reserved for children.

Gordon looked at Max, lying on the gurney. "Time to get him on his feet," he said.

* * *

MAX HEARD THE EXCHANGE. HE HAD NO IDEA WHAT THEY were talking about until he remembered the script. It was difficult to concentrate, but he needed to. In the script, there was a woman and her daughter. There was a killer, threatening them. Max was the hero in the scene.

He knew it was all made up. He wasn't sure how he was supposed to respond, but he knew that this was something planted in the back of his mind. He knew they were manipulating him, treating him like Pavlov's dog.

Freeze!

He steeled himself against the word. In his mind, "Freeze" meant move. It meant that he should fight back. And he would.

He was lifted off the gurney. It was a struggle to get him off. His feet skated under him for a moment before gaining traction. His blindfold was stripped away like a Band-Aid. The earmuffs jerked away. The light was so bright. He knew they were actually fluorescents, and dim. The lights that had been brought to the set weren't turned on yet. But after all the time in the darkness, anything was too bright. He squeezed his eyes shut. Whatever he'd been bundled up in came off. Hands pulling, unsnapping, ripping. He felt like a mannequin. It was hard to move.

Steel yourself.

He did. He gritted his teeth. He tensed up his body. Contracted every muscle group. Made himself as rigid as a board. He held the energy inside him, then let go. Everything flowed out. It left him empty. He waited for energy to fill him back up again, but felt like a deflated balloon.

No reserves, a voice cried in the darkness of his mind. You have no reserves left.

He tensed up again. Gritted his teeth. Tightened his muscles like a fist.

Heard Talia saying, "What's he doing?"

"Maybe it's some kind of stroke or something."

He could hear them. He could see. His eyes were adjusting to the light. He stayed tensed up. Ground his teeth. Held his breath.

When he couldn't wait another moment, he let go again.

This time, he felt the power. The power seemed to flow into him, filling every nook and cranny.

Hatred.

Channel it.

* * *

THE CONQUISTADOR OUTLET MALL WAS LOCATED ON Interstate 17 in Camp Verde, just off the exit for Distantdrums RV Park. The outlet mall had gone under. The anchor store, the Diane von Furstenberg outlet, was the largest in square footage; Tess estimated it at between ten thousand and fifteen thousand square feet.

The empty parking lot was enormous. Scattered here and there throughout, were sickly looking mesquite trees, all of them saplings tied down like small airplanes, offering sketchy shade in the summer.

Tess approached the Conquistador Outlet Mall from the front and saw nothing. The parking lot was empty. She drove around to the other side to get the lay of the land. She came in from the direction where she was able to see down the loading ramp to the anchor store. Sure enough, there were cars there.

She would check out the back entrance, but first she would make another sweep around. When she did, she saw a car turn off the freeway and cruise along Middle Verde Road. Tess was just at the edge of the farthest shop, the defunct shoe store. She thought it unlikely she'd been seen, since one of the trees blocked part of the view.

The car slowed and turned in to the parking lot. It was a green sedan, which matched the description of a car that had been stolen from a forty-eight-year-old man named Marvin Crowley, who had been found shot execution-style in the bushes below the Jerome-Prescott road. DPS and Yavapai County were at the scene, investigating not only the death of Crowley, but the burned truck down in the gorge.

Tess had known immediately that the truck would be a Silverado 2500HD registered to Sandstone Adventures.

The woman—the killer—was on the move.

Tess called Yavapai County Sheriff's Office for backup. She wanted them to come in fast, but silent. She wanted SWAT. This was an unusual request, especially from someone who had been a detective with a neighboring county for all of a day, and Tess understood the lieutenant's queasiness. He told her they would send a car when available, but they were shorthanded and it would take time to pull someone from the accident-slash-crime scene on Highway 89A.

Tess knew Yavapai County would be in touch with Bonny Bonneville. And she knew time was wasting. God only knew how much damage the woman could do in the meantime.

So she drew her weapon and left her car, skirting the building and looking for the green car.

* * *

SHAUN HAD DRIVEN TO THE CONQUISTADOR OUTLET MALL parking lot and once there turned left, heading for the back entrance. She'd known exactly where to go, because Gordon had told her about the outlet mall store when the plan was for her to shoot Max Conroy.

And she *had* come to kill Max Conroy, but she would do it her way. She would kill him slowly. She wanted him to beg for his life, and then, to beg for his death. Shaun's stolen 9 mm had a full magazine. She would shoot both kneecaps. Both elbows. Then one to the stomach. She'd stand over and watch him die by inches.

The kill shot—one in the ass.

Anyone who got in the way would die too.

Max Conroy had shot and killed her son. A silly movie actor, who wasn't worthy to be in Jimmy's presence. He wasn't worthy to speak to him or look at him or breathe his air, and yet Conroy was alive and Jimmy was dead. Her *boy*. Her son. Jimmy was brave, intelligent, ruthless, and strong. She could not picture life without him, yet now he lay at the bottom of the canyon in the dark, the whiff of brimstone rising from the broken truck. And she'd had to leave him.

The least she could do was avenge his death.

Shaun felt different. She was usually cool under pressure. She feared nothing. She did her job. But now she felt as if the world were rushing at the speed of light underneath her feet. Everything sped up, going so fast, whipping by. She was one long line of hatred and righteous fury. Her body was bruised and battered, and she still wondered if there were internal injuries. But the need was so great, so overwhelming, the well of anger so deep, she could not rest until she had him. She would finish this now. The closer Shaun came to her quarry the stronger she felt. She could sniff him out, she could find him anywhere. That solid, unbreakable cable, thin but tensile, ran from her to him; her hatred for him reanimated her, kept her going. One foot in front of the other. She could smell her own hatred. It was rank like the smell of an animal, enveloping her. Pure *need*.

He had killed her boy.

And now he would beg for her to kill him.

* * *

Tess stayed close to the building and peered around the corner. It was almost full dark now, thanks to the thunderheads covering the last sliver of sunlight. She spotted the green car and could see a shape—*thought* she saw a shape—sitting in the driver's seat. Just the sight of the old car, the sight of the silhouette in the car, touched something atavistic deep inside her—the urge to fight or flee. Tess could almost feel the woman planning, see the wheels in her head turning—the woman who had tried to kill her and tried to kill Max Conroy. Tess had dealt with many drug dealers, killers who made examples of enemies by torturing them and decapitating them. But she sensed this woman was worse.

She strained her vision against the reddish gloom, looking for headlights, looking for Yavapai County cars. Tess punched in the number for Laura Cardinal at DPS. Hoping that she or some of her people would be in a position to respond.

✳ ✳ ✳

SHAUN WAS READY TO MOVE. SHE'D WAITED FOR FULL DARK, waited to see who would come and go. She knew that there would be a woman and a child; she was supposed to kill them too. Whether they lived or died now was not the issue. If they got in the way, she would kill them. Otherwise, she cared about only one target—Max Conroy. She hunkered down to wait, keeping her eye fixed on the loading ramp, and saw a battered old rice-burner drive into the lot behind the store and park. A woman and a girl got out.

They were sticking to the plan.

Showtime.

✳ ✳ ✳

MAX COULD HEAR JERRY, GORDON, AND TALIA TALKING AS if he wasn't here. It could be because he just stood there like a dumb ox. He made sure he looked cowed and bewildered. Weak. And so their words drifted into him, and the more he listened, the more clear the words became.

"Where's Dave?" Jerry.

"Don't worry, he knows he's got to be here by seven." Gordon.

Talia: "Can he even speak? He looks like a zombie."

"Try Dave again." Jerry.

"He'll be here," Gordon said. "Do you have to worry everything to death?"

Talia said, "God, I can't wait until this is over!"

Max pictured their words, like hard gunshot pellets, cold and shiny. So much for true love.

He saw Gordon walk away from Jerry and Talia, phone to his ear. Gordon cursed, came back to the little group.

Then his phone sounded—New Age music. Gordon answered, impatient. "Yes?"

Gordon had been pacing, but now he stopped. He stared intently at the floor. Pressed the phone harder into his ear. "Are you sure?"

He listened. Max watched him listen. It was like watching a movie.

Surreal.

He needed to stay alert, ready. He needed to hold onto his anger, let it build.

Gordon was pacing now, talking into the phone in a harsh whisper. Max couldn't make out the words. But he felt the tension. He could feel that something had changed. Something had changed in a definitive way.

Gordon held the phone away from himself, looking at it in dismay. His face was gray in the fluorescents. He looked ten years older.

"There's a problem?" Jerry asked.

Gordon's gaze wandered to Jerry. "Yes, there's a problem. Somebody walked in and shot Jared."

"Jared?"

"The front desk man."

"At the Desert Oasis?"

"Yes! Where else would he be? The police are on their way."

"Holy—"

Gordon spoke over him. "He was shot by a twenty-two. Two to the heart. You know what this means?"

Jerry and Talia stared at him, openmouthed.

Max knew.

"Shaun," Gordon said. "One of my employees overheard what she asked him."

"What?" Talia demanded.

"She asked him where I was. She asked him if Max was here too. She's coming."

For a moment, everyone was quiet. Then Talia said, "This is getting too weird. I'm outta here." She shouldered her purse and started toward the back door, her boots clacking across the floor.

Jerry ignored her. "Maybe this is still salvageable."

Gordon turned to him. "Where's the Cadillac, Jerry? Where's Dave? We don't have a shooter. Somebody's been shot at *my* facility. You honestly think this can still work? Really?"

Again, Max watched the action unfold. Just like a movie. And he realized he felt nothing for these people—not even hatred.

"So what now?"

"What now? We abort the mission, Jerry. *We get the hell outta here!*"

"But what about Max? He knows!"

Gordon didn't spare Max a glance. "He's a druggie. An alcoholic. A nutcase. Who's going to believe him? And anyway, it's time to fold the tent. I don't know about you, but there are options. I'm part owner of the rehab center in Switzerland—"

Then Max heard it. A knock on the door.

"Who's that?" Gordon said.

"It's probably Talia," Jerry said, striding to the door. "Locked out."

He opened the door and a woman and a girl—she had to be all of eight years old—walked in.

"You're early," Gordon shouted.

The woman stopped, shocked. The girl stared at him.

Gordon stood over a small-caliber gun sitting on a rolling table. Max didn't like the way Gordon was eying the gun. He had the look of a cornered animal, and Max knew cornered animals were dangerous.

Max decided it was time to move.

He shoved the rolling table across the floor of the sound-stage, then went for the woman and the kid.

He reached them in six steps. Jerry jumped back, terrified. He yelled to Gordon, "Shoot him! Shoot him!"

Gordon looked at Jerry.

"The gun! On the table," screamed Jerry.

Gordon scurried over to the table and picked up the .22. He aimed it at Max.

Max wasn't worried. The gun was small. Gordon was agitated, scared. He was yards away. Max doubted he'd be able to hit the wall, let alone a human being. "You don't want to shoot anybody, Gordon," Max said. "You said yourself—it's over."

Gordon looked down at the gun. His hands were shaking, but he raised it. Pointed it at Max.

The little girl shrieked. Max whipped around to look at her, and that was when the gun went off.

Max looked down at himself. He was all right. He looked at the mother and the girl. They were all right. He looked at Gordon, who lay on his back on the soundstage floor, a look of sheer surprise on his face.

Gordon had shot himself in the head. The .22 had done its job, bouncing around inside his skull. Gordon appeared to be dead, but Max wasn't going to wait around to check his pulse. Jerry was screaming, and Max had no idea how he would react to his brother's death. Max yanked the heavy door to the outside open with one hand, and shoved the mother into the girl. He pushed them through the doorway, and pulled the door closed behind them.

The mother said, "What are you—"

"Move!"

He pushed them along. They stumbled across the pavement, up the ramp. "Which one's your car?" he demanded.

The woman stared at him, her face was white with shock. She seemed unable to move.

Max put his hands on her shoulders, more to steady himself than to calm her. He looked in her eyes. "Do you know who I am?"

She stared at him. "You're…you're Max Conroy."

"Do you trust me?"

"I…yes."

The child stared up at him.

"Listen. You've been set up. These are bad people. They want to kill me, and they probably want to kill you. You're witnesses. Get in your car and drive away now. Please."

The girl tugged at her mother's arm. "Mom…"

"What's going on?" the woman demanded.

"I don't have time to explain. Get in your car and drive out of here and don't stop until you get home. Do that for me."

She stared at him.

"Mom," the girl said. "We'd better do what he says."

The woman glanced at her daughter, uncertain. "I…"

And that was when a piece of stucco shattered above his head and almost took off his ear.

There *she* was, at the top of the ramp. Pushing past the side mirror of a big white truck, the light bouncing off the gun in her hand.

The woman. The woman they called Shaun.

Max shoved the door to the soundstage open. "Get inside!" he yelled, shoving the mother, shoving the girl. "There might be a bathroom. If there is, go in and hide."

They stumbled through the door and he pulled it closed.

If Shaun wanted them, she'd have to get past him.

* * *

ANOTHER SHOT, LOUD IN THE WALLED RAMP AREA, WHICH echoed like a vault. Max clung like a limpet to the wall and slowly eased around the side of the cargo truck.

"You might as well come out," the woman said. "I'll shoot you clean."

Liar!

Max resisted the urge to tell her what he thought of her.

After that there was silence. He couldn't hear her, couldn't see her. He had no weapon. His heart was pounding so hard he thought she could hear it. Could hear him breathing…

He did the only thing he could think of. He dropped to his knees and crawled under the truck.

The woman was stealth itself. But he saw her walk down the ramp. Saw her feet in the white athletic shoes. Whisper-quiet. There were three vehicles in line, and he saw her pause in front of the first two, crouch down, and look under. His truck was next.

* * *

TESS HEARD TWO GUNSHOTS, SPACED APART. THEY ECHOED, as if in a chamber. She came around the building, her 9 mm clasped in both hands and ready. She saw the long ramp down to the back entrance of the Diane von Furstenberg store, walled away from the parking lot, a loading dock partway down, and the two vehicles she'd seen on her first pass through: a box truck down at the end and a new Range Rover. The car closest to the top of the ramp and to her was a 1990s Nissan Stanza.

Squatting down beside the cargo truck was the dark figure of a woman.

Tess knew immediately who it was. *What* it was.

The woman.

As if the woman heard her, she stiffened. Her head whipped around in Tess's direction and Tess could feel the eyes drilling into her, although of course she couldn't see anything.

"Drop it!" Tess yelled. "Do it now!"

The woman laughed. She brought her weapon up and Tess fired.

Tess heard a yelp. Had she hit her? She squinted at the ramp, which was partially bathed in light and shadow.

Where was she?

The woman was gone.

* * *

MAX HAD BEEN WATCHING THE WOMAN'S FEET AS SHE walked to each vehicle, saw the way the heels came up and the soles bent as she squatted down to look underneath the cars. Then down to her hands and knees.

Come here, you bitch! he thought. *Come right over here.*

He watched as the feet approached. He could almost feel the animal strength of her, the confident, easy way she moved. He knew she was aware of everything, like a mountain lion in the wilderness is aware. Unafraid of any other animal. Scenting her prey. He'd come face-to-face with a mountain lion once in the boonies. The thing had stared him down.

But you're not going to get a chance to stare *me* down.

He willed her to come closer. Closer...

And she came.

The feet paused by the truck. He would grab her by the hands when she got down to look. By now, he had slithered under the oil pan and was positioned to strike.

Someone yelled, *"Drop it! Do it now!"*

The shout came from a short distance away. Max fixated on the shoes and saw the woman pivot. She was facing away from him at this moment.

He grabbed both ankles and yanked hard. She fell forward, landing on knees and elbows. Max felt the strength of ten men surge through him, a power line of adrenaline, his blood singing in his veins. With evil joy he dragged her effortlessly under, noting with pleasure how her head whacked the undercarriage of the truck.

Such sweet, *sweet* music.

* * *

Tess stared at the spot where she'd last seen the woman.

Gone.

No—she was down on the ground, stomach-down on the concrete. Tess watched as the woman moved, then struggled. She was being dragged under the truck. Twisting like a viper, the woman aimed her weapon at whatever had hold of her legs.

Tess suddenly heard the bark of a tire, and then two or three loud revving engines that could only come from cop cars.

They were here!

And then she heard the loud bang.

Tess strained to see. Heard the sound of a car door closing and an engine starting up, and at the same time heard several car doors open up behind her. She saw the Nissan Stanza charge up the ramp and fishtail sideways, straighten out, and race across the parking lot.

One of the two DPS cars gave chase.

Tess yelled at the other one, "Get an ambulance! Man down!"

* * *

Max had the woman in his grip. He had the sweet spot. She was his. Yes, she was twisting, yes she was fighting, but he had her.

He was so busy congratulating himself, he didn't see it coming.

He didn't feel it either.

But he heard it. The sound was a clang like a bell, only *louder*, as loud as the world. A massive thunderclap of sound, ringing in his ears, crumpling his eardrums. Everything got bright and then darker, like play sets shifting and expanding and retracting and dissolving, everything in motion at once, and all he could do was hang. . .on. . .to. . .her. . . shoes.

Hang on.

Time expanded.

Someone speaking into his ear. "Hang on."

But he realized he wasn't hanging on to her anymore. She'd already slithered away.

He heard a car start up and lay scratch. A distant sound. His ears still rang from the gunshot.

He'd had her. He'd held her fast in his grip, but now she was gone.

Hang on.

Did she *shoot* me?

Was he hit? He thought she might have shot him point-blank. But he didn't feel anything. He didn't feel any pain, but his energy level wasn't what it should be. All he could do was lie here on his side.

Someone was under the truck with him. Pulling at the waistband of his jeans, pressing something against him. He reached down to feel where the hand was. Where his stomach was. Blood oozed from a hole in his stomach. His stomach! Max knew he was in shock.

And then the pain came. Overwhelming, like a massive wave.

The person pushing against his stomach took the pressure off, and then put it back on. Something soft, like a cloth or a towel? Pressed hard against his lower body. And the person was saying, "It's OK, Max. Just don't move, OK? Just don't move." He knew the voice. Tess.

"Stay with me," Tess was saying. Her voice calm, gentle. He could see her. He could see her placing her neat, short fingernails on the place mat at the diner...Was that just yesterday?

"Stay with me, Max, just hold on. You'll be fine."

Bright lights. People around him. The harsh glare, rushing sound. Aware that he was being moved, just as he had been on the gurney. But Max didn't care now. He felt himself slipping away. He knew he was shot, because before there was the towel, his fingers had skated over blood—both wet and stiff at the same time. Like sticky red paint. It was him; it was his blood.

Sticky red paint.

* * *

THE MOTHER AND DAUGHTER BLUNDERED INTO THE STORE. Jerry barely registered their presence.

His brother lay on the floor. He'd shot himself. How could that be?

Gordon was dead. "Jesus," he muttered. "Gordon. *Jesus.*"

The mother and the girl looked at Gordon in horror, then scurried past them, headed toward the bathrooms. Jerry wondered what the hurry was.

But he didn't really care. He didn't care about them. His brother was dead. And he was busy. He had to find the new story line.

* * *

MAX COULD SEE THE STARS. THERE WERE A MILLION OF them. He was just rolling along. The pain was unrelenting, huge. People were talking around him, but that didn't affect him. His hands were numb. They didn't work. He felt cold. Something—blood?—pooled inside him.

Darkness lowered. He was in a tunnel. Up ahead was a light. *What was the joke?* he thought. It would come to him. He had all the time in the world. Something about the light at the end of the tunnel.

Then he had it. The light at the end of the tunnel was a *train*.

He smiled. He'd remembered the joke.

He felt as if he'd been wrapped up in the cocoon again, back when he was in the tank. But Tess, the deputy, was there. No, she was a detective now. She was talking to him in that calm way she had. She was telling him to hang on. *Hang on, Max, hang on.* But he didn't feel like hanging on.

The voices around him were loud and sharp. He'd lost Tess's voice; it had been submerged in all the babble. Where was Tess? He couldn't hear her anymore.

The lights were bright, annoying. *Leave me alone*, he thought. *I'm trying to die.*

Then the glare got brighter, and everything went white.

Epilogue

A TAP CAME ON THE DOOR TO MAX'S HOSPITAL ROOM. DAVE Finley ducked his head in, holding flowers.

"Can I come in?"

Max nodded. He'd been expecting it. Dave had kept a low profile and managed to stay out of the tabloids. The big story was about the crazy woman who'd tried to kill Max. The idea that she was still at large made people in Hollywood nervous. Did she have it in for just Max, or was she after celebrities in general?

Shaun Barron had led the Yavapai sheriff's car on a five-mile chase before she'd ditched the car in a field and escaped. They had searched everywhere, but she was gone.

Vanished.

Max hoped she'd died somewhere of one of her wounds. But he doubted it. They would have found her body.

And here Dave was, the Judas goat, holding a bunch of giant lilies from Trader Joe's. They'd already left rust-colored spots on his shirt.

Max would be released soon. Although he'd lost a lot of blood and needed a transfusion, he'd been lucky. The bullet had gone into the muscle just to the left of his stomach, a through-and-through shot. If it had been a half inch the other way, it would have been another story. As it was, he'd been in terrible pain and in and out of consciousness the first couple of days. They'd made him walk too—unbearable.

"Jesus, buddy, you look bad," Dave said, standing about five feet away. "You lost a lot of weight."

"A week in the hospital will do that to you," Max said, wincing. His muscles hurt like a son of a bitch. His voice was weak. He'd heard someone on some tabloid TV show comment that Max was a "shadow of his former self." Which was easy to see from the photos that had cropped up all over. Max in a backless gown, battered, bruised, sallow, and thin. One of them had caught him shuffling along with the rolling IV pole.

He didn't even look like Max Conroy anymore.

Detective Tess McCrae had been the one to tell him that Gordon White Eagle had committed suicide. Max didn't know how to react to this, so he didn't react at all.

To be honest, he didn't care.

Arrests had been made and bond paid. The wealthy didn't sit in jail like everybody else. A frightened woman told her story to the tabloids, citing Max as the hero who had saved her daughter and herself.

Max's life had been turned upside down, but he was heartened to know that Talia's life had been turned upside down too. And Jerry's. Instead of making millions on his estate, they were paying lawyers just to keep them out of jail.

But if Max had won, he didn't know exactly what the prize was. But he *was* improving. The doctor told him he would suffer no permanent ill effects from the gunshot wound.

"Hey." Dave was standing over him. "You got a vase, so I can put these in water?"

"Just leave them on the counter over there."

Dave laid them down and stared out the window. "Hey, man, I'm sorry about what happened. That was some really bad stuff."

Max said nothing.

Dave came over to the bed and stared down at Max. "It's unbelievable, what that woman—"

"Dave, don't do this."

"Do what?"

"I know."

Dave stiffened. A muscle in his jaw moved.

Max felt some satisfaction at Dave's discomfort. Although, of course, it was nowhere near the discomfort he felt all the time now.

Dave said, "You know what, man? I had nothing to do with what happened on the soundstage. I was gone. You can ask anybody."

"You set me up."

Dave's eyes got hard, bright. His face turned red. "What did you expect? You say 'you know.' Well, *I* know too. I know about you and Karen. I saw you—you and my wife screwing your brains out! You think I didn't have a *right*?"

Max said nothing.

"Look, I wanted to get back at you, I'll admit that. But I didn't expect for them to try and kill you! No way would I be a part of something like that. Sure, I'd hurt you. I'd screw you up if I could. After what you did? You bet I would. They used me. And if you think about it, all I did was drive out and pretend I was you. We used to do that all the time."

"You knew what they were going to do."

"No, bud. I swear. I swear to God. I thought they were gonna screw you over, maybe. Get you beat up or something. But I never thought they'd kill the golden—"

"Goose," Max finished for him.

"I swear. I'm looking you in the eye. I swear."

Max sighed. He didn't have the energy. And Dave could see it, because he came forward, up close to the bed, and peered down at him. "You're my *best friend*," he said. "I admit I hated you for what you did. Hated you. I've resented you ever since it happened. But I wouldn't do something like that."

Let it go, Max thought. *It doesn't matter anyway.* "I'm sorry about Karen. She and I both are. She loves you—it was just something that happened. It doesn't mean anything."

It doesn't mean anything. In his world, the person he used to be, it *didn't* mean anything. But now he knew what pain he'd caused. Dave hated him. He hated Max so much he'd conspired with Jerry Gold and Gordon White Eagle and Talia L'Apel to kill him.

When Dave walked out, he nearly ran into Tess McCrae, who was coming in with flowers of her own.

From where Max was sitting, the view had just gotten a whole hell of a lot better.

* * *

February—Los Angeles, California

JUDITH GOLDMAN WAS TOUCHING UP HER MAKEUP IN THE bathroom of Shabu Shabu when the door opened. For one moment, Judith thought it was a man behind her, dressed to the nines in a black tux. But no, it was a woman. Maybe one of the actresses who would be at the Oscars tonight—there were always one or two who liked to dress up like men. This one wore the tux like a second skin. Her hair was cut close to her skull, and she wore no makeup at all. Judith dabbed at her eyelashes with mascara, trying to scrutinize the woman without appearing to look at her.

The woman was fooling with her cummerbund. It had come undone, and although the woman appeared to be lean and athletic, there was a bulge there. A *pregnant* actress, maybe, Judith thought. *Hollywood.*

She glanced in the mirror and saw the woman in the tux looking directly into her eyes.

A goose walked over her grave.

As the woman stared into the mirror at her, Judith first felt uncomfortable, then nervous, then downright spooked. The woman held her eyes until Judith looked away.

For a moment, Judith caught a whiff of something rank, as if a wild animal had somehow gotten in here. Her imagination, of course. But the fear she felt when those feral eyes caught hers in the mirror—that was the word: feral. Judith started putting her makeup back into her cosmetic case, *throwing* the stuff in, her hands fumbling with the zipper, until she gave up and jammed the whole thing into her Fendi bag.

She mumbled an excuse for taking up room in front of the mirror, just aiming for the door to get *out*. The woman in the tux shot her cuffs and just looked at her, and suddenly Judith felt ridiculous.

It was only a woman in a tux, for God's sake.

* * *

MAX AND TESS WALKED ON THE BEACH IN PUERTO VALLARTA. It was just before dusk, and the sun looked like a blood orange melding with the water. Max was having a hard time regaining the weight he'd lost from his time in the hospital—he knew he looked like a skinny beach bum. He'd grown his hair long. Tess told him she liked his beard.

He'd just met her at the airport.

This was their first date. Neither of them knew where this was going.

It was still hard for Max to believe that Gordon White Eagle had committed suicide. The story had been fodder for the news outlets and celebrity sites. Psychiatrists and psychologists were interviewed ad nauseam, explaining that there was a grandiose type of personality that, when faced with the hard cold reality of prison or an end to fame or fortune, chose suicide. Apparently, it was a common solution for egomaniacal sociopaths.

And there was Gordon White Eagle's life, neatly tied up in a bow.

Talia had sued him for divorce. Since the moment she'd been picked up by the DPS outside the Sonic Drive-In across the freeway from the outlet mall—she'd been waiting for a taxi to come get her—Talia had been uncooperative with the police. She'd canceled the baby from Africa, moved in with Jerry briefly, then moved back out the following week. Jerry had retained one of the best defense lawyers in LA—which was saying something. He was charged with several counts, running the gamut from embezzlement, to conspiracy to commit murder, to accessory to murder. Jerry swore he had been framed, and his lawyer had asserted to Max that Jerry would not spend one day in prison. Max believed him.

It looked like Talia would soon be charged with conspiracy to commit murder as well. Her lawyer was not as good as Jerry's, but they played golf together.

Since Talia and Jerry wouldn't be getting their hands on Max's estate, Max had enough money to buy the one thing he desired most, the best *divorce* lawyer in LA. Scratch that: the best divorce lawyer in the world.

Max had been let out of his contract for the three remaining *V.A.M.Pyre* films. The young up-and-coming heartthrob, Dylan Harris, had been signed in Max's place.

He hadn't fought the studio. The only thing he really felt was relief. If he was going to continue on as an actor, he didn't want to be hamstrung by a part like Starker in *V.A.M.Pyre.*

Max *had* talked about his career with his psychotherapist, though. The psychotherapist, like his lawyer, was the best money could buy, and Max needed the best to untangle the snarl of strange thoughts, hallucinations, and night terrors Gordon White Eagle had planted in his mind.

"Look," Tess said. "The Oscars." She led him to an open beach bar and they took a couple of stools where they could see the television set.

Max glanced at the television set, but he felt like a bystander. At one time in his life, acting had been challenging and enjoyable. He had eaten, drank, and slept acting. And then it had morphed into celebrity, which had siphoned off the good parts of being an actor and left only the bad.

He'd loved acting.

Screenplays still managed to make their way to his door. Recently, Max had found himself thinking how he would play a certain scene, how he would develop a character that interested him. He was through with vampires. But there were some roles he found himself excited to contemplate. The kinds of roles that could get him nominated for an Oscar.

Max ignored the drinks, the beer, the parasols and olives, the smell of alcohol on the patrons' breaths.

If he even considered drinking alcohol, if he considered taking the meds he used to take, he would feel the ripping inside his gut.

It was the one positive thing Gordon White Eagle had ever done for him. The sensory deprivation therapy had indeed worked.

Gordon White Eagle would have reminded him of that, had he been alive.

May he rest in peace.

A blonde from *Entertainment Tonight* was color commenting on the red carpet, buttonholing actors male and female and asking, "Who are you wearing?" The Hollywood stars made small talk with the interviewers, posed for the cameras, and moved on.

"Maybe we'll see Dave," Max said.

"You're kidding, right?"

"No. He asked if he could give it a shot, and I said sure."

"But that's—"

"What? Fraud?"

"I don't know what it is," said Tess. "You're not up for anything this year?"

"The crap I've been in? No. Vampire epics don't get you Oscar nominations."

"So it's no big deal? He just does a quick interview on the red carpet and sits in the audience."

"Listen."

The young blonde interviewer cried out, "It's Max Conroy! Max, you're looking *great*."

"Thanks. I'm feeling great." Dave had his chin tucked into his neck and was careful not to look head-on into the cameras. But Max thought that unnecessary. He really *did* look like Max Conroy.

More than *I* do.

"I bet you're happy to be back here, after everything that happened. Even if you weren't nominated this year."

"It's good to be alive," Dave quipped.

"Well, enjoy the show!"

"I will."

He walked farther up the red carpet, then out of the shot.

"I still don't know why you let him do that," Tess said. "What a glory hound."

"He thought he could pull it off. It's kind of a high-wire act, but I think he did."

Suddenly, there was a loud bang. It came from inside the television, from offscreen, but dust and debris filtered back, and the video went haywire.

There were screams.

Fractured video. Blackness.

Then...

The feed was restored. Dust everywhere. People and debris scattered. The blonde who had interviewed the actors on the red carpet cried out, "Who was it? Who was it?"

Max and Tess stayed in the bar.

The bartender turned to cable news.

It took them twenty minutes to play the tape in full. But Max was patient.

It showed Dave Finley as Max Conroy walking up the red carpet. Suddenly, a woman wearing a tuxedo darted onto the carpet and grabbed Conroy, hugging him to her chest. There was something—a bubble of some sort—strapped tightly to her body.

It would turn out to be a suicide bomb.

They fell to the carpet—*pressed* into the carpet. Some people ran toward them, some pulled back, some stayed where they were, shocked.

Fortunately, most of the concussion from the explosion discharged into the red carpet—into the floor.

Two people in the crowd were killed instantly. Many others were injured, mostly by flying body parts and shrapnel from the bomb.

It was amazing that so few were seriously injured.

The man known as Max Conroy, and his attacker, were killed instantly.

* * *

TESS WAS QUIET. MAX FELT SICK INSIDE. THEY LEFT THE BAR and walked on the beach, this time with the full moon over their shoulders. Warm down here in the subtropics, even in

February. The waves came in. Endless waves, washing onto this beach, and onto the beach far north of here—in LA.

Max had suspected that Shaun wouldn't give up. He'd suspected she was going to try again. He'd gone as far as to hire a security firm.

But you didn't hire one for Dave.

How could he have known what would happen?

He didn't.

That could have been me, Max thought.

Instead, it was Dave Finley.

"You knew," Tess said.

"No. I didn't."

Tess stared at him.

"I thought at some point she would get to me. I never imagined she'd do it on the red carpet at the Oscars."

"You didn't?"

"No."

She held his gaze. There was still a question in her eyes. He didn't blame her. It looked bad.

Either she would believe he was the kind of man who would set his best friend up to be killed in his place, or she would not. He knew he couldn't sway her—she was too smart for that.

Abruptly, he thought of their motorcycle shop, and the realization finally came home. His best friend of almost twenty years was dead. He thought of all the adventures they'd had, how they'd grown up together. The many times Dave had had his back.

Now Dave was dead in his place. And he was culpable.

Tess said, "That woman. She was like a mother bear. You killed her cub. You never get between a bear and her cub."

"Wish I'd known that."

"She would never have given up until she got you."

"She got me."

"No. She got Dave." Tess crossed her arms and stared out at the ocean. "You realize what this means?"

"What this means?" Max asked.

"Yes, what this means."

Tess was beautiful. He didn't know where this would go, but he hoped, whatever happened going forward, his life would include her. The breeze lifted a strand of her hair (at least here, she didn't wear it in a neat bun) and he reached over and pushed it away from her face. She stared into his eyes, defiant. "You'll have to go back. There'll be an investigation and the police will want to talk to you."

He knew she was right—there were plenty of loose ends. But he would no longer have to look over his shoulder, thinking that at any time Shaun would jump out of the shadows, intent on killing him.

Dave took care of that, didn't he? The voice inside his head told him—the voice he knew he would be living with for the rest of his life.

Tess said, "What will you do now?"

"I don't know." But that wasn't entirely true. He wanted to continue his acting career. He'd lost track of that over the past few years, drowning his troubles in drink and drugs, but he was stronger now. It was as if he'd been given a second chance.

The strand of Tess's hair came loose again. He reached over and pushed it behind her ear once more.

She said, "You know this—"

"Shhh." He touched a finger to her lips. But he knew what she'd been about to say, that it wouldn't work. He would go back to his old life, and Tess McCrae would stay a cop. They belonged to different worlds.

"We can still see each other," he said. Painfully aware of the urgency in his voice.

She looked away.

Max said, "Long-distance relationships do work. We could try it out and see—"

"I guess we could try," she said. But there was enough doubt in her voice to sink a battleship.

He pulled her in to him. As they kissed, he could feel the beating of her heart.

Max closed his eyes and enjoyed the moment. Yes, he thought. They could try.

THE END

About the Author

Photograph by Ian Galley, 2011

J. CARSON BLACK IS THE BEST-SELLING, critically acclaimed author of eight books, including the Laura Cardinal crime fiction series. Born and raised in Tucson, Arizona, Black has found inspiration for her writing in everything from real-life horrors to the headlines screaming today's news. She is currently working on her next thriller.